The Mystical Gem

Chronicles of Datch

David Hallam

The characters and events portrayed in this book are fictitious. Any similarity to real persons, living or dead, is coincidental and not intended by the author.

ISBN: 978-1-917238-15-1

DEDICATION

To my wonderful daughter. You are always in my heart.

For all of my friends in the pub.

ACKNOWLEDGMENTS

I want to say thank you to all the staff in my local public house for putting up with me sitting in the corner typing away on my laptop.

I would also like to thank Jeff and Mick for fixing my TiPing errors and bad grammars :)

Datch and The Pack

Datch was now nine and a half years old (Nineteen in earth years). He was in his final year at school in Yuland City on the planet Bellatrix five. He had his own band 'The Pack' and over the last year had been catapulted into stardom along with his girlfriend Carina and his friends. Not only had they become a big hit with the masses but they had also manged to make interstellar headlines after they had saved the president from an assassination attempt. Datch is somewhat of a party animal and loves being on stage. He had perfected his singing along with a number of other things in the shower. He had also got the hang of his implant which was installed when he was six. Oh, and he had already died once and was only saved when his brain was transported to the starship Carpaycus. Thus, he now knows what it's like to die and no longer has any fear.

It was a sunny morning in Yuland city, Datch was sitting outside the Pancake shop having breakfast with Carina, Hagger, Dapo, Rosey and Tish. They were recovering from the previous night's gig at the Barbers Inn. They played there every week on the night before they were due at school. It was one gig they never missed unless they were too far away from home. It had been a good night and the place had been rammed as normal. It was where they started singing and they really enjoyed playing there. Also, they all had rooms overnight now to save them going home only to come back for school the following lunchtime.

"So, we have about three hours before we have to be at school so what are we going to do?" Asked Dapo.

"Well, I need at least one more coffee to wake up." Said Rosey who had been on the Old Man's Boots again with

Hagger. They both looked like they should have had another hour in bed, either that or they should be in a morgue.

"I thought we could head down to Clax's shop for a bit, he has a coffee machine in the back." said Datch with a grin.

"OK, I know that look lover boy." said Carina.

She looked straight into Datch's eyes with a look on her face that made him melt. He couldn't help it. With everyone else he could keep a straight face and not say what he was thinking but with Carina and that look, it just had to come out.

"OK." he said reluctantly. "He said he's decrypted the cube at last, he told me last night, and said he would show us when we went around."

"Oh wow, I thought it was a lost cause." said Hagger whose dad had hidden the cube in a drawer before he died.

"No, he said it was a lot older than he thought and because of that he had to figure out some of the language matrix first." added Datch.

"What else did he say?" Asked Hagger who had woken up all of a sudden.

"Not much else, but he did seem quite excited about it."

"Well, I think a trip to Clax's shop sounds like a good idea." said Carina now somewhat intrigued herself.

They all agreed to go and find out what Clax had found after eating their breakfast. Also, Hagger and Rosey had an extra strong coffee along with a couple of hangover cures. When they had finished, they all put on really dark glasses and hats before heading off towards the spaceport and Clax's shop.

Clax's shop was small but seemed to have everything you could imagine inside. It was just outside the spaceport and sold touristy things and also had a section near the front currently selling band memorabilia, namely 'The Packs'.

They went in and headed to the back past the fridge magnets, the place mats with pictures of the city and the surrounding area, the key rings and finally the cuddly toys. There in the corner was a side room. A hand appeared around the corner and waved at them to come so they followed it.

Clax's office was somewhat messy. It looked like it hadn't been cleaned up for two or maybe three hundred years. The books and bits on the top shelf had at least fifty millimetres of dust on them. It was one place you didn't want to sneeze. If you did, you would never find your way out without breathing equipment and a hand-held scanner. Clax was sitting at a desk and had a vid comm plugged into a strange piece of equipment which had a small black cube inserted into the top. The cube was glowing and data was scrolling up the vid screen.

"You came then?" he said without turning around.

"Yes, we had to, so what have you found?" Said Datch.

"This!" He pressed a button on the vid comm.

A hologram appeared in the centre of the room. It was a mess to start with and then something started to form in the air. A planetary system appeared in front of them. The fourth planet in the star system had strange writing around the edge of it and a red dot on the surface. More symbols appeared in a box next to the planet and then it stopped with a single light flashing under a green diamond shape.

"Err, why can't I read this?" Asked Carina.

"Yes, our implants should be translating it." added Datch.

Clax sat back in his chair and smiled.

"Well, your implant would translate it if it could but it doesn't know how."

"I thought the implant had all known languages?"

"It does, well sort of anyway. It knows all the ones that are used."

Datch thought about this.

"You mean it's a language that's not used anymore?"

"Not just anymore, it's not been used for a long time. Try twenty thousand years, it was in a time before implants and you only had one life. If you died then, you stayed dead."

They sat looking at the hologram for a few moments.

"So, it's not this star system the number of planets is wrong, so where is it?" Datch asked.

"I'm not totally sure as some of the stars have moved a bit but I think it's the Welly star system and the planet is Welly four."

"Oh man, that's the most boring place in the universe, why would it show that?" Said Dapo.

"I'm still trying to work it all out and can only partly read the text, but it does talk about a hidden Gem with magical powers, some of the script appears to be a version of one of the old religious texts. If I could scan a few pages, it would give me a translation key."

They looked at the text.

"Can we just request a viewing of the old books or something?" asked Hagger.

"Normally yes, they would send an image of them, but these are so old they only let you see them in person and then only at certain times of the year."

Rosey went over to the coffee machine and set about getting a round of coffees for everyone. She casually turned around and said,

"Well, we could just go there couldn't we, we do have lots of credits now after all?"

"That would be great, but you're forgetting one thing – school." said Datch.

"Yes, it takes three to four weeks to get that far and that's if you travel on the express flights." added Carina.

They all sat down thinking about the problem. Rosey handed the coffee out and they all sat looking at the images as they rotated around in sequence.

"Well, we can't say we're going there for a gig, I'm sure they don't know what rock music is, let alone have concerts" said Datch with a sigh.

"We don't even know if the gem exists or not." Said Tish

"Ah, well we do and yes, it did." said Clax; they all turned to look at him

"It does?" Said Hagger.

"Yes, I found it in one of the legends of Welly four. It is said that the gem had mystical powers and after one of the monks used it to gain power it was taken and hidden by the head of the order on a distant world. The monk died before passing on the location, there were rumours that a map existed but it was never found and the gem was lost forever."

"So, is this the map?" Asked Datch.

"Err, not that I can tell, but I think it is telling us where the map is, so I think we would need to go there to find out if it does exist."

“OK, let’s get this right,” said Rosey “We are at school and we need to take at least three months off to go to the most boring place in the universe to look for a lost map that is over twenty thousand years old and may not exist anymore.”

“Yes, but my dad did have the cube.” said Hagger in an encouraging way and then he tried Datch’s grin. It didn’t work.

“Does anyone have any ideas?”

They all sat looking at each other for a few minutes.

Datch thought about it. Hagger's dad had been killed by an arachnoid and they had found the cube when going thought his things. So, if nothing else he wanted to find the gem for him and after a while he started to smile.

“I might have an idea but need to run it by Jep first.” he said.

“Come on then, don’t keep it to yourself.” said Carina.

Datch spent the next five minutes explaining his idea and then after another coffee they left Clax and headed up to the school.

It was just before noon when they arrived at the school and Timbo was waiting outside with their bags. Timbo used to be a bouncer at the Barbers Inn but ended up becoming the band’s one and only fulltime member of the road crew. This also meant that he would now hang out with them a lot and do any carrying about that they needed.

“Hi Timbo.” Said Datch walking up to him

“Hi Datch, I’ve got all your stuff, do you need anything else?”

“Yes actually, can you come to the Barbers tonight for a beer?”

"Yes, seven ish OK?"

"That's fine, if we're not there yet, get a beer and put it on my tab." Datch smiled and Timbo started to think this wasn't just for a beer.

"OK, thanks Datch." He wasn't quite sure that 'thanks' was the right word. Knowing Datch, he was about to be talked into something that could involve long hours and a head ache.

The others came over and one by one took their bags and followed Datch into the school. He waved at the security guard on the desk. The guard gave him a smile and a thumbs up. It was strange coming to school at the end of the week. The last year had been during the week and finished with them doing a gig at the Barbers Inn. Now they went to the school after the gig. The second year however was a lot more interactive; they spent the afternoons being taught how to do this or that and then the evenings would be spent out in a bar or restaurants putting things into practice. In the case of Datch's team, it would normally involve the Barbers Inn.

Datch, Dapo and Hagger put their bags in their room and headed off to the games room. The Pack had sort of taken over a table in the corner out of the way. Being super stars was not easy. If you could be seen, people would come and want photos with you or an autograph etc. The Barbers Inn had put a big sign on the door 'Do Not Disturb 'The Pack' – you will be banned from the bar' Carina had thought it was a bit excessive but after a number of fans tried to take things like used tissues from her, she changed her mind.

The games room was quiet at the moment. The first-year students went home first thing in the morning and second year students were just arriving. It meant they could relax and soon the girls came in and headed over to them, they sat chilling out.

"So, when you going to talk to Jep?" asked Rosey.

“I don’t know, depends when he turns up.” replied Datch.

“I did see him five minutes ago walking down the corridor towards his office.” Said Carina.

“How did he look?” Asked Datch.

“Err, a bit hungover I think.”

“Hmm, that will be the Old Man’s Boots he was drinking with Hagger then.” added Dapo.

“It wasn’t just me, Rosey was egging him on as well.” Said Hagger defensively.

“Well, you suggested the doubles.” Rosey said.

Datch had seen this before, they both blew off steam when they were hungover, having a pop at whoever said anything they didn’t like so he stepped in

“Look, it doesn’t matter who had what, just chill while I go and find him.” They looked at Datch who stared back at them.

If there was one thing you didn’t want, it was that stare. Datch had learnt it from his dad and when he used it, you ended up feeling about ten centimetres tall and like a really naughty person. That look could stop an alien invasion let alone anything else. Datch got up and headed towards the door.

“Do you want me to come with you?” Asked Carina.

“No, I’m good babes, I need to do this solo, thanks anyway.”

Datch left them and headed for Jep’s office. He got there and knocked on the door.

“Enter.” Came a voice from inside.

Datch walked in and closed the door behind him.

“Oh, Hi Datch.”

Jep opened the desk draw and took out a very strong coffee that he had put in there when he heard Datch knock.

“What can I do for you?” he said trying to put on his tutor voice. This had no effect on Datch at all as he knew Jep far too well. He was after all one of the backing singers in the band.

“We want to go on a field trip.”

“Err, OK which city do we have a gig in now?”

“We don’t have a gig, well, not yet anyway.”

“What, you mean a proper field trip?”

Jep was surprised.

“Yes, Clax cracked the cube that Hagger's dad had. It has a map on it and showed us where to go.”

“Go, go for what?”

“The mystic Gem.”

“Right, let me get this straight. You want to go on a field trip to find a mystic gem using information that you retrieved from a cube which was found in Hagger’s dad’s drawer.” he paused and looked at Datch trying to work out what was going on. Datch nodded.

“OK, where to exactly?” he said picking up his coffee to take a sip.

Datch looked at him for a moment.

“Welly four.” he said.

A spray of coffee shot across the room. Jep blinked and thought about what he had just heard. No, he couldn’t have heard it right.

"Welly four, the most boring place in the universe?" he said still struggling with it.

"Yes, Welly four." Datch looked at him with the sincerest look he could muster.

Jep paused again. He knew he had a lot to drink last night and could have strange dreams sometimes but here was Datch the party animal asking to go to the most un-party place in the known universe. It just seemed so very wrong. At this point two things came to mind. One – Datch could cause permanent damage to the planets culture. Two – Datch could get deported from the planet for causing offence to the population in general. He looked at Datch again who was now starting to stare at him. He decided to try and put him off.

"It's not your sort of planet, you know that don't you?"

"Yes, but we still need to go."

"But you will have to be boring."

"Yes, I know."

"It could be really hard going."

"True, but we need to go."

Datch started to stare a lot more, which in itself was quite something.

"OK, OK, I'll talk to the principal." Said Jep starting to buckle under the pressure.

"Cool, we'll meet you outside later before we head to the Barbers."

"OK. Is it dark glasses tonight?"

"Sounds like a good idea, later dude." Datch smiled and left the office.

Jep sat looking at his desk trying to work out what had happened. No other student had ever been able to do what Datch did. They would come in all sheepish like and say yes sir, no sir and whatever you say sir. He had taken on Datch and the team because it sounded like it was going to be an easy two years. Now he was part of a band, the president of the planet was on first name terms with him and he automatically did whatever Datch said. Now he had to tell the principal that he wanted to take team Datch to Welly four on a field trip. He let out a very big sigh and tried to come up with an explanation why they needed to go.

When Datch got back to the games room the rest of the gang was sitting chatting. They stopped when Datch came in. He walked over to the table and sat down.

"Well, did he say yes?" asked Carina.

"Yes, he's going to talk to the principal about it."

"Great, so he'll let us know later then?"

"Yes, oh and it's dark glasses tonight."

"Good, it's nice not to be seen." Said Rosey.

"So, what's on for this afternoon?" Said Tish who was currently engaged with blowing in Dapo's ear.

"I think it's something to do with alcohol and what not to do with It?" Said Carina.

"Well, it's a bit late for that now." said Dapo looking at Hagger.

"Yes, I know what to do with it." said Hagger grinning.

"He just likes trying things out that's all, don't you?" Said Rosey rallying to her boyfriend's defence.

"Yes."

"OK folks, let's just chill, we'll find out all about it in a while, it should be interesting if nothing else." Said Datch trying to defuse any on coming argument before it started.

"Anyway, does anyone fancy a walk tomorrow morning? There's a shop in the mall selling alien clothes, I figure we might need to blend in." He added.

There was a pause while everyone else at the table tried to work out how Datch could ever blend into anything. Maybe a full-on city riot and even then, he would stand out in the same way as someone would driving a tank though your back garden while you were having a barbeque. When the universe created Datch it didn't just throw away the mould, it put high explosives around it and blew it up just to be sure it couldn't be put back together and then buried what was left of it in a place no one would ever look.

Now Datch was a really nice guy but he just had a knack of whenever he did something it just ended up being big in some way. Take lunch. He went over to the counter for the carvery, he ended up getting twice as much meat as everyone else. The joint was running out when he got there so they gave him the bit that was left and then they brought out a new one and gave him a bit more because he had to wait a moment. It wasn't timed or planned but it just happened, in fact it happened a lot.

Datch, looked at the others.

"What? I thought it would be cool to have the right clothing."

"Err, yes that would be a good idea, so what do they wear on Welly four?" Asked Carina.

Datch got out his vid comm and put up some images on it. The clothing was very plain at best, at worst it was very boring and seemed to be various shades of brown or dark green in colour. It consisted of various robes, tops and trousers. They all seemed to have pointy hats on with brown feathers sticking out the top.

“Is that it?” Said Rosey looking very disappointed.

“Mostly, but there are some dark purple ones as well” He put up another couple of images.

“Can’t we go in normal clothes?” Said Tish.

“I thought we wanted to blend in.” Said Dapo. Hagger nodded in agreement.

“Well, we could maybe vary the colours and use a bit of artistic license, we are tourists after all.” Added Carina after seeing the look on Rosey’s and Tish’s face.

Both Tish and Rosey liked bright colours and had developed their own styles. They were also currently in negotiations with a fashion manufacturing group for a clothing line.

Datch looked at them.

“OK, we’ll go and get some clothes. Rosey and Tish can be in charge of making them look cool.” There was a general agreement by all concerned.

“One question Datch,” asked Dapo. “How do you know the principal will say yes?”

“Because I sent him an email explaining that it was one of Hagger's dad’s last wishes that he wanted Hagger to go to see the spring festival there and meet his great uncle.”

They all turned to look at Datch with disbelief on their faces that is apart from Hagger who was grinning and really liked the plan.

“But he doesn’t have a great uncle living there.” Said Dapo.

“He does now.”

“Yes. I do and he’s cool.” Hagger said, the others turned to him.

“Hey, it’s a road trip, I’m sure my dad would approve if he hadn’t been eaten.”

There was a moments silence while the others took this in. Hagger was still smiling. Carina suspected Datch had been giving him lessons. After a few moments thinking about it they decided to go along with it. Anyway, Hagger was right, it was a road trip.

“So, are we going to the cake shop for breakfast tomorrow?” said Carina changing the subject before they could find even more complicated ways of getting into trouble.

“Yes, that sounds good, who’s turn, is it?”

“Mine I think.” Said Dapo.

It was good having a lot of credits, they could just do things. Yes, they had a lot of late nights or days away on tour but it didn’t matter because The Pack was one family now and when they were together, they felt whole. It was soon time to go to the first lecture, so they headed off to the lecture room.

That evening The Pack sat outside waiting for Jep. He finally came out and headed over to them. They got up and after a round of hellos they stated to head to the Barber Inn.

Jep was walking along side Datch

“So, aren’t you going to ask?” he said.

“No.” Answered Datch.

“Err, why?” Said Jep a bit puzzled.

“I don’t need to, he said yes, didn’t he?”

“Err, yes, but how did you....” his voice trailed off.

Jep realised Datch knew the outcome before he asked the question, in fact before he had even thought about asking it.

“Oh, we’re going shopping for clothes tomorrow morning so we’ll blend in.”

“We are? Oh yes, we’ll need to look the part.” Jep thought for a moment before adding “The principal asked if we could avoid starting an interplanetary war if at all possible.”

“Sure!” Said Datch smiling again which made Jep worry a lot.

They carried on down the street to the Barbers Inn. It was very busy these days but since Jim migrated the table up on to the balcony and had started keeping a barrier across the bottom of the stairs, they always had a seat. With the table being upstairs they didn’t get hassled now either. Before they started playing at the Barbers Inn, it was a quiet bar. A lot of the business had been in the form of food during the day. The evenings had been steady but you could always get a seat. Now days the bar had become a trendy place to be, partly due to The Packs continued presence and also the bar had become very well-known because of all the other celebrities that would now come in. The upstairs was for VIP’s and apparently the members of The Pack were now VIP’s and therefore counted, even Timbo was included. They walked into the bar past the bouncers that now seemed to live on the door and waved at Jim before heading up stairs. Timbo was sitting there with a beer.

“Hi Timbo.” They said sitting down.

“So, Timbo, do you fancy a road trip?” Said Datch.

“Err, I suppose so, where we going?” he said.

“Welly four.” Carina said.

“Is that near the mountains?” He asked.

Datch looked at him and wondered if he had ever been to school then decided to carry on anyway.

“Err, sort of. It will be a nice trip and not much to do but relax.”

“Oh good, I’m in.” Timbo picked up his drink and smiled.

At that point Jim came up with the drinks and food menus. It was a general rule that if they arrived before seven, food would be involved and it was only six thirty.

“Err, Jim” said Datch “We have a bit of bad news for you.”

Jim turned to them with a look of panic on his face

“What’s Happened, has someone lost their voice or something?”

“No, we’re going on tour again, only this time it will be about ten weeks roughly.”

“Wow, that’s a long tour, where are you going for that long?”

“Err, Welly four.” said Hagger.

Jim stopped and thought about this. That planet was not known for well, entertainment, let alone loud entertainment.

“Welly four, it’s boring why would you want to go there?”

“Err, we’re going on a quest to find a mystic gem.” Said Hagger helpfully.

Jim looked at them, he had known The Pack for over a year now and knew when not to ask.

"Oh… OK, so when do you leave?" He figured that was a safe response at this point.

"Not sure yet, but it will be soon. We'll give you a couple of week's notice. Oh, and I'll see if I can get The Snowmen to stand in for us." Datch added.

"OK, but that's going to be a hard gig. Welly fours idea of a rock concert is one guy in a barn strumming on two strings nailed on to a plank of wood."

They all looked at him. It was at that point he decided to ask for the food orders after which he headed back to the bar shaking his head.

The food came and they tucked in. After they had finished it, Peebop, Tank and Fred came in. After a round of how you doing dudes, Datch cleared his throat. This had the effect of silencing half the bar. Which considering that they were upstairs and the bar was now half full it was quite impressive. The rest of The Pack looked at him.

"Err, just to let you know, we're all going on a road trip and yes that includes you guys."

"Where to?" Asked Tank.

"Welly four." Answered Hagger who was now starting to enjoy the look on people's faces when they were told.

There was a pause while they tried to process what they had just heard.

"Welly four, what the hacks do you want to go there for?" Said Fred.

"Clax decoded the cube, it's the Welly four, star system." Said Datch.

"Yes, and we think it will lead us to a mystical gem." Added Hagger.

"Oh, of all the places to go to," said Fred, "I had to go there once for an insurance job, it was so boring I nearly fell asleep filling the forms in."

"Do we really need to go?" Asked Peebop.

"Yes!" Said The Pack in unison.

"OK, OK." Said Peebop.

"So, when do we leave, I have a couple of hair appointments to do early next week?" Asked Tank.

"Shall we make it the following weekend? I'll sort out the tickets." Said Datch who now was very keen to get the adventure started.

Just at this point Clax came walking up the stairs, the other bikers turned to look at him.

"Hi guys, what's happening?" he said.

"Welly four, really?" said Fred.

"Ah yes. When are we leaving?" he said with a grin.

"Next weekend apparently because Tank has a hair appointment next week." Said Peebop.

"Ah good, because I think we need to be there for a planetary alignment in five weeks' time, something I found on the cube."

"Oh right, I'd better book the express service then." Said Datch pulling out his vid com.

After a few minutes of looking, Datch found a flight on a small space liner. It had six stops on the way but would only take two weeks and it had suites available.

"Err, do you guys mind sharing?"

The bikers looked at each other and nodded along with Jep and Timbo

"Yes, that will be OK." said Fred.

"I take it you will all be OK with sharing as well," he said looking at Tish, Rosey, Dapo and Hagger, they nodded.

He tapped a few more buttons and the vid com beeped Datch passed it around so it could scan their ID's. After it had read everyone's, it was handed back to Datch.

"OK, I've booked two large three-bedroom family suites for the bikers along with Timbo and Jep. The rest of us have three double rooms, is that OK?"

They all nodded and Datch pressed a button, the vid com beeped again.

"OK, we are booked in. We leave at ten in the morning from the space port in the city and then meet the liner at the space station at eleven."

"Cool," said Carina, "We'll get half an hour to look around the space station."

"Err, are we going in space?" Asked Timbo.

Datch frowned, He was about to say yes in a tone that meant run for cover but Fred stepped in first.

"Timbo, come over here and I'll explain what's happening." he said.

Fred took Timbo to the table next to them so he could explain things to him. Timbo wasn't slow, he just needed to have things explained.

"OK, so tomorrow morning we'll meet in the mall just down the road at what, ten ish near the statue in the middle?" said Tish who had put herself in charge of clothing. The rest all agreed.

Then they turned to more pressing matters such as a game of Solar Ball. Half the bar ran for cover and the other half started taking bets.

The shopping mall was huge, with long streets lined with shops and restaurants. Here and there alleyways ran off to the left and the right. It was also two stories high with elevated walkways on both sides with stairs and lifts dotted about. The majority of people did all their shopping online but a trip to the mall was an experience. The shops were more tailored to items you needed to see more than what you needed. Like an invention for this or for that which you would not have thought of even looking for. Also, there were a lot of clothing shops and boutiques. Holograms floated in the air advertising the products on sale, trying to entice you into the shops.

At ten in the morning the mall was still quiet. Datch, Carina, Tish, Dapo, Rosey and Hagger were sitting next to the statue watching the fish in the pool at its base when Jep turned up shortly followed by the bikers.

There was the normal round of good mornings, that was apart from Tish who was insisting on saying "Good morning, Shoppers." in a very bright and jolly way.

After everyone was ready Carina turned to Tish.

"Please, lead the way."

"This way shoppers." said Tish waving at them to follow her.

They headed down one of the alleys to the right. They passed a toy shop, a baby shop and an alien food store which had some very strange smells coming out. Then on the left was a brightly lit shop with 'Alien Ware' written above the door. they walked in.

The shop was full of strange clothing, some of which had more than the normal number of holes for arms or legs while others had some missing. There was a lot a different colours and styles. It was a couple of minutes before a shop assistant came over.

"Can I help you?" She asked.

"Yes, we are going to Welly four on a field trip. We need some cloths so we can fit in." Said Tish.

"Why?"

"Why what?"

"Why Welly four?"

"Because we need too!" said Tish who was slightly annoyed.

"Oh... OK, please follow me." Said the assistant with a sigh.

They followed her over to the back of the shop. There along the wall was a small rack of very boring looking clothes. They had labels on them. One was listed as a ceremonial robe. It looked like a sack with sleeves and a hood, next to it was an evening suit and that looked similar to the ceremonial robe without the hood. They went along the rack and came to the conclusion that the entire clothing range had been created by someone with zero imagination and about minus two hundred for style. You almost went to sleep looking at them.

"Err, is this it?" Asked Rosey.

"Yes, this is everything that is worn on Welly four, I should point out that they do come in a number of colours." Added the assistant.

"And what would they be then?" asked Tish looking franticly for inspiration.

The assistant picked up a colour chart at the end of the rack

"Let's see. They come in light brown, brown, dark brown, black, dark green, green and light green, light grey and dark grey. Oh, and purple."

"The light green sounds better, what sort of light green is it?" said Tish hoping for the best.

The assistant showed her a piece of green cloth. It was not bright or bursting with colour and looked like very a faded version of normal green. Tish sighed and put her thinking head on, after a couple of moments she came up with an idea.

"OK, I have a plan, everyone chooses the one that looks the most comfortable and select light grey as the colour." She whispered something in Rosey's ear, Rosey nodded and grinned.

"You do know we want to blend in, don't you?" Said Datch who was now a little suspicious about the grin.

"I know, don't worry we will." she said.

"We had better get a selection. If there is a ceremony for the alignment, we want to look the part." Jep added.

They spent the next five minutes looking through the rack. It didn't take much, they counted thirty-five different items and some of them were gender specific. They placed the order and had their measurements taken. They were told they could have them by the end of the day. Datch asked for them to be delivered to the Barbers Inn and with that they left the shop.

"Right, me and Rosey need to get some bits, we'll meet you at school." Said Tish. With that she took Rosey and headed off further into the mall.

The rest of them went over to one of the cafés for a coffee before heading back to their various places of work or school. They had all gone to part time now apart for Clax who loved his shop but even that had shorter opening hours now. After all, the credits from the band were vastly more than any they could make from a normal job and if they could keep it going a few more years then they would be set up for all of their lives, well a couple of them anyway.

The rest of the week went by quite quickly, they all spoke to their parents and got the OK to go. Their mums and dads had by now gotten used to trips away and knew that Jep and the bikers would look out for them. Hagger was also living with Tank now because his dad had been eaten by a very big spider and his mum had died when he was young. Datch's dad had told him to keep in touch and if there were any problems to let him know as he had a couple of friends in the star system nearby and gave Datch their contact information.

They also did two gigs at the Barbers Inn to make up for the fact they wouldn't be around for ten weeks and told Jim they would do two nights when they got back as well which made him feel better.

Departure Day

The weekend came and Datch got his suitcase ready. For some reason Tish had kept hold of the Welly four clothing saying that it was going to be a surprise and Rosey wasn't letting on either. Instead, they were going to be given them when they arrived at Welly four. This worried him a little and he wasn't sure why. He took the suitcase out to his bike and put it on the back before going back inside to say goodbye to his mum and dad. Afterwards he got on his bike and headed over to Carina's to pick her up. All of The Pack now had bikes and when they flew together looked like a flock of demented monsters heading across the sky. Datch had paid extra to take most of the bikes. Dapo had left his as Tish was taking hers and Rosey had left hers at home as she wanted to annoy Hagger by cuddling him at the most inappropriate moments. The bikers all took theirs. Timbo would sit behind Clax and Jep would sit on the back of Fred's. This was because for some strange reason Jep felt safer sitting behind an insurance auditor but no one was sure why.

By the time Datch and Carina arrived at the space port most of the party were there. Only Tish and Dapo hadn't turned up yet so they sat outside waiting for them and a few moments later they arrived. They took their bikes to the external check in to get them transferred to the star liner. The automated assistant first scanned them and then the bikes disappeared through a hatch. They headed around to the main entrance and went in.

The space ports main concourse was a huge open space made of steel and glass with support towers reaching high into the ceiling. Holo screens floated in the air displaying the arrivals and departures. The place was full of aliens and humans alike all heading to their flights or the exits to get a taxi somewhere. They spotted the desk with their flight number on it and headed over. There was a small queue but it only took a couple of minutes to get to the desk.

"Hello sir?"

"Hi, I'm Datch and we have a booking for Twelve on the star liner Tar Gee"

The clerk looked at him and then at the rest before tapping a few keys on the terminal in front of her.

"I have five suites, two of which are family rooms is that correct?"

"Yes, that's correct"

"Can you all step up one at a time with your baggage and have your implants scanned. Can I have the family rooms first please."

Fred, Peebop and Tank stepped up and put their bags on the baggage transporter. The clerk looked them up and down raising an eye brow. As they were scanned their bags vanished in front of them. Then it was Clax, Timbo and Jep's turn. The clerk looked at Timbo and then looked up and up again before finding his face. They were followed by Datch and Carina and then the rest. After they had all been scanned and the luggage had all vanished including a very large bag that Tish had carried, the clerk turned to them.

"OK, that's all done, if you would all like to head down there to gate twenty-three your shuttle will be boarding in approximately fifteen minutes."

"Thank you." Said Datch.

They all headed down to the gate stopping on the way to get some sweets to eat on the flight. They sat and waited until the gate opened. This was new to Datch. He had been on continental shuttles but they all left from the shuttle port not the space port. He had been here before but that was with his mum and dad and that was a military transport that had a special gate.

“What’s it like?” Asked Timbo.

“What’s what like?” Said Datch.

“Err, going into space.” Said Timbo.

“Haven’t you ever been?”

“No, this is my first time.”

“Oh, well you know when we took the shuttle to the capital two months ago and it took off.”

“Yes, it went quite high.”

“Well, this shuttle keeps going up and doesn’t come back down.”

There was a puzzled look on Timbo’s face for a moment.

“OK.” he said and went back to his own thoughts.

Datch did wonder if he had a faulty implant or something as he always needed things explained to him. It wasn’t that he was stupid, far from it, it just seemed to take him a while to get new things into his head. As road crew he took great measures to make sure that the band had everything they needed. He would do anything to make sure things happened and as he was twice the size of everyone else, they always would.

The light came on above the gate indicating that it was open so they got up and went to the door. They were scanned again before being allowed to go through. On the other side was a long glass corridor going up a slight incline. They could see the outside of the shuttle. It was a lot bigger than the ones on the Carpaycus and had two rows of windows along the side. It also had wings and was like a long tube with a pointy bit at the front. They reached the door and Datch walked inside followed by the rest of them. There was a cabin assistant directing people to the seats and Datch was told to head to row thirty seat four. He made his way down the ship with Carina behind him. They found their seats and sat down and the others filed in behind.

“Err, these seats are a little small.” Said Timbo squeezing into the seat next to Tank.

Now Tank was not the smallest of people but Timbo made him look small.

“Timbo, when we come back, I'll get you the one with extra leg room OK.” Said Datch.

“That would be good. Thank you.” he said.

After a few minutes the shuttles captain came on the ship's intercom.

“Ladies, Gentlemen and other lifeforms I am Captain Lowly and would like to welcome you aboard the orbital shuttle. We will be taking off in five minutes and the trip to the space station should take a little under thirty minutes. Please note that the space stations gravity is only two thirds of the planet and you may find walking a little strange for a few minutes until you get used to it. Myself and the crew hope you enjoy your flight.”

After a few minutes the crew shut the door and went to sit in their chairs. Then the captain came back on the intercom.

“Ladies, Gentlemen and other lifeforms. We have been cleared for departure and will be lifting off shortly. please stay seated during the flight for safety reasons, thank you.”

The ships engines started up. The whine from the engines grew louder and then Datch felt the shuttle start to move. Slowly at first and then bit by bit it started to pick up speed. A vid on the front of the compartment displayed the view outside of the ship looking forward. He could see the space port, then the city and then the nose pointed up.

Datch remembered his first flight from the space port looking out the front of the ship as the sky went from light green to black and studded with stars. This trip was a little more sedate as the shuttle moved up through the atmosphere and towards the orbiting space station. Also, this time he had Carina by his side. She was holding his hand looking at the vid. Now the sky was starting to turn black and soon stars could be seen appearing in the darkness. The shuttle turned and there in front of them was the space station. Two huge rotating discs the size of cities spinning on a central shaft which was dotted with docking elevators and ports around its centre. The shuttle started to slow as it got closer to the station. On one of the docking ports was a star liner. It was a long sleek ship and was about thirty decks high and white in colour. It had two large interspace engines at the back and its own docking port on the side. Datch looked closer and could just make out its name 'The Tar Gee'.

"That's our ship over there." he said aloud.

"Wow that's big." said Carina.

"It's not as big as the Carpaycus but yes it's big." Said Tank.

"I think it looks cool." said Hagger who had stuck his head between the seats to get a better look. Rosey poked him in the ribs and when he turned around told him to sit down.

"Does that mean we have to go straight to it?" Asked Carina.

"No, it will be taking on supplies first, fresh meat, drinks and other stuff." Said Clax.

"Yep, we'll have time to have a quick look around the station. If you like we can always book a later shuttle to the planet on the way back?" Added Datch.

"Yes, that would be cool. We could all have dinner looking over the planet." Said Carina.

“Hey, why don’t we do a gig from here at some point. I bet the vid stations on the planet would love it.” Said Dapo who was now sitting with his nose pressed against the window. He somehow had got a window seat.

“That’s not a bad idea, it should make us some good money.” said Fred.

“Yes, we could do it at as home coming gig.” Added Hagger.

“Err, we haven’t left yet.” said Rosey.

The Vid screen started displaying ‘Docking in Progress – Please stand by’

“Well, let’s see how we feel then. For now, we need to research Welly four as much as possible.” said Datch trying change the subject.

“We have two weeks for that.” Said Tank.

“Not really, most of it will be spent chilling in the bar on the liner no doubt.” Datch said with a knowing look.

“Err, can’t we do the research in there?” Asked Hagger.

Datch raised his eyebrow.

“Well, maybe but Clax needs his kit for decoding the cube.”

The shuttle shuddered.

“Not anymore, I’ve manged to copy the data to my vid comm that’s running a data cube simulation program, I just need my vid comm”

Datch let out a sigh.

“They do say that some of the best plans are created in bars.” Added Dapo.

Datch was about to continue but the vid screen displayed 'Docking complete and the captain came back on the intercom.

"Ladies, gentlemen and other lifeforms, we have now docked at the space station. Please ensure you take all your belongings with you when you disembark. Please remember on exiting that the gravity is less than on the planet and might make you a little unsteady on your feet. I hope you have enjoyed your trip and on behalf of planetary shuttles thank you for flying with us."

People started to get up and head to the front of the shuttle

"Looks like our stop" said Peebop starting to get up.

Carina was up like a rocket.

"Come on guys" she said dragging Datch along behind her.

Carina loved space and wanted to see as much as possible. Datch did too, which was why they got on so well. Deep inside them they were both explorers. It didn't take long for them to reach the shuttle door and they exited into the space station. On the other side was a lift and it took them up to the main arrivals area. Once there, they were scanned again before being able to walk out of the main doors into the main part of the station.

The doors opened out into a large cylindrical space. It was like someone had got a city and rolled it into a tube that was five kilometres across. The floor curved around and up over their heads. Buildings bridged across the centre section. Above their heads was an array of lights shining like the sun. The air had the smell of a thousand worlds and every time you breathed in, a different scent would enter your nose. They all stood looking in awe at the sight and watched as transports journeyed back and forth between the main station hubs. It was mind blowing to think something this big was floating only two hundred and fifty kilometres above their heads. Carina spoke first

"Oh wow..." she said looking up.

"Yes, it's quite something isn't it." said Clax.

"Sure is..." said Datch.

The others just nodded slowly unable to take their eyes off the scene around them.

"Err, I know we could stand here all day looking at this but, we have a starship to catch and we are standing in the doorway." said Fred who had just been elbowed in the ribs by a woman trying to exit the arrivals bay.

"Yes, let's go and find the liner and then have a drink before going on board." Suggested Datch.

"Sounds like a plan." said Clax.

They started to walk through the central core of the station. After a few minutes they found an information point and Clax asked it which way to go. The liner was docked at port nine and they had to catch a transport pod and then walk to the departure bays before heading onboard the ship. They found an elevator and headed up to the transport tubes. As it took them up towards the central hub the view was amazing with the whole vista spread out around them. They could see the intricate lines running between the buildings and parks with people going from here to there. Then there were the alien zones which were areas that had domes over them to allow different atmospheres to be created. Strange plants could be seen growing inside some of them and some had weird coloured lighting.

They reached the transport tubes and entered a pod heading to the departure bays. The transport pods were small carriages that fitted inside clear glass tubes and ran on eight sets of wheels one in each corner which sat on four rails running along inside the tube. The tubes were also depressurized allowing for high-speed transit and the whole trip took only a couple of minutes to arrive at the elevators to the departure bays.

They got out of the transport and caught an elevator down or was it up to port nine. Datch tried to work out the up and down thing but because they were in space there was no up or down. He came to the conclusion that the outside of the hull was down due to the spinning of the station so therefore they were going down to port nine even though they had been looking up to it when they arrived.

The elevator came to a stop and the doors opened. In front of them was an open space with a few shops and cafés and behind them were the gates. They walked towards the gates looking for the one they needed. They all had large illuminated numbers above them and it only took a couple of minutes to find number nine. Just outside the gate was a large café and as they still had about twenty minutes before boarding, a snack was in order along with a cup of coffee to wash it down. They sat taking in the view while they waited and watched as people and aliens came and went. They had been shown various alien races at school along with their eating and drinking habits so it came as no surprise when a Tentacon who was sitting just over from them stuck his finger in his drink and sucked the drink through it.

"Did you see that?" Said Hagger.

"Yes, he's a Tentacon, don't you remember the lecture on Tentaca star system?" Said Datch.

"Yes. but it's the first time I've been close to a proper alien."

"And what about the barman in the hotel we stayed at in the capitol two months ago?" Asked Clax.

"What about him, He was a really nice friendly guy."

"One, he had three arms and two, he was a she."

"What. No. You're joking?"

"Why do you think she gave you, her ID?"

Hagger pulled a really confused face.

"I thought he, I mean she was going to send me drinks recipes."

They all burst out laughing and Hagger went red. Even Rosey couldn't help but snigger.

It wasn't long before they heard the first departure call for the Tar Gee. They finished their drinks before getting up and heading through the departure gate to port nine.

An elevator took them down to the docking ring and then a set of moving arrows directed them along the brightly lit corridor to the airlock at port nine. They were greeted by the crew who scanned their implants before welcoming them on board. The liner was very big and they had to wait in a reception area until a steward arrived to take them to their rooms.

They followed the steward though the corridors into the heart of the ship. It was a large open area with bars, clubs and restaurants. It also had a pool and a number of sport areas including a Solar Ball suite.

"Wow, I like this already." Said Carina.

"It's really nice." Added Tish.

"Datch, you've picked a good one dude." Said Peebop.

"It does look good, I hope the rooms are close together, I did ask for it." Said Datch.

“Yes sir, they are.” added the crewman.

They followed him into a lift that took them to deck twelve which was only three floors up. They walked out onto a balcony overlooking the pool. There were a few chairs to sit on and watch the scene below if you wanted a bit of peace and quiet. They headed past them and down a short corridor.

The crewman stopped.

“Can I have Tank, Peebop and Clax.” he said.

They stepped forward.

“This is your accommodation; I hope it is to your satisfaction.”

He pressed his vid comm and the ships computer scanned their implants and the door opened.

“OK, why don’t we all meet up in about fifteen minutes at the chairs up there.” said Datch.

“Sounds like a plan dude.” said Tank heading for the door.

They went in leaving the rest in the corridor. The next room was Timbo’s, Fred’s and Jep’s. The crewman turned to the opposite side of the corridor, Rosey and Hagger were next followed by Tish and Dapo and finally Datch and Carina.

“Thank you.” said Datch.

“If there is anything else that I can help you with while you’re on board, just let me know, my name is Clantry.”

“Thank you Clantry.” They turned and went in.

The suite was small but nice. It had a bedroom off to the side with a king size bed. To the side of that was a shower room combined with a toilet. The main area had a coffee table with two sofa’s and on the opposite wall a large vid screen. Back near the door was a drink’s making area and a communications panel. They sat down on the sofa; this was going to be home for two weeks.

“So, what do you think?” Asked Datch.

“I was hoping for a window so I can see the stars but the rest is OK.” said Carina putting her arms around him.

“The ship has a star lounge where we can sit eating and drinking looking out into space if that helps.”

“That would be cool, can we have dinner there tonight?”

“Sure babes.” he said and kissed her.

A force field appeared in the centre of the room as a column of light before slowly expanding out to make a large circle and then their luggage popped into existence in front of them.

“Looks like it’s time to unpack.” said Carina pulling herself away from Datch.

“Yes, we’d better or the others will be waiting for us.”

They set about putting the contents of the cases into the drawers provided. A message pinged on the vid com and Datch went over to look at it. It was a message telling him the bikes were in the hold. It beeped again. It was another telling them how to book the tables in the various restaurants and activities. They booked dinner in the star lounge and ten minutes later they were heading down the corridor to the seats near the elevator. Tank, Clax and Peebop were already there.

“How’s your room guys?” Asked Datch walking up.

“It’s OK but I wouldn’t want to live in it. it’s just a little small for my liking.” Said Tank.

“It is, what, it is.” Added Clax.

Just then Rosey and Hagger came up the corridor followed just after by Tish and Dapo

“Hi guys, are we going to get something for lunch? I’m still feeling a bit hungry.” said Hagger.

“Yes, we can do that. Why don’t we head to the star lounge, we should be in time see our departure.” said Datch.

Timbo came walking up the corridor with two pairs of extra legs walking along behind him. When he arrived, it turned out the extra legs were attached to Fred and Jep.

“OK, let’s go.” Said Hagger who had missed breakfast due to not getting up when he was told.

He turned towards the lift before realizing he didn’t know where to go.

“Go where?” said Timbo who was just getting the hang of being here.

“For food.” said Tank.

“Oh good.” he said smiling.

Datch called the elevator.

“I think if we go three floors down, we should come out on the main floor.” he said.

They got in the lift and sure enough, three floors down was the main promenade. They walked out and tried to get their bearings that is except for Timbo who just stood looking at the big ornamental water fall at the end of the pool.

“Come on Timbo. Lunch!” Said Clax.

“OK.” he said and followed them across to the promenade.

The Star Lounge was very big but narrow and ran down the side of the ship. It had large glass windows that looked out into space. As they walked in a waiter came over.

"Good day. Do you have a reservation?"

"Err no, we've just come on board and were hoping for a table to watch the departure?"

"Certainly sir. We have plenty of space at the moment. But may I suggest that in the evening you make a reservation as it can get very busy."

"I've already done it for this evening."

"Thank you, sir, it makes my job a lot easier. Please follow me."

He took them down the room to a very large table before taking their drinks orders.

They sat looking at the view outside. It was part of the space station and behind it the planet. Because the space station rotated so did the ships docked with it. This had a hypnotising effect as the planet slowly moved across the windows before going out of sight for a few minutes and then reappearing again at the opposite end. They finally got around to ordering food and it had just arrived when the captain came on the ship's intercom.

"Good afternoon, this is your Captain speaking. I would first like to welcome all the new passengers aboard the Tar Gee. We will shortly be releasing the docking clamps and departing from the Bellatrixian station before accelerating to interspace factor eighteen. Thank you for choosing the Tar Gee and I hope you have a pleasant trip with us."

"Oh cool, we can watch the departure." Said Carina getting all excited.

A few moments later the docking tunnel disconnected from the docking port and the ship started to move slowly backwards edging its way out until it had cleared the stations docking ring. The ship then turned to face the stars with the station alongside of them and the planet as a backdrop. The captain came back on the intercom.

"Ladies, Gentlemen and other lifeforms. We have cleared the station and we'll be leaving orbit shortly before heading to Datum three. Please pay attention to the lights, they will dim momentarily before we engaged the main drive system. You may feel a slight loss of gravity as we go to interspace factor eighteen, so when the lights dim, please stand still to avoid any accidents. Thank you."

The ship started to move again leaving the space station behind and soon the planet started to slip away as well.

"Wow we're leaving." Said Carina who was watching the view intensely.

Datch watched as the planet slowly disappeared and suddenly realised that he was leaving home behind. He had been to gigs on the other side of the planet but it was still on the planet. This was different, His mum, dad and home were on that planet. Now he only had The Pack. He was lost in his thoughts for a moment before Carina poked him.

"Hey lover." she said.

Datch looked at her

"Sorry babes. I was thinking"

"This is amazing."

Datch smiled and put his arm around her.

"Yes, our first time away from home." he said.

Dapo and Tish looked at him across the table.

"You OK Datch?" Tish asked.

"Yes, I'm good."

Outside there was now nothing but stars and then the lights dimmed. All of a sudden Tish grabbed the table, Timbo broke wind and Hagger burped along with Tank.

"What was that?" Said Tish.

"That was interspace factor eighteen." Said Datch.

"Is that going to happen a lot?" said Rosey.

"What Timbo breaking wind, quite possibly." Said Clax.

"No. The wobbly thing?"

"Oh that. No, only when we arrive at or leave a planet."

"Oh wow, look at the stars."

The stars had starting moving slowly past. They sat watching while they finished off their food.

"OK who's up for some Solar Ball?" asked Datch.

"I'm in." said Dapo.

Rosey, Tish, Hagger and Carina were also in but the biker's, Jep and Timbo went to the bar next door.

After the Solar Ball they headed back to their rooms to get changed for the pool. By the time they had got back the rest of The Pack were sitting around a couple of tables on the artificial beach next to the pool. They also seemed to be making the most of the bar as they had already polished off one round of drinks and were starting on the next.

"Datch." shouted Tank "There is a round of drinks for you dudes here."

The six of them joined the rest of The Pack to have a drink before getting in the pool. The pool area had its own outdoor bar and food area along with seating and even some changing rooms in case you didn't want to go back to your room. High up above the pool was a large glass dome and through it you could just about make out the stars going by. The pool itself was about thirty metres by twenty metres and at one end of the pool was the beach. The other end of the pool tapered down to 15 metres where there was a large waterfall cascading down an artificial cliff before crashing onto the rocks at the bottom and flowing into the pool. The area was so realistic and brightly lit that you could find yourself thinking you were outside on a hot sunny day. There was even a light breeze and you could get a sun tan if you sat there long enough.

Datch sat looking around and then he spotted Timbo staring at the clock with a puzzled look on his face.

"Timbo, are you OK?" he asked.

"Err. I think that clocks wrong." he said.

"No, it's not wrong. We're on ship time."

"Ship Time?" he said still looking very puzzled.

Datch decided to explain.

"Yes, ship time. It's a twenty-hour clock and is the same for every ship in space. That way everyone who travels a lot gets used to having the same length of day and night."

"Oh, I wondered that myself." Said Rosey.

"Yes, me too." Added Hagger.

"Do you get it now?" Datch asked.

"I think so." Timbo said giving the clock a hard look. The other two just nodded.

“You know when you’re puzzled by something you can just ask your implant.”

“No.” said Timbo.

“OK, I know you have an implant as you got ID scanned and you did go to school, didn’t you?”

“Err, yes, but I didn’t learn anything on account of getting into trouble a lot for not paying attention.”

There is always at least one in every class who doesn’t pay attention and Timbo appeared to be that one. Datch thought about this for a moment.

“OK. Look, as we are all together for the next seven to eight weeks at least, why don’t we all teach you how to use your implant?”

Timbo looked at the others who were now all looking at him.

“Do I have to?”

“YES!” They all said in unison.

“OK, when do I start?” he said reluctantly.

“I think tomorrow morning would be a good idea after breakfast. Then we can all do some research with Clax before chilling in the afternoon. How does that sound?”

“OK.” Said Timbo. The others all nodded.

Datch took another sip of beer before heading to the pool with Carina, Tish and Dapo. The rest of the afternoon went past very quickly and they had arranged to meet in the star lounge for dinner at 16:00 (19:30).

The star lounge was busy and they had to wait to get a table big enough to get them all on it. After ordering the food and drinks they sat watching the stars go by. Carina turned to Datch.

"If you had told me when I started school that we would be travelling across the stars in search of mystical gem, I would have laughed at you. But here we are on a starship flying through space. It's amazing."

"I sometimes can't believe it myself but it just seems to happen."

"You're telling me, we seem to be living life at a fast pace that's for sure." added Fred.

"Well, the rest of the lecturers back at home are taking bets on what we're going to end up doing this time." said Jep.

"Like what?" Asked Clax.

"Well, the list starts with us blowing up Welly four, then here's us severely damaging their culture, then us getting lost in space somewhere, as well as conquering the star system, and also another one we get thrown in jail and end up saving the Galaxy. Oh, and the last I heard, Welly four being blown up was favourite."

The others sat looking at him.

"Really?" Said Rosey looking at Jep in disbelief.

"Before anyone says anything, we are not blowing up any planets or star systems OK!" Said Fred.

Datch sat thinking for a moment and decided to add,

"No, we're here to find the gem not blow up a planet."

"What about a small moon?" Said Dapo with grin.

"NO!" Said Tish and then realised he was joking.

“I think we should focus on what we need to do when we get there. So, let’s just chill tonight and talk about other things. Tomorrow, we start learning about Welly four.”

They sat again looking out into space. The view was mesmerizing. They were drawn to the stars as they floated past outside.

“I wonder how many of them have planets with life on?” asked Carina in a dreamy sort of way.

“Statically its one in every hundred star systems.” said Fred without looking away from the view.

“It’s amazing that the universe is so full of life, it looks so peaceful and quiet.” Added Rosey.

“Yes, but lot of it is basic life. Intelligent life is one in a thousand.”

The food came out and they tucked into it.

In the morning after breakfast, it was still very quiet so they decided to sit in one of the bars taking over a couple of tables in one corner. The first hour was spent getting Timbo to use his implant. As soon as he found out how easy it was to find things out, he really took to it and couldn’t understand why he hadn’t learnt about it before. Then it was time for Welly four training.

“So,” Said Datch “let’s start with basics. I know we as students have had a basic guide to visiting Welly, but I think we need to go over it again for the others. Also, just to refresh ourselves a bit because we fell asleep in the lecture due to it being so boring. We never thought we would be going there anyway. Jep?”

Jep looked at them, they looked at him.

"Err, me?"

"Yes, you're the lecturer who did that piece on eating out there." Said Tish.

"Oh, yes, I suppose I did. OK." He paused for a moment and then cleared his throat.

"Right, to start with there is no music as such on Welly as it was banned thousands of years ago, no one knows why but it was, so it might be a good idea not to sing anything in public or we might get in trouble. The locals are very plain people and don't take kindly to outsiders breaking their rules."

"What no singing at all?" asked Dapo.

"No, not in public."

"Oh crap, that's going to be hard!" said Rosey.

"Yes, it does sort of go against who we are." agreed Carina.

"I know but that's their law."

At this point Clax put his hand up. He wasn't sure why but he felt he had to say something.

"Err, lucky for us we're going into the desert."

"Desert?" Asked Tank.

"Yes, the monastery which has the books we need to look at, is in the middle of the Jac-jar-jas-dabs-Hebis Desert."

"The what?" said Fred.

"I'm not going to say that again." Said Clax.

"I don't blame you." Added Jep.

"Let's just go with desert J."

"Sounds good to me. So how big is this J?" asked Tank.

"Err, about three thousand kilometres across."

"So, we have to travel across one thousand five hundred kilometres of desert to visit some monks who may not want to see us when we get there?" Said Rosey.

"Err, yes."

"OK. I think we need to do some basic desert training as well then. Any ideas?"

"Yes, I know what to do." Said Datch.

Everyone turned to look at him.

"My Dad told me what to do just in case my bike broke down in the desert at home."

"OK so, tomorrow can you give us a brief run down?"

"Sure."

The rest of the morning was spent going over some of the basic customs and then it was time for lunch followed by an afternoon chilling by the pool. This time though the bikers and Timbo joined them in the water. In the evening dinner was followed by the cabaret with some singer who was quite good but not The Packs style so they relocated to another bar to chill out watching the vid.

The following day they were just finishing lunch when the captain came on the ship intercom.

"Ladies, Gentlemen and other life forms we will be arriving at Datum three port seven in thirty minutes. Please can I asked that everyone leaving us at this stop ensures all of you luggage is ready for transport and that you do not leave anything behind. For those passengers staying on board the space station is above the third planet in this system which is a jungle world and can be seen out of the star lounge. Please be aware we will be disengaging the interspace drive in about fifteen minutes and the lights will dim just before. Please stand still while this process happens to avoid any accidents. Thank You."

"Oh cool. Are we going to stop here and watch?" Said Carina.

"I don't see why not, let's get another round of drinks in?" Said Tank.

Datch tapped the panel in the middle of the table and ordered another round.

"I believe that the planet is home to the Actora race who live in small villages suspended above the jungles or in cities high in the mountains. The temperature is about thirty-five degrees most of the time and very humid with it." said Clax.

"Wow, that's amazing how do you know that?" asked Carina.

"I stopped over here once to do some business and spent a few days sightseeing while I was at it."

"Was it good?" asked Datch who's only trip so far to another planet which had involved him nearly dying and the planet was a desolate hell hole.

"Yes, but the humidity gets to you. it's not a dry heat like it is back at home. You end up sweating buckets."

"So, what did you see there?" Asked Carina who was now really interested.

"Well, I took a flight across the great ocean, it goes right around the planet like a giant ring and is two thousand miles across. I also went into the jungle to see some of the animals there. It was quiet something. Their economy is based on food production, where as their sister world Datum six is very high tech."

“And we’re going to Welly four.” Said Tish who wished she was getting off at this point.

“Yes, but I’m sure that will be fun as well.” Said Tank.

Tish just looked at him as if to say really.

Clax continued his story and then the lights dimmed.

“Hold on everyone!” Said Datch.

Hagger burped and there was a feeling of butterflies in their stomachs for a moment and then the ship started to turn.

Slowly a large disc started to appear at the front of the ship getting larger and larger until it was a bright shining sphere in the blackness of space. You could see the great ocean that looked as if it cut the planet in two and on either side of the sea was a green lush paradise which slowly turned to browns and finally white at the north and south poles. Then the space station appeared. It was bigger than the one at Bellatrix five and was shaped like a large cylinder with docking ports dotted along the hull. The Tar Gee matched the stations speed and slowly dropped towards the cylinder. It took a couple of minutes before the ship docked. The docking ring was staying still while the rest of the station was rotating creating gravity for everyone inside. They watched for a while as the planet rolled by in front of them before going off to have a game of Solar Ball.

The two weeks were taken up with Timbo’s training sessions in the morning which took place in a small bar that served breakfast. After that it was learning about Welly four and what they could expect to find when they got there. Also, some of the greetings and customs as well as how to ask for directions in the local language in case anyone got lost. Then it would be lunch time which was spent at the bar next to the pool. The Pack had sort of taken over a number of tables near the bar so they didn’t have to move far for a refill. This was followed by Solar Ball and swimming in the pool in the afternoons. In the evening would be a choice of the disco bar, Karaoke bar, Sports bar or the cabaret depending on what they fancied. If nothing else it was a relaxing trip.

Welly four

The two weeks passed very quickly and then it was time for Welly four. They got up early in the morning and had breakfast before heading back up to the balcony overlooking the pool to wait for Tish and Rosey. They were going to give them their Welly four clothes. It wasn't long before Rosey and Tish came walking up the corridor with a large bag.

"Are we ready for the adventure?" Said Tish smiling.

"I don't know yet." Said Datch "you've got our clothes."

They laughed.

"OK Mr Datch, you're first then." Said Tish reaching into her bag.

What she pulled out was not a surprise. It didn't look like they had done anything. Datch took it and looked at it.

"I thought you were going to fix it up a bit?" he said looking at her.

"We have, turn it inside out." said Rosey

He did and the top transformed into a brightly coloured shirt with The Pack embroidered on the lapel. It also had the bands logo on the back in big green flaming letters.

"Oh wow." Said Carina.

"Not only that but they have full climate control systems built in so we won't get too hot or cold. The climate control has a link to your implant so it will keep you at a happy temperature. Oh, and they have their own sound systems."

Datch turned it the dull side out and tried it on.

"What do you think, will I pass for a local?"

They looked him up and down.

“Well, you look like one, I’ll say that.” Said Fred.

“Yes, not bad to be honest.” Said Jep.

“OK let’s see what we all look like. Let’s head back to our rooms and all get changed.” Said Datch.

With that Rosey and Tish handed out all the clothes and everyone headed back to their rooms to put them on. Five minutes later they were all back and looking like a large group of really boring people with zero taste in clothes.

“Well, at least we should fit in.” Said Datch.

“Yes, but it doesn’t feel like us.” Said Dapo.

“I know but we need to look the part.” Added Tank.

“OK, let’s head to the bar and go over the plan again.” Said Datch.

Two minutes later they were in the bar with a round of drinks in front of them.

“Right, everyone, listen to Jep. We need to get this right.”

Jep cleared his throat.

“OK, so we’re here on a field trip from the university of Mangolla on Bellatrix five and we are studying the rituals and customs of other cultures. We are here to find out more about the ancient religious order of monks living in the High desert. OK so far everyone?”

There was a round of nodding

“Right, the bikers and myself are senior faculty members and you are all post grad students, finally Timbo is our support manager. We are going to head to the desert using the bikes. Everyone did bring the desert-coloured paint, didn't they?"

There was a number of blank looks.

"It's all good." said Datch "I have extra in my case."

"You mean we have to paint the bikes?" Said Peebop looking horrified.

"Don't panic, it's only a temporary paint made of nano bots and to get rid of it, I just touch your bike with a little device and it all goes away. The nano bots will even clean your bike in the process."

There was a sigh of relief from the bikers.

Jep Continued,

"OK. Does everyone know their titles and field of research?"

Everyone got little cards out and waved them at him, that is apart from Timbo who got a little badge out and pinned it to his shirt.

"Another round of drinks before departure I think." said Fred.

They sat having the drinks and going over things when the captain came on the ship's intercom.

"Ladies, Gentlemen and other lifeform. We will be arriving at Welly four in approximately thirty minutes. Can everyone leaving us please here ensure you have all your items ready for transport. The lights will dim before the ship slows for arrival. Thank you for travelling with the Tar Gee and we look forward to seeing you again soon."

"OK, Looks like our stop." Said Clax "Drink up everyone."

They finished their drinks and headed back to their rooms.

“Are you ready for this Babes?” Asked Datch when they got back to their room.

“Yes.” said Carina “I can’t wait to step foot on another world.”

“I’m buzzing a bit too.” he said.

He was also trying to put the thoughts of the last world he had been to out of his head.

They put their baggage in the centre of the room just as the lights dimmed.

“Well, we’re here, time to go.” Said Datch.

They waited until the lights came back up before Datch pressed a button in the ships coms panel to let them know their luggage was ready for transport. The bags disappeared and they stepped out into the corridor to wait for the others. They soon appeared and they headed down to the docking port.

They left the Tar Gee and headed along the docking corridor and into the space station. It was a lot smaller than any of the other space stations they had seen on the way. It was more of an orbital platform than anything else. It had about twenty floors and they mostly consisted of cargo decks. The station was dimly lit and reminded Datch of the alley at the back of the Barbers Inn. It had piles of junk sitting outside of the bays just like the rubbish waiting to be collected by the disposal droids. They went through to the shuttle area and found the ship to take them to the surface. It wasn’t hard to find as there was only one of them. After all the luxury of the past two weeks it was very basic and was more like a bus station. They got onboard the shuttle ready to head down to the surface.

The shuttle was a cargo shuttle with a passenger bay added on and it seemed to be an afterthought. Yes, it had seating and a vid screen to watch the view outside but that was it. They had just sat down when the shuttle took off and started to head for the planet.

“Are you sure this is safe?” said Tish looking at some paint that was peeling off the wall.

“Yes, it is a bit of a rust bucket but I’m sure it’s fine.” Said Fred just as the shuttle lurched to the side.

“Are you sure?” Said Dapo.

“All the shuttles are like this here,” added Clax, “it was one like this I went on a hundred years ago.”

“Looking at the state of this one, it might be the same one.” Said Tank.

The shuttle lurched back the opposite way.

The shuttle took about fifteen minutes to descend and all the way down it lurched from sided to sided. Finally, it reached the surface and landed. They all breathed a sigh of relief and then disembarked.

The space port was very small with the main arrival’s hall being about the same size as a small supermarket. They came to the immigration station and waited until an officer came out. Jep stepped forward to speak.

“Good afternoon, sir, we are the research party from Bellatrix five.”

The officer looked blankly at him and then at the others.

“Welcome to Welly four, I’m afraid I haven’t been told you were coming. Is it a state sponsored trip?”

“No, the university on Bellatrix five is paying for it. I hope it’s not going to cause any problems; we have come a very long way.”

“What is it you have come to research sir?”

"We're here hoping to meet with the monks in the great desert and learn about some of their ancient rituals."

"Hmm, well I'm not sure if that will happen but you're welcome to try. Can you please follow all our laws while you're here? We don't have many visitors but we do like the ones who come to behave."

"Oh, most certainly sir. We have been researching all of your customs while on the way here."

"Excellent. Now please can you take me through the members of your party so I can fill in the paperwork."

"Yes, I am Professor Jep Doji leader of the party and head of religious studies."

"Thank you and this gentleman is?" he said looking at Tank.

"Dr Bertrum Angor. He's our Professor in Religious statues."

Datch, Carina and Tish had to turn around to hide the grins on their faces. Everyone knew Tank was a nickname but now they knew why. He waited until the officer had written it down.

"And this is ..."

He went through the gang until everyone had been noted down.

"Thank you very much. If you please wait a minute while I enter you on the computer and print out your visas."

The officer went back into the office.

"Err, why didn't he just scan us?" Asked Hagger when the officer had gone.

"Most people don't have implants here so they still put things on paper. You'll find some places where the implants don't work." Said Clax.

There was a moment while everyone tried it just to check.

"It does seem slower than normal."

"Yes, there seems to be a bit of a delay before it comes back with the information."

"So, what's the name of the hotel we're going to then?"

"Err, The bucket." Said Clax who had booked the hotel for them.

"The Bucket!" Said Tank.

"Well yes, they don't have very good names here and the hotel is the highest quality."

"How many stars?" Asked Tank.

"Well, three stars and that is the top of the range here."

"Three stars?" Asked Tish.

"Well, they don't have much in the way of visitors."

"So, what do we get?"

"The room and a small bar."

"What about food?"

"Well, it's a bit basic but OK to eat."

"Oh, why did we come here!" Said Rosey.

At this point the officer came back out of the office with a number of bits of paper.

"Can I have your attention please."

The others all turned around.

"Here are your documents, please keep them on you at all times. Your visas will last for one month. If you require to be here longer then you must get your papers renewed before they expire. I've listed your place of residence as the Bucket, it's a very posh hotel and I'm sure you'll enjoy your stay there. Welcome to Welly four."

He started handing out the paper work to the various members of the party. When he had finished, they thanked him for his help and headed to collect the luggage. They had to go to the outside collection point because of the bikes. Datch showed everyone how to apply the temporary paint to them. They loaded the bikes up with their luggage and got on.

After a few minutes of messing around they finally got the bikes nav com to except 'The Bucket's' location and took to the sky. As they increased in altitude Carina said.

"Look at the sky it's blue."

It was a light blue not a light green as it was on Bellatrix five.

"It's because of the gases in the upper atmosphere, these are different to ours. Don't worry though. It's still OK to breathe." Said Jep.

"It looks cool." Added Rosey.

The bikes reached cruising altitude and levelled off.

The landscape below was somewhat uninhabited and was mostly farm land. Most of the trees had large leaves and resembled palm trees similar to the ones at home. Here and there was a farm house or a small village tucked away in amongst the trees and fields. Linking between them were a network of roads. Bellatrix five had roads but they tended to be only main roads in the countryside as most vehicles flew everywhere. Here on Welly four things were a bit more ancient and most people got around on small electric vehicles or horse and carts. No one was sure what happened to Welly four but around twenty thousand years ago the whole planet went from being a very proactive space faring culture to a stagnant one overnight. It was as if the population's spark had been taken from them. The whole planet went back to the dark ages within a few years.

In the distance a town came into view. As they approached the outskirts the place looked very old with none of the bright lights you would see back home. The houses were very plain looking and all the shops just had their names painted above the doors and a window to look in. No Holo screens trying to entice you in with brightly coloured displays or vid panels showing the latest offers. The streets were clean but empty and the place was very quiet. The bikes dropped lower and came in for a landing in front of a four-story building with an ornate wooden front. Above the door was a sign saying 'The Bucket' with a picture of a bucket underneath. They got off the bikes and walked in through the main door.

The hotel was somewhat dated to say the least. The main lobby had a number of chairs that were so old even the moths had moved out of them for better premises. There was a small bar to the side of the lobby which had a bartender who looked as if he was gathering dust for a living and had the sort of personality that would make you want to move planets. The reception area was a small desk and behind it was a small old man with a long beard. They walked up to him.

"Good morning, sorry afternoon, sir. We have reservations for The Pack." Said Clax.

The old man looked at them for a moment eyeing them up and down.

"One second sir, I will check the book."

He opened a large book on the desk.

“Ah yes, here it is. six double rooms. How long are you going to be staying?”

“We are staying until after the planetary alignment but will be going into the desert for a few days on an expedition and maybe a few other places from time to time. We will however be using the hotel as a base of operations while on Welly four.”

The old man looked unimpressed.

“We will be paying for the rooms until we depart for home.” Clax added.

“Can I see all your visas please?” said the man.

They all handed their papers to the old man. He looked at them and wrote down some details in the book.

“Thank you. Here are your room keys and you’re all on the first floor. Dinner is served between seven and nine at night and breakfast is eight to nine thirty in the morning. We would also like to have your meal orders as soon as possible so the chef can have the food ready for you.”

“Err, do you have any menus?” asked Datch.

“Yes sir.”

The old man gave them all a bit of card with menu printed on it.

“Is this todays menu?” Asked Carina.

“No, that is the menu.” Replied the man looking at her as if she was stupid.

It suddenly dawned on them that the menu didn’t change.

“Oh.” Said Tank.

“We’ll just take our bags to our rooms then and come to the bar to discuss it before ordering if that’s OK.”

“I’m sure it will be OK, sir.”

With that the old man shut the book and went to a room behind reception. Datch wondered if it was for a nap. He looked like he needed one.

“Well let’s meet back in the bar in say fifteen minutes.” Said Clax.

They picked up their bags and headed for the stairs. The hotel didn’t have a lift.

“When you said this was a three-star hotel, I take it the stars are the stick-on type that fall off after five minutes!” said Datch trying to carry both his and Carina’s bag up the stairs.

Clax looked around the hotel just to be sure it wasn’t some sort of a joke and then looked up at Datch who had reached the first landing.

“Yes, I think they were but I would hate to see a one star.” he said reluctantly.

A corridor ran the length of the building with another flight of stairs going up. They turned left down the corridor and headed towards their rooms. Datch’s and Carina’s room was first, the door had a proper key and they had to unlock the door before they went in.

The room was basic and that was making it sound good. It had two single beds and a dresser in the corner. The dresser had a bowl on it with a jug of water and a small mirror along with a number of little leaflets. Datch picked them up and found one detailing the facilities that were available in the hotel.

“Err, where is the en-suite?” Asked Carina.

"Well, according to this, the en-suite is down the corridor, second on the right, first left and please knock first."

"Oh, I really wanted a shower."

"Looking at this, the only shower we're going to get is if it starts to rain or we find a water fall somewhere."

"And this is one of the better hotels." She added.

"I think a one star must be a tent or something. Anyway, we had better hurry up so we can head down stairs."

They pushed the two beds together and sorted their backpacks out before freshening up by splashing water on their faces, after which they headed down to the bar.

The bar was basic and had only bottled beer and a few spirits that had to be measured out. There was no vid and the seating was somewhat dated and would have not been out of place in a museum. Well, let's be honest, it looked like no one had touched it in a hundred years. There was almost as much dust on them as there was in Clax's office.

Datch and Carina walked up to the bar and the barman came over to them.

"Can I help you?" he said in a way that made you think he had been dragged away from something important. The room was empty.

"Yes, two beers please." Said Datch.

"Please can I have your room number."

"Yes, it's six." He turned to a fridge behind him and got out two bottles with rubber stoppers in. He turned back to face them placing the two bottles on the bar along with two glasses.

"Thank you." Said Datch.

"You're welcome." said the barman and then turned back to the really important job of starring out of the window.

Datch looked out the window in case something interesting was happening. There wasn't.

They sat down and Datch opened his beer and poured it into his glass. They both looked at it. It was dark brown and looked nothing like the nice light golden coloured beer they were used to.

"Well, go on then." Prompted Carina who wanted to see the look on Datch's face before she tried hers.

Datch took a sip and pulled a really odd face.

"Is it that bad?" She asked.

"Err, well its different that's for sure. It tastes more organic I think but I think it will grow on me." he took another sip.

"Yes, I think I can live with it."

Carina opened hers and was just about to take a sip when Clax walked in.

"I see you're trying the local ale. Barman, four beers please the room number is nine."

Tank came walking in followed by Fred and Jep. They went and collected their beers from the barman before sitting down.

"So, what do you think of it?" Said Clax pointing at the beer.

"It's OK, but I prefer the stuff we get at home." said Datch.

It wasn't long before the rest came down and they started to discuss what the next move was. By dinner time they had sorted out the details of the next part of the trip and headed to the dining room for food.

The dining room was in better shape than the bar and the food was again basic but did however taste good and they all had asked for a large portion as it was going to be a few days before they were going to be back. The main course was a selection of steak, a stew, cabbage type pie and a fish salad with cabbage. Everyone had gone for steak apart from Hagger who had the stew and Rosey who had gone for the salad. They sat looking at the food. The stew appeared to be potatoes, some sort of meat, carrots and cabbage. The salad had the normal things with some sort of fish and grated cabbage.

“They like their cabbage, don’t they?” Said Jep looking at his steak which had also come with a small helping of cabbage.

“Yes, it’s a local past time growing cabbage. They even have cabbage growing competitions.” Said Clax.

“I’m really starting to see why this is the most boring place in the universe. Even the food looks dull.” Added Fred.

They finished their meals and headed out to find a shop. The shops were open late so all the farmers could get things they needed. The Pack were after supplies for the trip. Clax had got hold of some military rations but they were looking for something to spice them up a bit. The shops did seem to have a variety of food and they got hold of some fresh fruit and a few vegetables that Clax said would go well with the rations. They decided to have a walk around the town and then afterwards decided not to do it ever again. The houses all looked the same as did the streets. In fact, the only remotely interesting place was the town centre.

All the roads ran into the centre of the town where there was a large circular area with strange symbols carved into the ground. There were nine concentric circles with a large obelisk in the centre. Datch stood looking at it.

“What have you spotted?” Asked Carina who had noticed his interest.

“The symbols, the three over there look similar to the one’s on the cube. Clax?”

“What?”

“Look!” he said pointing at them.

“Oh, yes they look like the ones on the cube, one second.” He got out his vid com and scanned the symbols, it bleeped.

“So?”

“Yes, they are the same, but there are not enough for the vid to decipher them. It needs some points of reference.”

They all stood looking at the obelisk. Then one of the locals came walking by.

Clax turned to him and asked him what it was.

“That’s one of the old mystic spires that legends say use to bring happiness and prosperity to the planet. All rubbish of course. It’s just a symbol of times gone by.”

“Hmm, Interesting… Thank you.”

Clax said and the man trudged off.

“Do you think it is connected?” asked Datch.

“I don’t know.” said Clax.

They scanned all the symbols in the area just to be sure they didn’t miss anything.

Then they headed back to the hotel bar to try some more beer in the hope that it might start tasting better.

Sand Gets Everywhere

The sun came up and a number of cockerels decided to make sure the population was awake by making as much noise as possible. Datch opened an eye. Carina was in bed with him and as it was a single it was a bit cramped. He lay there thinking that it might be handy to have a plasma canon right now and cancel the external alarm call. Carina lived on a farm but the roosters there were a lot more discrete and knew when to shut up. She opened an eye and looked at him.

"Morning lover boy." She said and got off the bed.

"Morning babes."

"What time is it?

"Not sure, but it just got light I think."

"And where is the toilet?"

"Down the hall, second on the right, first left and please knock first."

"Oh. I had better get dressed then." She put her clothes on and trudged out the door.

Datch got up and then followed her. There was a queue.

The breakfast was going to be served in about an hour so people had a chance to get themselves ready for the day ahead.

After breakfast they went to reception and informed the hotel that they would be gone for a few days. They fetched their bags and headed out to the bikes. It was going to be a three-day ride into the desert and it was going to be hot. They all had extra water bottles and extra food. The bikes had all been fitted with extra racking on both sides and now looked more like pack mules with the amount of extra equipment and supplies on them. They mounted up and started the engines.

“So, who’s on lead?” Asked Tank.

“I think Clax should as he’s been to this planet before.” Said Datch.

“Err, I’m not sure how that qualifies me as it was only here for two days and the opposite side of the planet.” said Clax.

“Yes, but a least you have been here before. None of us have ever set foot on this planet.” Said Carina.

“Fred has.”

“Sorry, I only visited the space station to fill out some forms. I never came down to the surface.”

“Oh... OK, point taken. I’ll do it.”

The bikes took to the sky and a lot of the local wildlife ran for cover. They set the bikes for follow and after a few seconds they formed up in a row and headed out over the fields with Clax in the lead. The navigation system was not happy. This planet didn’t have a full planetary navigation grid and therefore it was not sure where it was. It had to rely on the pilot knowing where he was going. The navigation system also knew how The Pack flew and was very worried in an AI kind of way. Clax wasn’t sure either and had spent that last two hours looking at maps just in case they got lost. He was now hoping he had worked it out correctly. The bikes flew over fields, forests, towns and villages. There were no big cities at least not on this part of the planet. After a few hours they landed for a bite of lunch. Clax had spotted a town with a bar that did food and surprisingly it was marked in a guide book. The bikes swooped down landing outside.

The bar was a bit brighter than the rest of the buildings nearby with brightly painted windows and a decked area outside which had benches and sun parasols. They went in and up to the bar. Behind the counter was a middle-aged man who smiled when they came in.

"Can we have a beer please?" Asked Clax

"Sure thing. Do you want import or local?" the barman said in a cheerful way.

"Import!" they all said in a hurry.

"I take it you're from off world?" he said pulling the first beer.

"Yes, Bellatrix five." Said Tank.

"I'm from that part of the universe myself. Only a hundred or so light years from there."

After they had got the beers, they went and sat outside apart from Clax who stood at the bar. After Clax had a good drink of beer the barman enquired.

"What are you folks doing here? you're a bit of the beaten track."

"Oh, we're on our way to the desert on a university trip to meet the monks."

"What monks?"

"The ones at Quaki."

"Oh, that weird bunch."

"What do you mean?"

"Well, on this planet people don't sing or dance and are generally very boring. Them lot, they chant a lot and have a strange dance. They say it was from before the dark times. Weird if you ask me."

"Are we on the right track?"

“If you’re heading south, yes. I take it them bikes can move so you should hit the desert just before night fall.” He paused “That is if you stop for another beer and food.”

“I think you can say we will. Err, I hate to ask but do you do any food without cabbage?”

“I have a good chicken curry.” The barman said in a quiet voice.

Clax nodded and walked over to the table were everyone had sat down. he said quietly.

“Err, anyone want a good curry?”

There was a lot of nodding. Clax walked back to the bar.

“Curries all round please.” He wasn’t sure why he was whispering because the bar was empty.

The curries came out along with flat bread. They had bread sticks and dips as well. They all tucked into the food and it didn’t last long. After the food they had another three more beers each apart from Clax who needed to navigate. They thanked the owner for the food and drinks before heading back to the bikes.

Six hours later the terrain bellow started to turn to scrub land and soon the desert was in sight. They slowed the bikes and came into land where the sands started and the scrub finished. The sun was starting to set and it would be dark soon. They got their tents off the bikes and placed them on the ground. A quick press of a button and a tent appeared. They had seven two-man tents. This was because Tank and Timbo had one each.

They set up the camp in a circle so all the tents were facing each other. The bikers went and got some wood so they could have a fire in the centre. After all, it could get cold in the desert at night.

Carina and Rosey sorted out some food and Clax got out some beers from his bike and handed them around.

"Hey, proper beer." Said Dapo.

"Yes, I have a number of packs in the back of my bike."

"That's a good idea, I should have got some too." Said Timbo.

"You don't think I would leave out the important supplies, do you?"

They all got handed a bottle and sat around the camp fire eating and drinking.

Datch turned to Carina.

"So, we're on an alien planet what do you think?"

She looked up at the stars, none of them looked at all like the ones at home. Yes, they were still stars, but all the patterns were different and there was a nebula visible cutting across part of the sky with pink, purple and blue patterns of light which lit up the sky like a bright neon light.

"The sky looks strange, none of the stars are the same. It's very different from home. Even the people don't seem to be very happy."

"Yes, I know what you mean. But see that star there, the dim one just below the bright one. That's home."

Datch had just spent five minutes with his implant working it out.

"Wow, it looks so small." She said and then they were all looking at home.

They sat chatting till about nine at night and then headed off to the tents. It was going to be a long day and they needed to be up early in the morning so they could get moving before it got too hot.

The next day they headed off into the desert. They flew high up to try and avoid the heat from the sands. If they were on course, they should be able to land at an oasis and stay there overnight. Then it would only be another eight-hour flight to the monastery. They had been checking up on the monks and it turned out they were quite welcoming to visitors. Mainly because they didn't get many.

After a short stop for lunch and drinks, they ploughed on across the sky. After a few more hours, in the distance they could see trees sitting in a bit of a dip. They slowed down and dropped lower. As the oasis got closer, they could see a small number of tents and some strange animals. The animals look like Jaxx's but with long fur that seemed to reflect the sun. This had the effect of making them look as if they had coats made of glass.

They landed on the opposite side of the oasis to the animals so as not the scare them. Moving the bikes under some tree's so they were in shade and set up camp. A couple of the group on the other side of the oasis came to see who had landed. Carina smiled and said Hello but they didn't answer back instead they had puzzled looks on their faces. Clax spotted Carina and came over and spoke to them but used an alien language. Luckily the implants translated.

"Greetings to you and your friend. Sorry but my friend here does not speak your language."

"Greetings, are you not from our world?"

"No, we're from across the stars."

"So, why are you here?"

"We are on our way to see the monks at Quaki."

"That is many days travel from here but I see you have machines."

At this point one of the other men came walking over.

"Err" said Carina "Don't they have implants?" the man who had just arrived turned to her.

"No, they don't. Greetings I am Tajiquay the leader of the tribe and yes, I have one as do my family."

Carina breathed a sigh of relief.

"Sorry, I didn't mean anything. It's just everyone on our world has them."

Tajiquay laughed.

"Please come and join us for dinner. Maybe you can tell us some of your world and we can tell you about ours."

"We would be honored, please let us freshen up first as it's been a hard ride." said Clax.

"We feast just after dusk." he said and with that he called to the other men and then headed back to their camp.

The evening air was starting to cool down and was a nice 32C instead of 50C. There was the smell of smoke from across the oasis. The Pack came out of their tents and started to make their way over to the other camp. As they approached the sound of chatter could be heard. The tribe had laid out large blankets on the sand and lit a large fire in the centre of the camp. They walked in and straight away Tajiquay shouted something and they were brought over to him to sit on a rug next to him and his family. There was the smell of meat being cooked and an air of excitement about the camp.

"Welcome!" Said Tajiquay as they sat down. "May the gods bless you."

“Thank you and may the gods bless you and your tribe.” Clax said in his best native tongue. Tajiquay smiled at him

Clax then introduced then and Tajiquay did likewise before turning to all of them.

“Time to eat.” he said, “Please enjoy the food, then we talk.”

He clapped his hands and a number of trays of food appeared in front of them. There were vegetables, fruits and meat. All of which had different spices on them.

“Please take a bit of each and try it.” Tajiquay said.

“Thank you, we are very honored.” said Clax and gave a little folded hands gestor. The rest of them tried to copy him, some with more luck than others.

Soon they were all tucking in. This was a lot better than rations. With all the spices and rich flavours their mouths were watering.

“This food is amazing.” Said Datch without thinking.

Tajiquay converted it into the native language and a cheer went up. Datch went a bit pink but luckily the fire light stopped anyone seeing it. They ate like kings and then some strange bottles appeared.

“I take it you drink on your world?”

“We sure do.” said Dapo.

Small cups were handed around and then a small amount of a clear liquid was poured into them. Hagger had a sniff.

“Wow, it smells like Old Man’s Boots”

The Chief gave him a hard look. Clax stepped in.

“Old Man’s Boots is a drink back home and Hagger tends to drink a lot. In fact, maybe a bit too much.”

Tajiquay looked at Hagger who now had a grin on his face and then laughed.

“To guests from a far.” he said and lifted his cup.

They lifted their cups and had a sip.

“Wow, this is good stuff!” said Fred with a slightly hoarse voice.

Tajiquay looked across to Hagger whose grin had just got a lot bigger.

“I take it you like it Mr Hagger?”

“Yes, it’s very nice thank you.” he said with a big grin.

Now the talking started, it was all about Bellatrix five and what they did there. Music, Bars, School and even what they watched on the vid. The tribe was hanging on every word as if they were speaking from the gods or something. Finally, Tajiquay said.

“Do you have any of this music?”

“Err, I thought it was illegal on this world?” said Jep.

“Well, let’s just say we do things a bit different in the deep desert. Old habits die hard.”

He looked at Jep and winked.

“We do have some on the sound systems on the bikes.” Said Datch.

“Can we hear it?” he asked and then sensing the apprehension added “There is no one in 200 kilometres of here.”

“OK, Sure.” said Clax and got out his vid.

Thirty seconds later there was a roar of engines from the other side of the oasis and Clax's bike appeared over the trees. It came in low over the camp before landing at the side of them. He then selected a slightly less noisy tune and told the bike to play it. The camp listened and then when the track had finished, they all clapped.

"OK, now you listen to ours." Tajiquay clapped his hands.

Some of the tribe had been sitting on boxes which they now opened. Inside them were a selection of instruments. Even some small drums. They were handed out to various members of the tribe and soon they started to play a folk song. It wasn't rock but it still had a really good rhythm and soon some of the tribe was up and dancing. As the tempo increased Datch was sure he could see little sparks in the air around the dancers. Yes, he could.

"Tajiquay, why can I see sparks in the air?" He asked.

"All I will say Datch is that is old magic." He tapped the side of his nose and turned back to look at the dancers.

The dancers were spinning and Carina, Rosey and Tish had been pulled up by them. Soon Datch, Dapo and Hagger were up there as well following the dancers. As Datch moved to be with Carina the sparks around them started to get stronger and it felt so good. The song finished and as they walked back to the chief there were sparks buzzing around their heads like little fire fly's and then slowly, they disappeared.

"Wow, that was amazing." Said Fred "I really thought your head was going to catch fire at one point."

"Yes, we need some of this for the gigs back home." added Tank who was now checking for hair damage on Rosey's head.

Datch looked around the camp. Everyone now had big smiles on their faces and looked really happy.

"So, I bet you don't get much of a chance to do the music here."

"Sadly No, but here in the great desert when we are away from the prying eyes we can dance and sing as much as we like. It is all part of the old ways before the dark times."

"Did Welly four have singing and dancing then?" asked Jep.

"Oh yes, many thousands of years ago, the planet was alive with it. Then the dark times came and the music was taken away from us."

"What you mean the mystic gem?"

Tajiquay went quite for a moment and then turned to Jep.

"How do you know about the gem?" he said in a way that made Jep think he had said too much.

Jep thought quickly.

"When we were researching Welly four it came up in one of the old stories and said that when it was stolen the light vanished from the planet."

Tajiquay gave him a funny look as if trying to work out if Jep knew more than what he should. Jep had learnt to hide a lot of things, mostly from the principal of the school. He had also got very good at it because of The Pack. Tajiquay made up his mind and continued

"Yes, so the legends say anyway. But tell me more about your world."

Jep let the conversation swap back to Bellatrix five and the tribe wanted to know everything about this strange far-off world. It started to get late and they thanked Tajiquay for the evening and the tribe's hospitality before saying goodnight and heading back to their camp.

The next morning, Datch woke up to find that sand had blown into the tent and had manged to get not only in his blanket but also in his mouth. He spat it out and Carina woke up.

"What time is it?" she said and coffed up a small pile of sand.

"I don't know but it's getting light."

"My mouth is full of sand."

"Yes, mine was too along with a number of other places."

"Oh, I see what you mean." She said trying to remove some from inside her top.

"I think it came through the tents flap. Anyway, do you fancy some breakfast?"

"Sure."

Datch put his clothes on before heading out to the bikes for supplies leaving Carina to put hers on. Datch was just getting out a bottle of water for Carina when Fred and Jep appeared.

"Morning guys."

"Morning Datch. You the only one awake?" asked Fred.

"No, Carina's awake and getting dressed."

"Well, let's get some food going, I'm sure the rest won't be long."

Sure enough, one by one the rest of The Pack started to appear. Quite rapidly in fact when Fred started cooking Jeader slices.

Soon, Breakfast was over and it was time to go. It didn't take long to pack up the camp and put it on the bikes. They took off and after flying over the tribe's camp and waving goodbye to them Clax set course for the monastery. The bikes climbed up to cruising altitude before levelling off. The desert stretched out in front of them and they settled back for the eight-hour ride. Only Clax was watching his instruments. Everyone else's bike was on auto and following his in formation once again.

Carina seemed to be a bit happier today and full of life as they flew across the desert. Even Datch was feeling full of beans and he wasn't sure why. The bikes flew on and finally after a few thousand sand dunes there in the distance was a small town and siting on a hill in its centre was the monastery. It was a large structure with a huge tower in the centre with an obelisk sticking out the top like some sort of demented radio tower.

They came in low, landing outside what looked like a small inn and got off the bikes. They had the feeling they were being watched by just about everyone but casually walked into the building. They were pleased to find it was indeed an inn.

"Good afternoon, sir. Do you have any rooms available?" said Clax.

"Yes, we do, we have four double rooms."

"Err, there's twelve of us." Said Clax hoping that there were some rooms that the owner had forgotten about.

"We have four rooms."

"Are you sure there's not a spare one anywhere?" added Clax.

"No Sir, you misunderstand, we only have four rooms in the building."

"Oh, I see." He turned to the others. "The inn only has four rooms in total so we might have to share a lot."

There was a lot of whispering and muttering then some nodding.

"We'll take them all please and is there any chance of having that room over there as well?"

"You mean the bar sir?"

"Yes please."

"Well, as you have booked the whole hotel I don't see why not, for a modest fee of course."

"Why of course." Said Clax and smiled.

After a bit of negotiation, it cost three credits for the whole inn for three days. The bikers would sleep in the bar, Timbo and Jep would have one of the rooms and the other three rooms would go to the rest of them. They paid the inn keeper another six credits to sort out some food for them that didn't have cabbage in it before heading out for a walk. They headed through the narrow streets to the monastery. It was surround by a very high stone wall that could stop an army and had a set of huge wooden gates that had a smaller wooden door on the side. Clax knocked on it. A hatch opened and a head stuck through it.

"Yes?" Said the head in a squeaky voice.

"Err. Hello. We have come from the university on Bellatrix five and would like to have a meeting with one of your monks?"

"Why?"

"Well, we want to talk about some of your ancient scrolls."

"Why?"

"Err. We want to learn about the old stories."

"Why?"

Clax was starting to wonder if the head knew any words but yes and why

"Because they interest us very much?"

"Why?" Clax thought about it for a moment

"Why do you keep asking me why?"

The head looked at him and then at the others.

"OK, please wait." The head disappeared.

They could hear muttering behind the door then someone running off down a corridor that had a big echo.

"Do you think he just ran away?" Said Hagger.

"I Don't know." Replied Clax.

A door slammed somewhere inside and then a bell rang

"Well, that's odd." Said Jep.

"The man at the bar said they were odd." Added Tish.

"I think he was right." Said Carina.

There was the sound of shouting from somewhere behind the gate.

"Err, should we stay here?" Asked Rosey who was now feeling a little nervous.

"We'll give it a few more minutes then try again tomorrow." Said Datch.

"Do you need me to open the door?" said Timbo.

They looked at Timbo and then at the door. After a moment's contemplation they decided the door would lose.

"Err, not just at the moment Timbo, but maybe tomorrow." Said Fred.

They were just about to turn around when there came the sound of a door banging and footsteps getting closer. They stopped behind the door. There was muttering again and then the hatch opened.

"Hello?" said the head.

"Hello." Said Clax.

"Monks are all doing things now. Come back tomorrow."

"Err what time?"

The head turned to a voice behind the door. There was more muttering before it turned back again.

"Two bells in morning."

Clax was just about to ask when two bells was, when the hatch closed.

"Two bells it is then." Said Clax.

"Err. Anyone know when two bells are?" Asked Tank.

There was a long silence while everyone tried to use their implant. They didn't work.

"My implants not working." Said Datch.

"No, it won't. This is the deep desert, no chance of a link here unless we are near the boosters on the bikes. We'll just ask the owner of the inn when it is. He'll know." Said Clax.

"Hold on a minute." Said Datch "Aren't bells musical instruments?"

"Yes." Said Carina.

"Well, why do they have them then?"

“That’s a very good point Datch.” said Jep.

“Err, maybe we shouldn’t ask why.” said Clax looking a little worried.

“Hmm, maybe not.” Agreed Jep.

They walked back to the inn and went through the door. The inn keeper had tried to rearrange the bar for the bikers. He had made some beds on the floor from some mattresses that had appeared from somewhere and judging by the state of them, would find their own way back afterwards. From what they could tell it was the only inn here so they didn’t have much choice. The owner showed them to a big table that had been made from a number of tables that appeared to have come from the bar.

“Welcome back, I hope you had a nice walk.” He seemed to be happier now.

“Yes, it was very nice after the ride to get here.” Said Clax.

“Would you all like to sit down, I have food for you.”

“Err, dare I ask what we are having?” Said Tank.

“Yes, we have roast err, how do you say it ‘Jeader’?”

“Yes, Jeader.” Said Clax.

“With onions?”

Clax nodded

“And Weagee sticks and salad no cabbage.”

“You mean Weega and it sounds very good.”

“Please sit. I fetch.”

They sat down and the food came out. The meal was basic but very nicely done. It didn’t take long to finish it off and when they were done the owner came over.

"You want proper beer?"

They weren't sure what a proper beer was around the desert but figured that it might be worth a try. The man vanished behind the bar and a few moments later came out with some glasses. It did look like normal beer. Tank took a sip. It wasn't ice cold or even a bit cold but it did taste like beer. He smiled. The others all took a sip. Yes, they could drink this. The first drink didn't last very long and when the owner came over, they asked him about the bells and he told them it was about mid-morning.

They sat at the table for a couple of hours chatting and Clax got out his vid comm. The barman watched as the hologram appeared in front of them. Clax added the images into the program and it put up the I'm thinking sign. The barman was watching them intently. The program pinged and two characters changed slightly. The owner came running over.

"Hide! Bad place! Not Good!"

Clax shut the vid down.

"What do you mean Bad Place?"

"Yes, Bad place, not you show! It is forgotten."

"You know that place?" asked Jep.

"Yes, it's up. Not good, People die."

The owner was getting quite worked up so they decided to change the subject. After he went into the back Tish turned to the others.

"Err, was that weird or what?"

"Yes, it was a very strange reaction." Said Jep.

"He looked scared." Said Carina.

"Yes, very scared." Added Datch.

"He said it was up, do you think he meant in space?"

"I don't know, maybe I should send my dad's friend a message. I'll tell him to meet us back at the town. It will take him a few days to get the message so we should have time to get back." Said Datch.

"Yes, we might need a lift." Added Hagger.

The rest of them looked up and sighed. This trip seemed to be getting more complex by the minute, err, well, by the bells anyway.

They asked the owner if they could sit outside for a bit as it was starting to cool down now. He went out the back and came back with some fold up chairs for them to sit on. Clax gave him a one credit tip as a thank you and the man's face lit up again. They sat outside the front of the inn next to the bikes which had been fitted with planetary comms units. This allowed their Vid Comms to connect to the planetary network and therefore would work correctly when near the bikes. Datch sent his dads friend an email asking if it would be possible to meet them at their other hotel in six days' time and to bring his spacecraft. They sat taking in the cool night air and as soon as it got dark the multi legged creatures that had been hiding from the sun came out and started chirping loudly to makes up for the fact they had been quiet all day. Before long it was time to head off to bed.

Next morning Datch got up and went to the window. He stretched and was sure several of his bones popped back into joint. The bed was just a wooden board and the mattress was more like a bag filled with something small and lumpy. He tried not to think what it could be.

Carina woke up and came over to him.

"Hi lover." She said putting her arms around him.

"Morning babes. Did you sleep OK?"

"Most of the night but this mattress is not the best."

"Yes, I know what you mean. I think I'm going to bring my sleeping bag in tonight with my mat."

"Good plan."

They got dressed and went down the stairs. The bikers had already brought their sleeping gear in and were still snoring away. They went and sat at the table in the other room. One by one the others appeared and then the owner appeared.

"You want breakfast?" he said.

"Err, what do you have?" Asked Clax.

"Jeegee slices, bread and coffee."

"Looks like Jeader sandwiches all around."

The owner went back through the door and Peebop tried to see into the back.

"Err, you do know he's killed a Jeader to feed us all." he said.

"I sort of guess by the amount of Jeader that seems to be on the menu." Clax paused. "Well, it would be on the menu if we had one. Do you think we can have Jeader steaks tonight?"

"More than likely judging by the size of that Jeader." Added Peebop.

The owner came back with some sort of bread rolls and a plate of Jeader slices. He turned and went back for the coffee. After a few moments he came out with a large coffee pot and a tray of small cups. Clax asked him if they could have Jeader steaks, onions and chips for the evening meal and gave him another credit. The man's face lit up and after Clax explained what chips were, he went off into the back grinning from ear to ear.

"Err, he seems very happy when you give him a credit." Said Datch.

"A credit here is like a month's earnings." Said Jep.

"Wow, we spend that on a single drink." Said Rosey.

"Yes, their economy is pretty much at a full stop so we get a great deal money wise."

There was a sudden cough from the other side of the table.

"Wow, this coffee is strong!" Said Fred going a bit red.

"Oh, I should have warned you. The coffee is more like liquid Caffeine and will most likely kill anything known to man." Said Clax.

Rosey took a small sip of hers.

"This is good coffee. I need this at home." She took another sip.

"Oh yes, so good."

The others looked at her.

"If you drink Old Man's Boots trust me, you need this."

"I wonder if he does takeaway?" Said Hagger.

"What? To Bellatrix five?" Said Fred.

They finished breakfast and sat outside in the chairs waiting for two bells. The owner came out and told them it was almost time so they put their intelligent faces on and headed up to the monastery.

They knocked on the door and the head popped out the hatch.

"Yes?"

"Err, we came yesterday and you said to come back now?"

The head looked at them and went back inside. There was some muttering and the head popped out again.

"Yes. Father Jamby will come for you. Please wait."

The hatch shut.

They stood there for a few minutes and then footsteps were heard from inside. There was the sound of large bolts being pulled back and then creaking as the large door was opened.

Inside was a monk dressed in fine robes and looking like a rabbit in the headlights.

"Err, welcome. I understand you wish to talk about the old scriptures?"

"Yes, we're from the university on Bellatrix five. We have come a long way to hopefully see one of the ancient texts." Said Clax trying to sound as intelligent as possible.

"Hmm." he said looking at them all. Then after a moment's thought. "OK, follow me please."

They walked through the large doors and into a long corridor heading up a slope to another large gate. The whole place echoed with their footsteps as they followed the monk. They got to the second door and it opened. This time behind the door was a courtyard with seating all around the edge and hear and there, monks were sitting reading, praying or just relaxing. They crossed it and came to another wooden door.

The monk opened it and they went in. It was a large office and looked very old.

"Please be seated."

They all found chairs and sat down.

"So, you wish to see the ancient texts?"

"Yes, if it is at all possible." Said Clax.

"Why?"

"Clax, tell him we want to understand more about their old culture." Said Jep.

"That will not be necessary, I do have an implant and can understand you."

"Oh, my apologies. I'm professor Jep Doji. We didn't know you would have implants."

"Accepted. So, what has sparked this interest so close to the alignment?"

"We have been looking into ancient cultures and Welly four came up. It dawned on us that we knew so little about your culture and after a few meetings we decided to come and find out. Also, as the alignment was due, we thought it would be nice to combine the two."

"Hmm." The monk looked thoughtful for a minute.

"Well, which parchments did you have in mind?"

"We were interested in the ones before the dark times. The really old ones." Said Jep.

"OK, please follow me."

He got up and walked to the door with The Pack following along behind. They went outside and headed to the central building through another set of big doors into a dimly lit corridor.

“Please, try not to make too much noise, it is a quiet place for study and contemplation.”

“We understand.” Said Jep.

“You do realise that the parchments are in a very old script.”

“Yes, we have a Vid Comm with us. Once it sees a few parchments of text, we should be able to translate them for us. We have set it up so that it we be able to send the translation matrix to our implants.”

“That’s quite impressive. normally it takes months for a system to do that.”

“Yes, we were lucky enough to find bits of the old language in an old parchment that had been copied. It didn’t make much sense but we think we have about half of the alphabet.”

They came around a corner and headed down a corridor. There were little rooms on both sides with small glass windows in the doors.

“Can I hear singing coming from that room?” Asked Rosey.

“Err, no that’s one of the monks reading an old script. It can sound tune full at times.”

Ahead of them was another set of huge doors.

“When we go in here, please do not touch anything. If you ask me, I will fetch it for you.”

They all nodded. The Monk opened the doors and they walked in.

It was a very large circular room filled with shelves and tall racks. The shelves covered the walls and the racks ran from the walls to the central area of the room. All of which had tubes on them. In the centre was a number of tables and desks. The monk took them over to a number of the large tables and sat them down.

"Who would like to start?"

"I need to, I have the vid and until it decodes the text the rest can't read it." Said Clax.

"So, what would you like?"

"I need a script with as many different letters as possible."

The monk thought for a moment and then went over to a shelf. He picked up a large tube and brought it back.

"Try this?"

He carefully laid out the parchment in front of Clax who got out the vid comm. It beeped and then scanned the document.

He waited while it analysed it.

"No. it needs more."

The monk fetched another big script and laid it out. The unit beeped and again. Clax muted the volume.

"And another please?"

Another parchment was laid out for the unit.

"Err, how many letters are in the old alphabet?"

"There are two hundred and eight." Said the monk.

"Hmm, that's strange, it's found them all. But can't seem to get the context. Can I have one more please?"

The monk went and fetched another.

It was scanned and the vid comm was still not getting the context then Datch had an idea.

"Clax, can you overlay the alphabet with musical notes?"

"Yes, but why?"

"That monk in the corridor was singing the text."

"I'll try." He pressed a few keys on the vid comm.

The vid comm started working hard.

"Well?" Asked Jep.

"It's doing something but I'm not sure what."

Then the scroll appeared on the screen with its translation.

"That's it. They're all musical. That's the key some of the characters are musical instructions."

"What?" Said Jep, Peebop and Fred in unison.

"All the scripts are musical. In fact, the whole alphabet is musical. No wonder the cube was gibberish."

There was a sudden silence.

"What cube?" Asked the monk suspiciously.

Clax thought quickly.

"Oh, that was what got us interested. We found a very old cube with writing on it and we could never decode it. The rest of the faculty are going to be so annoyed that we have done it."

The monk relaxed a bit.

"OK, building the matrix now." He pressed a few buttons and the vid comm did the whole 'Please wait I'm busy thing.'

Five minutes later it finally said 'Matrix complete'.

"OK folks. Who is first?"

"I'll do it." said Datch.

"OK, get ready to except the file."

Datch waited and a file transfer box appeared in his mind. He accepted it and the file downloaded. Then another box appeared in his head asking if he wanted to install. He accepted and his implant said ready. He turned and looked at the parchment. It took a moment and then he could read it. The strange thing was that as he read it, it started singing in his head.

"Oh wow!" he said.

"What do you mean?" Said Jep.

"Just accept the matrix and then look at the parchment." he said.

"You see it?" Said the monk.

"Yes, and hear it!"

"You hear it as well?"

"Yes, its singing to me in my head."

"What, its singing?" said the monk who was looking taken a back and surprised at the same time.

"Yes, singing."

"Can I hear it?"

Datch looked at the others, Jep and Clax nodded.

"OK, get ready to accept the file."

The monk pulled a funny face and then looked at the parchment. It took a moment and then a very big smile appeared across his face. He moved on to another one and the smile tried to get bigger. The look of pleasure on his face said it all.

"This is amazing. If you folks need anything, just ask. You have opened my mind and I now feel one with the gods."

He walked over to the nearest rack and started looking at the parchments. He couldn't stop looking at them it was like a drug. Then Datch noticed it.

"Look at the monks head."

They turned to look. Sparks were coming from his head like a waterfall.

"Err, do you think he's going to explode?" Asked Carina.

"I don't think so. But we need to see the script about the gem I think."

"Err, you know you have sparkles as well."

Datch looked around at the rest. As soon as they took the download and looked at a text they started to sparkle.

"We all do."

There was a moments pause.

Datch got up and walked over to the monk.

"Can we see the parchment about the gem ceremony please."

The monk walked over to a rack and handed Datch a large tube. He was in some sort of trance or daze.

They got it out and placed it on the table. The scroll sang to them and as it did bright sparks danced around their heads.

It told of a ceremony of music and singing which reacted with the gem charging it up. Then at the right moment a priest would release the energy across the world bringing happiness to the planet.

"Wow. I feel good." Said Peebop.

"Me too." Added Fred.

"Yes, but it's not helped us find the gem." Said Datch.

"Hmm, there must be something else here." said Jep looking around.

"Yes, lets spread out and look for anything that doesn't look totally religious."

They started looking around the room. Father Jamby seemed to be in a world of his own and totally oblivious to them. They went up and down the racks looking at just about every tube. They also checked the racks for markings or anything that could resemble a map. After three hours of looking, they went back to the table and sat looking around in case they had missed a bit. Father Jamby was looking like some sort of fire work and was slowly working his way through the scrolls.

"I don't know, we must be missing something." Said Tank.

"Yeh, I don't see anything." Said Datch.

"Well, I checked nearly every inch of the rack I was looking at and found nothing." Added Tish.

"Yes, but there must be a clue here somewhere." Said Hagger.

Datch leaned back in his chair and sighed. He sat staring up at the roof thinking.

"So, what do we do now?" Said Fred.

"I don't know." Said Clax.

"What do you think Datch?" Said Fred.

Datch was sitting looking up with a grin on his face that was slowly getting bigger.

"Datch?" Daid Fred.

The grin was now right across his face.

"Datch!" Daid Carina and Rosey at the same time.

"I've found it." he said slowly.

"What, where?" Said Clax.

"Look at the lights."

They all turned to look up. The whole ceiling was covered with rings and clusters of lights with a large bright light at the centre.

"Oh, bloody hacks, the lights are the planetary system."

"Yes, and look at the fourth's planets satellites." Datch added. "One is green and not white. The gem. It's on one of the moons."

"Yes, but which one?" Said Fred.

"I think we need to go somewhere and let the cube show us the satellites. It looks to be the third one out. but I'm recording it just in case we've missed something." Said Datch.

They all sat looking at the map. After a few moments Datch got up and went over to Father Jamby.

"Can I ask you something?"

He turned to Datch. The top of his head looked like a roman candle with all the sparks crackling around it. He also had a very big grin on his face.

"Yes, anything."

"Before the dark times was there anything on the moons?"

"There was a number of small bases so I believe."

"Do you know which ones?"

"No, sorry. I only know that because one of the old parchments mentioned a visit to a small temple up there."

"OK, I think we are going to go now, we need to make notes on the texts that we have been reading." Datch paused for a moment "Oh, and can I suggest you try to think of something other than scriptures before you go outside as someone is likely to throw a bucket of water over your head."

The monk looked at him and then looked up at the sparkles.

"Oh, I see what you mean. Wait one minute and I'll show you out."

Datch went back and sat with the others until the monk calmed down enough to take them back to the main door. As they left, he turned to them.

"If you people want to come back in just tell the door staff Father Jamby said it is OK."

"Thank you very much for all your help." Said Clax.

"Your very welcome. Now, if you'll excuse me, I'm going to head back to the library."

The monk turned around and the door closed behind him. They could hear the sound of someone running away from behind the door.

"Do you think he's going to be OK?" Asked Carina.

"I'm not sure, but I have a feeling he's going to be walking around with a grin stuck on his face for the next six months." said Jep.

They walked slowly back to the inn discussing what had happened. It was by now late afternoon and the sun was starting to drop in the sky. In the desert it was dark by seven in the evening and just to confuse things this planet had a twenty-six-hour clock or ten bells in the desert. The desert time seemed to start at sunrise and stop at sunset. This meant you could never be late for bed unless it was getting light.

They arrived back at the inn and had a warm beer and some food.

Later that night when the owner disappeared for a while to get some more beers. Clax turned his vid comm back on and displayed the cube data. This time the data was different. They could read it!

Data streamed across the hologram. Clax pressed some buttons that he could now see and the cube zoomed into the moon and then back to the planet and the tower in the centre of the monastery. Then it showed an expanding curtain of energy circling the planet.

"Wow. Is this saying what I think it is?" Asked Carina.

"Yes, it is. The gem is on the third moon and if I'm reading this right, we need to bring it back to the monastery for the alignment."

"Err, do you think that's wise, it looks like it explodes." Said Timbo.

"Well, in which case it will bring life back to this planet and everyone will party or, the planet will explode and put everyone out of their misery." Said Datch with a grin. "I'm going for the party one."

"Err, You would." Said Fred.

"Well, if it does blow up professor Ploons will win the pot back on Bellatrix." Said Jep.

"I thought we said no blowing up of planets." Said Rosey.

"We did." Added Tank.

"We're not going to blow up the planet. The gem goes in the top of that big tower over there." Datch said pointing in the general direction of the obelisk at the monastery.

"Why?" said Hagger.

"Why what?" Asked Fred.

"Why can't we blow up the planet?"

"Because people live on it. I sometimes worry about you. You should really lay off the Old Man's Boots."

The others let out a sigh.

Datch cleared his throat and there was a scream from somewhere in the street. He raised an eyebrow.

"OK, I have a plan. We'll hang out here for a couple of days and sus out how to get it up there. Then we should head back to the hotel in time to meet my dad's friend. On the way we should call in at that bar we stopped out on the way here to find out if he knows about the moon and also have another curry. Then once back at the hotel, we should chill out and go and look at the town centre again. I have a feeling it will look a little different now."

The others looked at him.

"Well, that sounds like a plan and Hagger there is no blowing up planets. Now remember that!" Said Tank.

"OK." Said Hagger slightly annoyed about the fact.

They turned off the vid and sat back in their chairs. Shortly after the owner came back with a crate of beer. He also had got some crisps from somewhere. They decided to give them a try and avoided reading the use by date.

The next two days were spent looking around the town and checking out the monastery with the tall obelisk. There was no sign of any way to get up. Datch concluded it must be inside it but the others weren't so sure. It came time to head back across the desert. They gave the inn keeper another ten credits as a tip and said they would be back in a week or so. Then headed off into the sky. The trip back was uneventful. The oasis was deserted so they took the chance to have another look at the cube data before going for a swim in the pool under the palm trees. Also, a musical sing along session was called for around the camp fire which made them all feel more themselves.

It took all of the next day and a half of the day after to get to the bar they had stopped at for a curry. They arrived and parked up outside before heading inside for beers and curry.

The owner had seen them land and was standing behind the bar waiting for them.

"Welcome back, I take it a round of import is in order?"

"You bet." Said Fred walking up to the bar with a big smile on his face.

He fetched a number of large glasses out from under the bar and started filling them.

"So, how did you get on in the desert?" He asked

"Very well, the monks were very helpful and we were given access to all of their ancient scrolls." Said Jep taking a very large drink.

"Wow, you must have impressed them."

"You could say that." Added Datch with a grin.

"Do you happen to have any more of the that curry be any chance?" Asked Carina.

"Not today, but I do have a very good chilli on the go."

"With rice?" Asked Dapo.

"Of course, it is quite a hot one though."

"We have just flown across the desert in blazing heat so a bit more won't matter." Said Tish.

"Point taken. Twelve chillies coming up."

With that he escorted them into the restaurant section and sat them down before going to fetch the food. It didn't take them long to demolish the food and then afterwards they sat there drinking.

The owner came over and started talking to them. After a few minutes Datch turned to him and asked.

"Do you happen to know anything about the third moon, I thought I saw some buildings on it when we arrived?"

"You may have, there is an old base up there but I don't think anyone's been there for a few thousand years. I only know about it because I have my own telescope and do a bit of star gazing."

"Oh, I just wondered if anyone would know about it?"

"I don't know if anyone would, it's been a long time since it was used."

They carried on talking for another hour before thanking him for the beer and telling him how much they enjoyed the chilli. They mounted the bikes for the final part of the trip back to the Hotel. They arrived late in the afternoon and then took turns to have a shower in the bath. It was so good to get clean. After they had dinner and a couple of beers they headed off to bed.

Moon's Galore

The next morning, they had breakfast and decided to go out for a walk to the town centre. They headed down the street and came to the obelisk. The rings looked the same but they could just about make out the text. The years had taken their toll on the carvings and some were barely readable but if you looked hard enough you could still read them.

Datch walked up to the obelisk in the centre and started to read the markings on the stone. He had got about five lines down when Fred tapped him on his back.

"Err. I think you should stop that."

"What? Why? I'm only reading it."

"Yes, but look." He pointed to his head and then at the first ring.

Datch looked up. There were sparks around his head and then he looked at the first ring. It had started to glow faintly.

"Oh. I see. Are you sure it was me?"

"Yes."

They watched and as the sparks disappeared from around Datch's head the ring stopped glowing.

"So, when we read the texts here the rings light up. Maybe we should all read it?"

"I think that would be a very bad idea." said Jep.

"Why?"

"You weren't reading it. You were singing it."

Datch looked at Carina, she nodded.

“Oh wow. I so want to see what happens when we give the gem back.”

“We’re giving it back?” Said Hagger.

“Yes, it is theirs.” Said Fred.

“I thought it was mine?”

“Err, No, it’s theirs.”

“Oh, well can I hold it at least once then?”

“I’m sure that will be OK.” Said Rosey trying to make him feel better.

Datch nodded.

“Anyway, if we took it home, I suspect that everyone would think we were strange walking around with sparks coming off our heads.”

There was a general consensus of agreement about that.

“So, what did it say?” Asked Carina.

“What?”

“The obelisk.”

“Oh, it said Bring happiness and joy to the chosen. Let the light shine and energies follow. Let…” Carina was pointing at his head.

“Well, it seems any time we recite these texts we start to sparkle.” Said Jep.

“Can I have a go?” asked Hagger.

“NO!” Everyone said in unison.

“Let me explain. We’re trying to blend in, aren’t we?”

"I'm wearing the clothes."

"Yes, but walking around looking like you have a firework stuck in each ear would sort of make you stand out a bit don't you think?"

Hagger thought about it.

"Err, yes." he said reluctantly.

"So, if we say to stop doing something then it doesn't mean you can have a go, OK?"

"I suppose so."

Datch didn't like to see Hagger like this.

"Look Hagger, if you stick with the plan and we are able to put the gem in place. I'll let you do it OK?"

Hagger brightened up at the sound of this.

"OK." he said.

"But, no more wanting to do things, just do the same as the rest of us?"

"You got it Datch." Said Hagger.

Rosey was about to say something, changed her mind and started smiling again.

"I've had an idea, everyone spread out and use your implants, try to take images of every part of the area. Clax can use his vid comm to put them all together. Just don't read anything." Said Jep.

"Err, how do I do that again?" Asked Timbo.

Carina went over to him and whispered in his ear.

"OK, thank you." he said and walked off to take some pictures.

Later that day they were sitting outside the hotel having a beer when a pickup truck landed in the carpark. They watched as the driver got out with another man. The driver was a tall stocky build with red hair and his comrade was a slightly smaller build but still looked like he could do ten rounds with a heavy weight wrestler. They went inside the hotel and then two minutes later they came back and looked at them.

"Err, do you think we should run or hide?" Said Jep.

"No." said Fred.

"Err, who is Datch?" Said the driver.

"I am." Said Datch standing up.

"Hi, I'm Dag your dad's friend and this is Shiner my first mate."

The next five minutes were spent introducing everyone and then Dag turned back to Datch.

"So, I got your email and your dad asked me to come if you needed help?"

"Yes, we need a lift to the third moon and back."

"Why?"

"It's a bit of a long story but basically we believe that a gem is hidden there and that it could bring life back to this planet."

"Err, really?" he said looking very sceptical.

"Yes, Jep can you explain please."

Jep spent the next half an hour explaining what was going on and at one point they uploaded the matrix to Dag's implant and then had to tell him to read the images in his head and not sing it. His head started to sparkle and he felt good about life.

"Wow, this is strange."

"Well, if just reading the text can do that, just imagine what the gem can do."

"So, what makes you think the gems on the moon?"

They carried on explaining about the monastery and the map. The end result was that after an hour of chatting they had got a lift to the moon. They carried on talking and drinking until after midnight apart from a short pause for dinner. Dag and his mate Shiner had got rooms in the hotel for the night and plans were made for the following day.

Next morning after breakfast they went outside to the bikes. It was going to be a short trip as Dag had landed in a field a few kilometres out of town. The planet only had a couple of space ports and the local security forces were very relaxed when it came to people landing on the surface. This was mainly because no one ever came to the planet and secondly it gave them something to do when it came to checking that the ship was where it was meant to be. Soon, in the distance they could see a small spacecraft. It was a cargo ship shaped like an eagle with two large boxes under its wings and on its back the familiar shape of the interspace drives.

They landed at the back of it and Dag opened the cargo bay for them to put their bikes in. The inside of the ship was quite small and had a main corridor with a number of rooms off to either side. They followed Dag up to the command deck. It wasn't like the Carpaycus. It had windows and four chairs facing forward. The more Datch looked at it the more it looked like a very large shuttle with rooms. Dag opened a cupboard and handed out some chairs. Datch looked at them.

"Err, what if it gets bumpy?" He asked.

"Don't worry, they are magnetic and will stick to the floor when I power the systems up."

Datch looked at the chair and then at the view. 'Well, this was different if nothing else' he thought. They sat down and Dag powered up the systems. Datch tried his chair just in case and found that it was stuck to the floor.

"OK, here we go."

The ship lurched forwards and up before pointing its nose skywards.

"Sorry about the shaky take off folks. She's a bit of an old ship and can groan a lot but she can do interspace eight when I want her to."

The ship started to accelerate upwards and soon they were going through the clouds. With the large windows at the front the view was incredible and it felt like you were flying yourself. The ship shook a bit as it went through the high clouds and then the sky started to change to a darker blue. The stars started to appear one by one and then the nebula came into view. They had gone from the dayside to the nightside but unlike Bellatrix five there were no brightly lit towns and cities below. Only one could be seen and Clax said it was the capital.

"Won't we get seen going to the moon?" Asked Carina.

"No, they have planetary radar but the orbital systems shutdown thousands of years ago. All they have now is some early warning systems for tracking meteors and asteroids." replied Shiner.

"Oh, so we can just go and look around and nobody will know. Cool." Said Datch.

"Talking of the moon, any idea where we need to land?"

"I think it must be at the old base if it still exists." Said Clax.

“It’s still there but I think we will need space suits as I’m not sure its air tight anymore and there are no power readings.” Said Shiner looking at the monitor in front of him.

“Oh. We don’t have any.” Said Fred.

“Don’t worry. We have some spare ones, so we’ve got you covered.” Added Dag.

“Would it be possible if I could stay here.” said Jep not liking the idea of walking around in a suit.

“Yes, me to.” Said Tank and Fred in unison.

“I’ll be staying here so that will be fine. We can watch what is happening on the vid in the comms room.” Said Shiner.

Tish also wanted to stay behind but changed her mind when Dapo said he was going.

“There it is folks!” said Dag.

They turned to look out of the window and there in the distance was a moon. It looked like any other moon, whiteish in colour and covered with craters. They could see a flat circular area towards the top of the moon that was about five hundred kilometres across at a guess. As they got closer structures could be seen dotted about. In the centre they could make out a number of landing pads of various sizes that had almost been consumed by the lunar regolith. At the top of the area a large structure was visible and appeared to have been built into the side off a large hill. It had two sets of large doors and to the righthand side of them a number of smaller doors.

“That’s the main complex there.” Said Dag pointing at the large structure. “I’ll bring us in to land outside the main airlock and we can enter through that door to the right. You never know it might still work.”

The ship flew in close to the front of the base. There were no lights or signs that anyone had been there for hundreds of years. The moon's surface regolith was nearly half a metre deep and as the ship came into land the dust and rock were blown across the area creating a cloud that floated above the surface until the moon's gravity pulled it back down. The ship touched down in a small pit created by the thrusters.

Dag turned to the party.

"Are you ready for a walk folks?"

"We sure are." Said Datch standing up.

"OK follow me. The space suits are in the cargo bay."

The exploration team followed him to the cargo bay leaving the rest to head to the comms room.

The space suits were very light weight and were basically low power forcefields which stayed about twenty centimetres away from the body. This meant it was easy to move around and the only heavy bit was the oxygen and field generators that you had on your back like a rucksack. They all suited up and moved to the cargo bay doors.

"Right, everyone! Turn on your suits systems." Said Dag.

They all pressed the panels on their arms. There was a flash of sparks as the suites powered up and the pressure was stabilised.

"Is everyone's system, OK?"

There was a round of people nodding.

"OK. I'm going to depressurise the bay. If there are any problems, shout and I'll stop it."

He pressed a few buttons on a console and alarms sounded and lights flashed. There was a hissing noise as the air was removed from the bay. A light turned green above the door.

"Everyone OK?"

There was another round of nodding

"Right. Opening the door."

He pressed another button and the main doors opened.

"Follow me." said Dag waving at them.

The lunar surface was very bright. It was like looking at a white sheet of paper in the sun light. The visors adjusted their tint to stop some of the light and avoid any retinal damage. They moved down the ramp and onto the surface. The dust felt like they were walking on a soft rubber mat and it compressed as they stepped on it. Here and there were areas which had been cleared by the thrusters and you could see the original surface below. In some places you could even see markings that had been protected by the dust and therefore hadn't been destroyed by the years of neglect. They moved slowly over to the large doors and then cross to the smaller door they had spotted to the side. Dag brushed off the dust at the side of it and found a small panel. It was dead. He brushed a bit further down and found an emergency release. He tried pulling it but it didn't move so he tried a twist but it still didn't want to move.

"I can't get it to work! It must be jammed." Said Dag pulling at it one more time.

"Timbo, we want to get in." said Datch.

"OK Datch." said Timbo walking over to it.

He looked at the door and the locking mechanism before grabbing it with both hands. There would have been the sound of screaming metal if there had been air around it to transmit its pain. Instead, the door opened and there was a blast of dust as the air inside rushed out.

Dag looked at Timbo and then at Datch.

“Your dad said you might need help but looking at Timbo I’m not sure why?”

Timbo went in the door and the rest followed behind. That way if anything was inside it would hit Timbo first and then regret doing it. The suits helmet lights came on lighting up the air lock. It was clean and also was void of power. Dag fetched out a big light and turned it on. It lit up and hovered just above him.

“Err, we need to shut that door before we open that one or if there is any air in there it’s going to come through like a hurricane.” Said Dag.

“Timbo?” Said Datch.

He went over to the door. It closed!

“OK, let’s see if this opens?” Dag tried the emergency release.

The door grunted but didn’t open. He tried it again but still no luck.

“I think we need Timbo again.” he said.

Timbo walked over and hit the door. The door decided it was a good idea to open and there was a loud hiss as the airlock filled up.

“Can we take the suits off now?” Asked Rosey.

“No. we don’t know if the air is breathable or if there are any twenty-thousand-year-old viruses in it.”

“Oh, good point.” Said Clax who now was starting to have visions of arachnoids trying to eat him.

They stepped into the darkness on the other side of the door. The lights on their helmets flashed up along the corridor and the floating light lit up the area around the door. Dag looked around.

"What are you looking for?" Asked Datch.

"Well, I'm hoping there is an emergency power connector here somewhere. It should be a small green panel with two yellow lines running diagonally across it. All bases in the IPSF have them."

They all started looking for it and after a lot of wiping of dust off the walls Dapo shouted.

"Is this it?" he said pointing to a little faded green area on the wall in front of him.

Dag went over to him.

"Yes, that's it. I don't know if this is going to work though."

He got out a large box from his back pack. It had a thick power connector mounted on the side of the box and a small panel. He prised open the panel on the wall. Inside was a mating connector for the one on the box. He plugged it in and pressed a few buttons on the panel. The box bleeped and started to hum.

"What's that?" Asked Hagger

"It's a portable power system, I'm hoping it can deliver enough power to get some of the emergency systems online."

The humming got louder and then one of the corridor lights started to flicker into life, then another a bit further down the corridor and another. Soon there were about a third of the lights working. Then there was a bang and one of the lights went out again.

“OK. Looks like we will need to be as quick as we can. I don’t think the base systems will work for long.” said Dag.

There was a fizzing noise and a shower of sparks from the light that had just gone bang and then it fell on the floor.

“I see what you mean.” Said Datch.

“Try not to touch anything we don’t have to or it may go bang as well.” Added Dag.

Now the corridor was lit up they could see it ran down to a junction about fifty metres away. It had quite a bit of fallen debris on the floor. Most of the bits were broken light fittings and parts of celling panels with the occasional air duct hanging down for good measure.

They started to pick their way down towards the junction.

“Do you have any idea what we are looking for?” Asked Dag.

“We think it will be in one of the temple areas but it will be well hidden were ever it is.” Said Clax.

They got to the junction and decided to split up into two teams, Datch, Carina, Clax and Timbo in one and Hagger, Rosey, Tish, Dapo and Dag in the other. That way they could cover more ground and do twice as much damage.

Dag got another floating light out and programmed it to follow Datch. Even though the lights were on it was still quite dimly lit with areas where none of the lights had survived.

The teams split up and Datch’s team started to head down the corridor carefully stepping over anything that may go bang. They entered a side room that looked like some sort of recreation area. There were old style pool tables and some sort of gaming vid on the wall along with what looked like a holo suite in the corner. They headed back out into the corridor and followed it down to where it joined another one.

It became a lot wider and also a lot higher here. Off to both sides large doorways were visible in the dim light. Datch stuck his head though the first doorway before gingerly going inside to have a look with Carina following behind him. It was very dark inside as none of the lights had come on. As Datch's and Carina's head lights shone across the room, they could see a lot of tables and chairs scattered about and at the back was a long counter with a serving area.

"This must have been a café or restaurant." he said.

"Yes, it looks like it." Added Carina.

Some of the roof had collapsed partly burying some of the tables. They went back out into the main corridor to join the rest.

"You two take that side and we'll take this one." Said Datch.

"OK, but careful what you touch. This place is in a bad way." Added Clax.

They started to pick their way from room to room. Some of the rooms were shops of one sort or another. A hairdresser, a couple of bars and a small theatre. One by one they worked their way along the area towards the far end. They had almost got to a large set of stairs when they spotted lights coming from the other direction.

"Is that you folks coming towards us?" Said Datch aloud.

"No, it's you coming towards us." Came a voice that could only have been Hagger's.

They stopped and waited for the rest to come walking up the corridor.

"Any luck?" Asked Datch.

“We found the main power plant and the command centre and also the recreation areas but no temple. What about you?”

“Nothing, just a load of shops and bars mostly.”

The extra light from all of the lights had made the whole area a lot brighter. Behind Hagger was an ornamental staircase. In fact, now they could see it clearly, they noticed it curved up towards a grand entrance to something. Above the entrance was a huge green gem.

“Err, that’s not it, is it? because if it is, we’ll never get it out the door.” said Dapo looking up.

They all turned to look at it.

“No.” said Clax after a moment. “The gem from what I can tell is about the size of a football. Anyway, that’s got light fixings inside it.”

They looked and sure enough there were cables running inside it.

“Well, at least we found the temple. Let’s go and check it out.” added Datch.

They gingerly headed up the stairs making sure the steps could support their weight. At the top was the entrance to the temple there was a set of double glass doors with an image of a green gem on them. They pushed one of the doors and it opened. Inside it was a circular room with a roof support in the centre which was covered in the same symbols as the obelisk on the planet. There were also various small rooms around the edge of the main room and places for incense to be burnt. They started to look around for anything that could contain a football sized gem. The side rooms turned out to be mini prayer rooms for private meditation and didn’t have anything in them except for a few mats on the floor.

They found two private rooms that looked like they were used by the priests to get ready for ceremonies and had a number of boxes that had various garments in. The robes looked ceremonial and were a lot brighter than anything they had seen on the surface including what Father Jamby had been wearing. They searched the temple from top to bottom even under the podium which was in front of the centre post.

“Well, it doesn’t appear to be here.” Said Dag.

“It must be here somewhere.” Said Datch.

They looked around again in case they missed something.

Then Datch looked at post and went over to read it in case it had a clue.

“Hey the text isn’t glowing?” he said.

“Well maybe it’s because we’re not on the planet?” Said Clax.

Datch thought about one of the scripts back on the planet and read it in his head. Sparks appeared around his head.

“Err. Look” he said and sure enough sparks were going around his head.

“So, this text is missing the sparks, but why?” Asked Hagger.

Datch looked closer at the post. Some of the characters had been changed.

“If the gem reacts when someone starts reading, sorry, chanting the text and you wanted to hide it, you wouldn’t want it to start lighting up like a beacon every time the text was read would you.”

“So, you’re saying it is here somewhere.”

“Yes, these characters have been changed. Look I know this might be a long shot but start reading the chants in your heads and walk around looking for anything glowing.”

“OK, we’ll give it a go.”

The next ten minutes were spent walking around the temple singing the scripts out loud. The result was that everyone had sparks appearing in the air at the side of their heads but still nothing was glowing.

“Maybe someone beat us to it?” Said Dag.

“Yes, maybe.” Said Clax with a sigh.

They started to head to the door.

“Look!” Said Dapo pointing at the door.

There was a bright light shining outside.

“Do you think the security services have come to find out who is here?” said Carina.

“No, Shiner would have told us over the comms.”

Timbo and Dag slowly moved closer to the door.

The light was starting to dim a bit now and by the time they reached the door it had almost gone. They put their heads through the door. The area was empty and the only foot prints in the dust were theirs. They all came to have a look.

“Well, that’s weird.” Said Tish.

“Yes, just a bit.” Added Rosey.

Carina looked at Datch. He was thinking and the look on his face was very complex.

“Are you OK?” She asked, there was a pause before he answered.

“Yes. I think so.” He now had a grin on his face.

“Everyone, start singing the texts again.”

“Why?”

“Just do it.”

They started to chant one of the scripts and the large gem outside the temple started to glow lighting up the whole area.

“Bloody Jaxx! it’s in there.” Said Fred.

They stood looking at the gem, inside the plastic casing there was something shining brightly.

“So, what do we do, break a religious symbol to get to it?” asked Rosey somewhat apprehensively.

“Err, I hate to point this out but technically we just ransacked their temple. So, breaking a bit of plastic is in my book OK.” Said Dapo.

Everyone thought about this and then started looking for large blunt objects.

Soon everyone was back and after a number of failures Timbo came up with a large metal bar. It looked like he had pulled out a roof support and everyone was now looking up nervously for signs of structural collapse. He walked up the stairs with the bar going thump as it went up each of the steps.

“Err, please stand back!” he said

Everyone moved a long way back. He lifted up the bar with both hands and thrust it towards the plastic casing. There was the sound of splintering plastic and the front of the gem fell off.

“We can add destruction of religious symbols to the ransacking of temples now.” Said Dag with a smile.

Inside the casing was a lot of lighting panels and tucked behind one of them was something with a green glow.

"So, who's going to get it?" asked Dag.

"I'll will, but I'll need a boost." Said Hagger.

"OK, Timbo give Hagger a boost. Hagger don't drop it, no matter what, OK?"

"OK."

Hagger was lifted up and inside the plastic casing. After he removed one of the lighting panels, he could just reach the gem. He carefully took hold of it. It was very heavy and took a couple of attempts to lift it away from the metal work that it was sitting in. Then slowly Timbo lowered him to the ground. The gem was slightly bigger than a football and was cut in the shape of a diamond. It was light green in colour and glowing dimly. They stood looking at it.

"So, this is the mystical gem." Said Clax.

"Yes." Said Datch.

There was a long pause while they took it all in.

"Err, so what do we do now?"

"Well, we can't just walk into the monastery with it and say 'hello we just ransacked your temple on the moon and found this' can we?" Said Carina.

"No. but can I suggest we get back to the ship before which ever part of the base that is missing Timbo's crowbar falls down." Said Dag.

"Yes, that sounds like a very good plan." Added Datch looking around.

Rosey decided to leave a note saying sorry about the mess and explaining that it was necessary.

With that they started to head back to the ship with a bit more pace while checking for missing support beams as they went. They had to pick their way along the corridors but eventually they got back to the airlock in one piece. Timbo then did the honours and opened the doors for them and ten minutes later they were all back on the ship. Jep and Tank were waiting outside the cargo bay when they came in.

"Let's see it then?" said Jep excitedly who was looking like a kid in a toyshop.

"Wait till we get to the rec room." said Dag.

They headed up to the room and went inside. Hagger lifted a heavy bag onto the table and then slowly opened it revealing the gem.

"That's incredible." Said Jep.

"Not half." Added Tank.

"And watch this." Said Datch.

He started to read one of the scripts in his head and sang it out aloud.

The gem started to glow brightly.

"Wow that's amazing." Said Fred.

"Err, I wonder if it likes our music?" Said Rosey.

They all stood and looked at each other for a moment.

"We could try but we don't have our music." Said Dapo.

"Yes. We need our music." Said Hagger.

Rosey and Tish had a grin on their faces

"What?" said Carina.

"Press the button inside your right collar."

Carina did and a holo screen popped up in front of her face.

“Oh wow. Can we do star lovers?” she said.

“Err, maybe not, we don’t want to overload it.” said Clax.

“What about ‘Shoot for the Stars’, it’s a good song and not too heavy?” Said Carina hoping for a yes.

“OK, we’ll give it a go.”

“Well, this should be entertaining” said Dag to Shiner.

They pressed a few buttons in the holo screens that had now popped up in front of everyone’s face.

“So how does this work then?” Asked Datch.

“Well, we’ve programmed each garment with the instrument belonging to that member of the band. So Datch, yours will play the guitar and Tish will have drums etc. They are all programmed to follow Tish’s drums and should all work in sync.”

“Remind me never to get you to make me a business suit.” Said Fred.

“Is everyone ready?” Said Tish ignoring the comment.

There was some nodding and then Tish nodded and the beat started up. To start with the gem didn’t light up. They started to sing and the gem started to glow dimly but didn’t do much else. They stopped.

“Hmm. Let’s try ‘Wild Wind’.” Said Datch.

The song started to play and the gem glowed a little brighter.

“I think we need to try ‘Star Lovers’.” Said Carina.

“OK, Let’s try.”

They started to play and the gem started to glow. Then Datch and Carina started to fire off each other and the gem exploded with light. Once everyone could see again Jep turned to Datch.

"Let's not do that again. I think I might need to have new retinas fitted when I get home."

"Yes, let's not" added Shiner who was blinking and still trying to see the rest of the room.

"That's amazing," said Fred "Its reacting to the emotional content of the music."

"That's what is in the scripts, emotions and when you read them the emotions come through. Datch couldn't help but to sing them when he was reading in his head." Said Clax.

"So, what happened to the monk then?" Asked Rosey.

"Err, I think it was emotional overload. He was reading scrolls so fast his mind went into meltdown."

"Well, at least we know why they put it at the top of the obelisk, it was so people didn't go blind." Said Carina.

"Yes, just imagine the whole planet chanting at the same time. It would be brighter than the sun." Added Clax.

"Err, so how are we going to put it in place without being blinded by it? When we get anywhere close to monastery it's going to light up with all the monks chanting. Let alone when we try and drop it on the top of the obelisk." Asked Tank.

"I don't know but I think we need to talk to the monk. He might have information that may help us." Said Datch.

"You do realise that if the monk sees it and starts chanting, we'll all get really bad suntans!" Said Fred.

"Yes, maybe we can kidnap him and take him to the desert before putting him close to it?" Said Hagger.

“That’s nearly as bad as blowing up a moon.” Said Carina.

“Well, we did vandalise their temple.” Said Hagger.

“What moon did you blow up?” Asked Dag with a slightly worried look.

“We didn’t, nor do we intend to!” Added Carina while giving Hagger a hard stare in case he had any more ideas.

Dag looked slightly disappointed for a moment

“Well, I think we should first find something to put it in that does not let light out and then head back to the planet as quick as possible just in case Hagger finds a big gun from somewhere!” Said Datch.

“I second that.” Said Jep.

“I have a metal box that should do the job.” Said Dag.

They followed him to one of the other rooms and he pulled out a metal box from one of the racks. The gem fitted inside but it was a little loose.

“Err. We don’t want to chip it. Can we pad it with something?” asked Jep.

“Hmm. And it had better not be flammable just in case.” Added Fred.

“The box has holes in it.” said Tish.

“Hmm...” said Dag thinking.

“I know,” Said Shiner “What about the lagging for the reactor coolant system. That’s got to be able to cope with the radiation from the gem.”

“Yes, that should work.” Added Dag

He went and pulled out a large box from one of the shelves and brought it over. In the box was a large roll of some sort of insulator. He pulled out a section and placed in the box.

"OK, let's try it now."

They placed the gem in the middle. It fitted quite snuggly and seemed to be quite securer. Datch picked up the box and shook it. It seemed to stay put in the middle.

"I think we need to do another test." Added Datch.

"What?" asked Clax.

"We need to test it against it lighting up."

"Oh, I see what you mean." he said.

They closed the lid and turned the light out.

"OK, everyone sing Star Lovers."

"Are you sure?"

"Yes."

They did and the box didn't seem to let out any light.

"OK. That works." Said Jep.

"Right, back to the planet and the hotel bar I think." Said Datch.

They headed up to the command deck. Well, cockpit and sat down.

The ship lifted off and headed back towards the planet.

"Err. Can we avoid going too close to any moons." said Peebop looking at Hagger.

"I don't have a gun." Hagger said sarcastically.

They all laughed.

Outside the planet looked like a large black circle that was slowly eating away at the stars as it started to get bigger. As they approached the planet Dag altered course to take them to the daylight side of the world. Down below an ocean could be seen running across the middle of the world and a small city could be seen on its shores.

"That's the capital down there." Said Clax pointing out of the window.

The ship dropped into the outer atmosphere and the comms bleeped. It was planetary security asking who they were. Dag answered and told them they had been giving some tourists a flyby of the moons. Then after a couple more questions they were cleared for planet fall and started to descend towards the surface. Below them were light fluffy clouds and as the ship entered the thicker atmosphere it started shaking.

They cleared the clouds banking to the right and then followed the flight corridor before heading back to the same field they had taken off from a few hours ago. There was a farmer leaning against the gate as they touched down. Dag secured the ships systems before they headed down to the cargo bay to exit the ship. As they came out the farmer came walking over to them.

"You can't park that there." he said pointing at the ship. "This is my field."

Dag walked over to talk to him. There was a lot of muttering and Datch could tell by the tones in the farmers voice that the negotiation was not going well. He had an idea.

"Clax, do you have about ten credits of the local currency?"

"Yes. Why?"

"Just give me it please."

"Oh, I see."

He did and Datch walked over next to Dag. They were arguing about the ship.

"Err, sorry to but in Dag but may I just talk to this chap for a minute?"

"Go ahead, I'm not having much luck."

Datch walked off with the farmer and after a couple of minutes the farmer started to smile. Datch carried on talking and then did some pointing and the farmer nodded. Datch then gave him something and the farmer had a very big smile. They walked back to the group.

"The farmer, Mr Gimjee, has kindly agreed to let us park here for the next four weeks if we wish to."

"Yes, you are very welcome." Said Mr Gimjee grinning,

"Thank you." Said Carina.

"No thank you lady. I will see you around." he said and walked off out of the field.

"Well, how about that." Said Dag.

"It just needed a few credits, that's all."

"A few?"

"Yes, ten and we have the field for a month. Oh, and he asked if we could move the ship around the field every few days so he doesn't get any brown patches."

"Remind me never to play poker with you." Said Shiner.

"OK, let's head to the hotel." Said Tank.

"Err, are we taking the gem with us?" Asked Jep "It's just that it might start glowing."

"Hmm, good point. Dag is it OK to leave it here or do you have to get back home?" Asked Datch.

"Yes, sure, I'm not going anywhere. I haven't had this much fun in years and can't wait to find out how much trouble you can get into."

"You do know I died last time, don't you?"

"Well, your dad did say something about it and asked me to bring along a stasis unit and transporter just in case. But I figure it won't be necessary as I'm here and this planet is about the only place in the universe where nothing happens ever."

"Yes, but we're now talking about kidnapping a monk and storming a monastery." Added Tank.

"Good point." said Dag thoughtfully "Shiner, did we put that life pod in the ship?"

"Yes, it's in the corner of the rec room."

"Good. Maybe we should plug it in."

"OK, I'm on it."

"So, let's get going, we have a planet to destroy." said Datch.

"Oo, that's much better than a moon." said Hagger.

"That's a metaphor!" Said Carina giving him a hard stare.

They went to move the gem and found it was now glowing very brightly in the box.

"Err. Why is it doing that?"

"I don't know, maybe it's because the gem is back on the planet. Still, that farmer looked very happy, a bit too happy if you think about it." Said Clax.

“Do you think it’s the gem?” Asked Rosey.

“Could be, maybe even in its current state it can have a local effect.”

“I think we had better put it in the centre of the ship to make sure no one can see it.”

Everyone nodded and they moved it next to the reactor core. It was the most heavily shielded area of the ship and they figured the extra shielding would stop things leaking out.

“Do you think it will be OK?” Asked Carina.

“As long as no one starts chanting outside the ship, it should be fine.” Replied Dag.

Half an hour later they were sitting outside the hotel with a beer in their hands and chilling.

“So, how are we going to get the gem to the top of the obelisk?” Asked Jep.

“Well, we need to get to the monk first and try to talk him into helping us.” Said Datch.

“Yes, but how the heck do we do that?” Asked Tank.

“I’m thinking we need to get him alone and out of the monastery.” Said Datch.

“He’s a monk, how do we get him out?” asked Jep.

“Hmm. Can I have a gun?” asked Hagger.

“NO!” everyone said together.

“OK, let’s ride out to the edge of the desert tomorrow and then into the desert the next day camping at the oasis before heading to the monastery the following day. We can stop at the same inn.” Said Datch.

"I'm taking my inflatable bed with me this time." Added Timbo.

"Err, we can take the ship. It will only be fifteen minutes flight time."

"That would work but we need to keep the story straight for the monk. So, let's take the ship to the oasis and leave it behind the trees near the water hole. It will only be a short trip on the bikes from there to the monastery. That way no one will see the ship and also people in the town should not be affected by the gem." Said Datch with a grin.

"Err. I've seen that grin on your dad's face." Said Dag.

"Where do you think I get it from." Replied Datch now grinning even more.

This normally had the effect of making people think that he had an evil plan or was about to bite their necks. They ordered another round of drinks and the barman came out with a smile on his face.

"Here are your drinks ladies and gentlemen. Please enjoy them and if there is anything I can get for you please just ask."

He gave them another cheerful smile and went back inside.

"Err, that was weird." Said Carina.

"What do you mean?" Asked Dag.

"Well, last time we were here, he just grunted and spent his time starring out of the window."

The others all nodded.

"And your point is?"

"Well, look at him now."

They looked back at the hotel. The barman and one of the other staff were cleaning the bar and also humming as they did it.

"OK. That is odd." Said Clax, "They never hum. It's meant to be illegal."

They watched as they cleaned and vacuumed the bar including the windows. Then a couple came down the street also smiling, laughing and chatting as they walked along.

"You don't think it could be the gem, do you?" Asked Tish.

"Err, no, err maybe…" Said Clax, "It's quite a distance from here."

"Yes, but given what we have seen so far. It could be leaking out somehow."

"It's behind a metre of radiation shielding and a force field!" Added Dag.

They sat looking around. People seemed to be a lot happier all of a sudden.

"Err. This is not normal." Said Clax.

"It's a good job it's inside the ship and not just in the box or they might be dancing down the streets." Said Dag.

"Yes, it must be the gem." Said Jep.

"But how?" Asked Peebop.

"Maybe they are linked mentally to the gems frequency or something."

"Could be. That would explain why it was hidden on the moon. The monk couldn't hide it on the planet because it would still work and the people near it would give its position away." Said Clax.

"You mean like some sort of humanoid happiness meter?" Said Jep.

"Yes. I suppose so."

A man came walking down the street and said good day to them before cheerfully carrying on down the road.

"This is really strange. They wouldn't even look at us yesterday." Said Rosey.

"Yes. it's sort of really creepy." Added Tish.

"OK, that gem leaks a happiness field or whatever it is for at least ten kilometres. We need to come up with an idea of how to get the monk to it without him lighting up like an emergency beacon." Said Datch.

"Well, he has an implant, can't we show him it?" Said Clax.

"You know what he was like with the scrolls. His head might explode." Said Hagger.

"What is it with you and blowing things up?" Asked Carina.

"I don't know, I just want something to go bang I guess."

"Well try not to think about it please."

"I don't think his head will go bang. However, he won't need any happy pills for a year or two at least." Added Datch.

"OK, what about this. We go into the monastery and talk to him. We'll tell him that we have it and show him via the implant. It will get his interest up if nothing else." Said Clax.

"Yes, that should work." Said Datch.

"Yes, and as soon as he leaves the monastery, we can put a sack over his head." Said Hagger.

"Why?" Asked Dapo.

“Because that’s what they do in all the movies.”

“There will be no sacks, guns or blowing things up. Does everyone understand.” Said Datch.

There was a moment while everyone gave Hagger a hard stare.

“Right, so we get him out of the monastery and then take him to the ship to show him the gem. We’ll then come up with a plan to get the monk and the gem back to the monastery in time for the alignment in five days’ time. How does that sound?” Said Datch.

“OK. But let’s have another beer before dinner and double check what we’re going to do.”

They sat drinking and after going over it a number of times they changed the subject and ended up telling Dag the story about saving the president.

The rendezvous

The next morning Datch and Carina got up and headed down to breakfast. The dining room also seemed to have been cleaned and even had fresh flowers on the tables.

“Err. This is weird but nice.” Said Carina sitting down.

“The flowers are a nice touch but I bet we still have cabbage on the menu.”

The waiter came walking over with a smile.

“Good morning, I hope you have slept well.”

“Yes, we did thanks”

“Myself and the chef have been talking and if you wish we will try to give you a breakfast like home.”

Datch and Carina were a little worried about this with images of cabbage being included.

“Err, Like home?”

“Yes, we have done a little bit of research and if you like we can do, Jeader slices and sausages, Hacks eggs, Parlly fruit and mushrooms. We can also do how do you say, Fried bread.”

Datch suddenly realised that the waiter was speaking Bellatrixian. He put a big smile on his face.

“Yes, Fried bread. Think that sounds wonderful. I’ll have it. can I have coffee with it as well?” Asked Datch.

“Certainly sir, Local or Import?”

“Oh, import please.”

“And for you, mam?” he said turning to Carina.

"Err. I'll have the same please."

"Certainly mam."

With that he disappeared into the kitchen.

"Was he speaking Bellatrixian?" Carina asked.

"Yes, pretty well too."

"Wow, that gem is really good."

They sat waiting and after about fifteen minutes the waiter came back with two plates. The food looked like a Bellatrixian breakfast.

"One moment, I shall return with the bread and coffee."

"Thank you." Said Datch.

Datch turned to Carina.

"Well, it looks good." he said taking a bite of a Jeader slice.

The waiter came back with the bread and the coffees.

"Is everything OK for you?" he said.

"Yes, it's very nice thank you. Please put a two-credit tip on the bill for you and the chef." Said Datch.

"Why thank you sir."

He went off to the kitchen to tell the chef.

They had got about halfway through breakfast when Timbo, Tank and Jep walked in.

"That looks good." Said Tank.

"Yes, and the waiter is trying to speak Bellatrixian, we tipped him two credits." Said Carina.

It wasn't long before the rest turned up and soon everyone was having a full Bellatrixian breakfast. Also, as everyone had tipped the waiter and chef. The waiter now had a very big smile on his face and was bending over backward to please everyone.

They finished their food and headed out to the bikes.

"It's sort of a shame to take the gem to the monks, the service at the hotel is so much better now." Said Carina getting on behind Datch.

"I know what you mean, but if we get the gem to its rightful place then everyone on the planet will be like that."

"I suppose so."

The bikes started up and they headed off to the ship. They landed at the back of the cargo bay and put the bikes inside. They were just about to close the door when the sound of singing was heard from behind the hedge.

"Do you think we should go and tell them we're about to take off?" asked Datch.

"Yes, I suppose we should." Said Dag, "But be quick."

Datch went over to the hedge. On the other side was a young couple and the young woman was singing to her boyfriend. Datch coughed. The woman turned around startled by the noise.

"Err, Sorry to disturb you but we're about to take off and thought it might be an idea if you were to move back a bit."

The woman looked at him with a puzzled look. Datch thought for a second and then had an idea. He pointed at his chest, then behind him and then up. The woman looked through the hedge and nodded. She grabbed her boyfriend and took him across the field. Datch went back to the ship and disappeared inside.

A few moments later the thrusters fired up and the ship took to the air. It turned before flying off into the distance leaving the young couple with a ringing in their ears.

Onboard The Pack relaxed for the fifteen-minute flight. The ship got flight clearance to head to the desert and went up to thirty thousand feet before accelerating. The land could be seen below going past very quickly and soon the desert could be seen in the distance. A moment later they were flying over it and then the ship started to drop down again. The breaking thrusters fired and the ship slowed. Before long an oasis could be seen and a matter of seconds later, they were over the top of it.

"So, where do I park?" Said Dag.

"Just put it over there near the trees at the back." Said Clax.

"OK."

The ship touched down neatly between a couple of palm trees.

"Right, if you stop here and look after the gem, we'll go get the monk." Said Clax.

"OK. But what do I say if someone one turns up while you're gone?"

"Oh, if they do just say you're prospecting for oil or something. Also, if a tribe turns up with a lot of tents, camel things and their leaded is called Tajiquay. Be nice, their OK sort of people." Added Datch.

With that they headed down to the cargo bay and got on the bikes.

Eight hours later the monastery was in sight and soon they were over the town. They brought the bikes in for a landing outside the inn.

The owner came running out.

“Welcome, welcome, pleased to see you here.” he said.

“We’re here for a couple of days. Do you have rooms?” said Clax.

“Yes, Yes, for you, anything.” he said and shouted something at the door.

There was a lot of noise from somewhere inside.

“You want err, Hacks for dinner?”

“Yes, that sounds good thank you.”

He shouted something else at the door.

“OK. We sort out for you.”

There was a lot of squawking from somewhere behind the inn followed by silence.

“Well, that will be dinner sorted then.” Said Tank.

“Yes and at least we know its fresh.” Added Jep.

“I hope it was a fat one.” Added Timbo.

They went inside and sat down. Timbo came in with a large box that he had picked up from the hotel. He opened it in front of them. Inside was a number of cans of beer which were all sitting with ice on them.

“I thought you may like these.” he said.

“Timbo. You’re a star!”

“They all reached in and grabbed a can each.”

The owner came back out and looked at them and at the box.

Clax gave him a beer and smiled at him. He opened it and took a sip. You could see the lights come on inside his head.

“Thank you.” he said and went running into the back with it.

There was a lot a muttering and then he came back out.

“Where from?” He asked.

“The big city. It’s imported and you need to cool it down to drink it.” Said Timbo.

Clax sort of translated it. The owner went running into the back again and more muttering. He came back out again.

“I get some for next time.” he said and went running out the door into the street.

“Err, I’m not planning for there to be a next time, but still, at least he’ll have good beer for any other guests that might turn up.” Said Fred.

“So, when are we kidnapping the monk?” Said Hagger.

“We are not kidnapping the monk!” said Datch.

“No, we’re just going to talk him into coming with us and hope his head does not explode when we show him the gem.” Added Tish.

“Why is it that most of this trip has consisted of comments about things exploding or being blown up?” said Dapo.

“Don’t forget ransacking of temples, destruction of religious symbols and kidnaping.” Said Hagger making sure they didn’t miss anything.

Datch gave out a long sigh.

“OK, we may have sort of ransacked a temple, broken a symbol and put a monk into some sort of religious coma. But we mean well and once the gem is back in place, I'm sure everyone will be happy."

"So, when do we nobble the monk?" Said Peebop.

Datch gave up and just carried on.

"I think we should go at two bells again. Clax can nip to the monastery in a minute and tell the doorman we're coming and to let Father Jamby know that we have more information for him. That should get his attention."

"OK. I'll go as soon as I've finished enjoying this beer. Oh, and don't drink them all while I'm gone." Added Clax.

"OK, let's chill out. I think it's going to be a long day tomorrow." Said Tank.

The next morning, they got up and had leftover hacks for breakfast. Then, after a couple of very strong coffees, they headed up to the monastery. The street was hot and dusty even at this time in the morning and they were all sweating by the time they reached the big door. Clax knocked on the hatch and it opened.

"Ello?" Said a head.

"Hello, we're here to see Father Jamby." Said Clax.

The head looked them up and down.

"He is very busy."

"Please go and tell him the people from Bellatrix five are here to see him."

The head looked at him. Clax reached into his pocket and gave the head a credit.

"OK." The head said and the hatch shut. There was the sound of feet running behind the gate.

A few moments later the feet came running back and the big door was opened. There was the head attached to a very small man. They all looked at him, then at the door and back at him. The hatch was about half a metre higher than he was and there was no sign of steps or ladders.

“Please hurry, this way.” Said the little man and waved for them to follow.

They headed up the corridor and into the courtyard. Then crossed it to the big office. Father Jamby was sitting at his desk with sparks around his head. There were scrolls and texts scattered all over the place as if someone had been trying to read them all at once. They walked over to him and sat down.

“Hello again. How can I help you?” he said smiling.

“Well, it’s more what we can do for you.” Said Datch.

The monk remembered the last time and started smile some more.

“In what way?”

“Hmm. Let me come straight to the point. You know the gem in the old stories?”

“Yes, we have some of them here, but if you’re hoping to find it. I’m afraid many have tried to find clues to its where abouts but no one has found anything that would help them.”

“Well, they should have looked up.” Said Tank.

“What do you mean?”

“The map showing its position is the lights on the ceiling of the library. They show the planetary system with a little green gem on the light that represents the body it’s on.”

“How do you know this?”

"Can we trust you?" asked Datch.

"I'm a monk, of course you can trust me."

"OK. I'm going to send a file to your implant. Please watch it."

"And don't let your head explode please." Added Rosey.

Datch sent the vid to the monk and waited.

The monk's face was a picture. First a puzzled look. Then a slowly expanding smile that spread right across his face and then if it had been possible to smile any more the monk would have managed it.

"Is it real?"

"Yes." Said Datch.

"Do you, have it?"

"Yes. But not here. Do they let you out?" asked Jep.

"Why?"

"Let's just say that the gem has a strange effect on this planet's population. Therefore, we have got it in a safe place away from anyone." Said Jep.

"What do you mean?"

"Well, if it is near anyone and I mean within say ten kilometres, it seems to make them all really happy and motivated."

"It does?"

"Yes. We parked the spaceship ten kilometres out of town and when we got to our hotel everyone was smiling and humming. They were even cleaning the place from top to bottom as well." Added Dapo.

"Oh... The stories are true then."

The monk thought about it for a moment and he walked over to a stand in the corner and picked up a staff and a small parasol.

"Normally, I would not venture out but seeing as this is a very important religious matter, I'll make an exception in this case. Please lead the way."

They got up and headed out of the office and down to the main gate.

The man at the door came over to the monk.

"Everything alright sir?"

"Yes, I'm just going for a bit of a walk with these fine people. I must attend to a religious matter that has just been brought to my attention. Oh... I may be very late back so if you could pass on my apologies to the others, it would be appreciated. Thank you."

"Yes sir." Said the man and opened the door.

They walked out and down the road to the inn.

"Err, you're not scared of heights, are you?" Asked Jep.

"No. why?"

"Peebop, can you stay here and watch things."

"I'll leave you, my beer." Said Timbo.

"OK. I'll prop up the bar till you get back. Oh, and you better bring back more beer if we have any, as I may have drunk them all."

"What are we doing?" Asked the monk.

"Going for a ride. Get on the back of Fred's bike. Tank you take Jep." Said Datch.

The monk gingerly climbed on behind Fred.

“OK father, hold on tight.” Said Fred.

“Are we going to go fast?”

“Yes, it’s a long way father.”

The bikes took to the air. Peebop watched them go and then walked into the bar. He opened the cold box and pulled out two beers. Then he knocked on the counter and the owner came out of the back room. He turned to him and gave him a beer. The owner pulled out two glasses and sat down next to him.

High above the desert the monk was holding on to Fred for dear life. The bikes were at full throttle and flying in formation. The trip took seven hours coming but that was at half throttle. They were at full throttle on the way back and were planning to do it in four. The desert sands went past below and a thunderous roar filled the air. The bikes systems were pushed to their limits and four hours later they could see the oasis in the distance. The bikes slowed, losing altitude as they did. As they got closer, Datch spotted the tents first.

“Err guys. We have company.” Said Datch.

The bike dropped lower and they could see people dancing about.

“Well, they look happy.” Added Tank.

“I’m not surprised,” said Clax.

The bikes touched down next to the ship and Dag came walking over.

“Hi Datch. I see you have the monk.”

“Yes, and I see you have friends.”

“They said they know you.”

Datch thought for a moment

“Err, Tajiquay by any chance?”

“Yes, I think that was his name.”

“OK. Let us take the monk inside and we’ll be out in ten or fifteen minutes depending on if he explodes or not.”

“OK?” he said and headed back over towards the tents

“Am I likely to?” asked father Jamby.

“We don’t know father?”

“OK Father. If you would like to follow me. We’ve put it in the reactor room to try and stop it leaking out so much.”

As they entered the ship the sparkles around the monk’s head intensified. They walked down the corridor to the reactor room and entered it. There on the floor was a box and it was glowing.

“OK. We’re not sure what’s going to happened when I open it.”

“I’m ready.” Said the monk.

“And so am I.” said Tank holding a fire extinguisher.

Datch opened the box.

The gem was glowing brightly.

“Oh, my word. It’s true.”

The monk moved closer to the box and lifted the gem out. sparkles flowed down his body and he became a column of light.

“This is wonderful. Such joy and happiness.” he said.

He slowly put the gem back in the box. There was a dazed look on his face.

“We need to put it back on top of the obelisk.” He added.

“I think we need to go outside. It will reduce your brightness a bit.” said Datch helping the monk out of the room.

They headed back towards the cargo.

“I can’t believe you have it after twenty thousand years. It must be the legend.”

“What legend?”

“There is a story about a warrior that would come and bring back the light.”

“Yes. But we’re from Bellatrix five and also rock stars not warriors, so how does that work?” asked Datch.

“It doesn’t matter where you’re from. You’ve brought the gem back to us.”

“We all have.” Said Datch.

“You’re a rock star? You make music?” Asked the monk suddenly realising what he had said.

“Err yes. We found the clues to the gem’s location on a cube in Hagger’s dad’s drawers.”

“Which one of you is his dad?”

“None of us. His dad got eaten by a big spider.”

“Spider?”

“Yes, it’s a long story but Jep is a real professor and also does backing vocals.”

“You all sing?”

"Yes."

"So, you're music warriors."

Datch gave up.

"Yes, I suppose so."

"Have you tried singing to the gem?"

"Err. Yes."

"And what happened?"

"We nearly went blind. That's what." Added Tank who was walking along behind Datch but had now put the fire extinguisher down.

"That's wonderful. It likes you."

"What. It's a gem."

They came to the cargo door.

"Err, yes, but it's a psychic gem that responds to powerful emotions and then passes them on to everyone on the planet."

"What sort of song did you sing to it?"

"It was a love song that me and Carina sing together."

"Sorry to ask, but are you and Carina a couple?"

"Yes."

"That's why everyone near it is feeling happy and in a loving mood. The gem took your emotion and amplified it a million times."

"So, you're saying that if we sing Star Lovers to the gem when it's back in place the whole planet will be happy and full of love for each other?" Asked Datch.

"Basically. Yes!"

Datch started to think about it and a grin spread across his face.

"Datch. No. I know that look too well." Said Fred.

"But it would be so good to do a gig."

"Yes. You have to sing to it." Said the monk.

"But we don't have our instruments." Said Carina.

"We have the sound systems in our clothes and we can sing to it like before we started playing the instruments. We can even make mock instruments to make it feel more real."

They started to walk over to the tents. The tribe did seem to be much happier now. They all had smiles on their faces and were laughing and having a great time doing whatever. Datch then spotted Dag and Shiner along with a number of the tribe making a wooden shack.

"Err, What's Dag doing?" Datch asked.

"I think he's making a bar." Said Fred.

"OK. I didn't ask."

Just then Tajiquay came walking over.

"Datch!" he said as he approached.

He had a big smile on his face and then he spotted the monk and stopped. Datch looked at him and then decided that he needed to say something.

"Tajiquay, how are you?"

"I'm good Datch. who is this?"

"This is Father Jamby, he is a friend of ours and he is cool."

"OK."

"No, trust me. He is really cool."

"Well, welcome to our camp father."

Father Jamby tried to put his mind at rest.

"Yes, I'm here in a relaxed way only. Please carry on."

"OK father but it may get noisy later."

"I'm sure it will be fine."

They walked over to the circle of tents.

"Please sit with us. We have killed a lamb today and tonight we have kebabs."

"Kebabs?"

"Yes, and your friend is doing a free-bar. I'm not sure what that is but he says we won't get sand in our drinks. I'm not sure why we haven't done this before. I don't remember having kababs before either."

"I have a feeling they are going to be perfect." Said Datch.

"Yes. me to." Added Tank with a knowing look on his face.

"Datch?"

"Yes father?"

"I've been thinking. We need to try the song out."

"What, now?"

"Yes, it won't spread to the planet until the alignment and then only if it's in place on top of the obelisk."

"What about these people?" Asked Carina.

"They will be fine. They have already been exposed to it."

"Can I at least have my kabab first. Just in case." Said Tank.

"Just in case what?" Asked Tajiquay.

"Err. It's nothing. Just we may have a surprise for all of you later."

"What sort of surprise?"

"A musical one. We're hoping to sing for you."

"Excellent. We will look forward to it."

Datch called Timbo over.

"Yes, Datch?"

"We need some supplies..." and he started to whisper in his ear.

Timbo nodded and walked off in the direction of the 'free-bar'.

Dusk came and so did the kababs. For a tribe of people living in the deep desert and never having had kababs before they sure tasted good. The camp site became a hive of activity. People were chatting and laughing. The whole camp was totally out of place with the rest of the planet. The evening went on and Timbo came over.

"Datch. I have the things you wanted."

"OK. Thanks, Timbo. Tell the others to meet me in ten minutes behind the bar." He turned to Tajiquay

"Tajiquay, we will sing for you in about ten minutes. We just need to get ready. Father Jamby, please follow me, I need your help."

With that Datch got up and headed for the ship with the monk in tow. When they were out of ear shot Datch turned to the monk.

"OK. We're going to take the gem to the free bar and place it in the shack. That way we can see what happens. Your job will be to open the box when we start singing."

"OK. I can do that. But I'm sure it will be good."

"I don't doubt it."

They headed into the ship and went into the reactor room. Dag was there and gave them some very black cloth to hide the box until they were ready. They picked it up and took it to the shack. Timbo had put some speakers up. Dag did have a look around the ship but couldn't see where he had got them from, also, he was wondering where the microphones had come from that Timbo was now handing out. He decided not to ask for two reasons. One – Datch's dad had warned him about things happening around Datch and two – Timbo was about the size of a house and most likely wouldn't need a removals company to move one. They walked over to the shack and placed the box inside under the make shift bar.

The Pack was assembled and walked out the front of the bar.

"Hello. Err. Desert." Said Datch.

"Are we ready to rock?"

There was a moment while the population caught up.

"YESSSSS!" came the response in some sort of broken Bellatrixian.

Datch nodded to Timbo and Star Lover started. The monk opened the box. What happened next was first the dancing began and then every member of the tribe started to light up like a column of fire. Not only that but the shack was lit up with beams of light shooting into the sky.

They finished the song and looked at the crowd.

"More. More. More" They were shouting and apparently their Bellatrixian was improving.

So, they did Wild Wind.

At the end of the song, they stopped. The shack was a glowing like an exploding star and the monk was in a trance. The rest of the population were all wearing the biggest smiles that they could get on their faces and looking like you could saw their legs off and they wouldn't care.

"OK?" said Datch "I think we can put that down as a successful test."

"Yes, and no one has gone bang." Added Carina.

"Err, guys look at yourselves." Said Jep.

They were all shining columns of light.

"I think I need a new set of sunglasses. These don't seem to be working anymore." Said Dapo.

It took a couple of minutes to die down and then the monk came out of the trance. He looked at them blinking from their glow and closed the box.

"Oh my." he said, "That was incredible. You are incredible. We so need to get the gem on the tower and you need to play to it again."

They put the gem back in the ship and went and sat back down with Tajiquay. He was looking at them in an odd way.

"That my friends, was very different."

"Yes. did you like it?"

"Yes. But tell me my friend, what is in the box?"

Datch looked at the others one by one, they all nodded in turn including the monk.

"Can we trust you? I mean really trust you?" asked Datch.

"I give you my word as a nomad that nothing will pass my lips or a thousand fly's will plague my tent."

He picked up a glass and took a sip.

"It's the gem." Said Datch.

A jet of spray shot out of his mouth and he coughed and spluttered.

"The gem!"

"Err yes. We found it or according to father Jamby it might have found us. Either way it's the gem."

"Praise to the gods. It will be an end to the darkness at last."

"Yes. Father Jamby can just take us into the monastery and we'll put it up the tower and play to it."

The monk went quiet for a moment and was deep in thought.

"Yes, about that. I'm not sure it will be that easy."

"Why?"

"Well, the other monks might not understand and might want to try singing to it themselves. Mainly the ones without implants. Also, the head of the order might not like it and over time the order has lost sight of the music. They try but they don't have the emotional content."

"Oh... OK, what are we going to do then?" Asked Datch.

“My tribe will help you, my friends. We must bring the light back to the land.”

“Well, we could blow something up?” Said Hagger.

Datch and Carina stared at him and he went quiet.

“How long do we have?” Asked Rosey.

“It’s four days until the alignment and it’s at six bells.”

“Oh, so about two in the afternoon then.” Said Carina.

“It will take longer than that for us to ride there.” Said Tajiquay.

“That’s not an issue, we can put you all inside the cargo bay and fly you there.” Said Dag.

“That would be very interesting, I have never been up before.”

“But how are we going to get in without the gem being discovered? The doorman is bound to notice it.” Asked Datch

“Maybe we can sneak in while he’s having a nap.” Said Carina.

“No. He’s always there.” Said the monk.

“What if he was to take a nap and someone else was on the door?” Said Tajiquay.

“Why would he do that?”

“Well, we have some stuff in my tent. It is used for when we have visions. If you smell too much of it you won’t wake up for a day.”

“I’m not sure I can condone hurting anyone.” Said the monk.

“It won’t and they’ll have a really great dream.”

“If that’s all. Then OK.”

“So, what’s next?” asked Datch.

“We’ll need to cross the courtyard and through the main building to the base of the tower. But there will be people in both areas. I may be able to get some of my fellow monks to help but we need to keep the others away somehow.”

They sat thinking for a while and then Datch started to grin.

“How much of the smelly stuff do you have and can it be put in food?”

“I have a full bottle but I’ve never tried it in food?”

“Well, if it does work in food. I was thinking that Father Jamby could put it in their lunch and then we would only have to deal with the odd rouge monk or assistant.”

“I would need to know it was safe first though. I don’t feel right about hurting people but if they’re just going to have a nap, I’m alright with it.”

“Hmm, I’m not sure it will work in food but I will be back in a minute.”

Tajiquay got up and went in his tent.

“So, what do you think so far?”

“It might work. We have another problem though. The wooden platform that went up to the gem’s resting place has long since fallen down and rotted away. How do we get it up there?”

“I can do that.” Said Datch, “I’ll fly it up there on my bike and put it in place. You just need to tell me how to do it.”

“Well, If I remember my scripts the gem sits in a round pit on the top that is cut out in its shape, also there are two clamps that lock it in position. These should be placed over it.”

“OK, sounds simple.”

Tajiquay came walking back over with a wine bottle in his hand. He sat down.

“Is that the bottle?” asked Datch.

“No. This is wine but I have put three drops in it. We will try it now.”

“Err, we don’t want anyone dying.”

“It will not hurt anyone. It is how do you say err… made from all-natural ingredients.”

He waved at one of his men to come over and poured out a small glass of wine

“Please drink this my friend and tell me what you think.”

“Thank you.” he said and took a sip. “This is good wine but does have a little tang.”

He took another drink and sat down, they sat watching him for a moment while he finished off the wine.

“Do you feel OK?”

“Yes, I feel, wow this is good wine. Can I have some…” with that his eyes rolled backwards and he passed out.

“He’s still breathing.” Said Tank going over to him.

“Yes, and he’s also got a grin on his face.” Added Rosey.

“Tajiquay, which tent does he sleep in?”

“That one there, I’ll get a couple of my men to take him to it.”

“That’s not needed. Timbo, please do the honours.”

“OK Datch.”

Timbo picked up the man with one arm and carried him to his tent.

“Do we need to drug the doorman? Can’t we just get Timbo to walk though it?” Asked Tajiquay.

“Yes, but then we would need to get them a new door afterwards.” Said Carina.

“Good point.” he said.

“So, let’s recap the plan. One – We go back to the inn outside the monastery and Father Jamby goes back in with a couple of bottles of the special made from all-natural ingredients wine. Two - On the day of the alignment, Father Jamby gives all the unfriendly monks a glass of wine as a toast to the start of day saying he found it in an old scroll. Three - When they are all sleeping, he comes down to the main gate where you’ll all be waiting and will have given the doorman a happy sniff of ‘made from all-natural ingredients. Four - You will make your way to the platform with Tajiquay and his men running shotgun in case of any suicidal monks. Five - While you’re doing that, I will put the gem in position and then meet you on the platform for the songs.”

The others all looked at him.

“Well?” he said.

“Sounds about right.” Said Fred.

“Right, let’s carry on with the party.” Said Datch.

They went back to enjoying the night.

The next morning the man who had the wine seemed fine and didn’t even have a hangover. Datch and The Pack helped to load the tribe into the cargo bay and the gem had an extra layer of insulation in the hope that anything leaking out would not be too bad. Once the oasis was cleaned up and everyone was accounted for, Dag shut the door.

The Pack along with Father Jamby and Tajiquay followed him up to the flight deck. They were given chairs. They looked at them and then at The Pack who had sat down. They followed suit. The engines started up and they grabbed the side of their chairs.

"OK. We're carrying a bit of weight now so it's going to be a shaky take off. Hold on."

The ship started shaking as the engines increased thrust. Slowly but surely, it lifted into the air. The nose pointed forwards and then the ship accelerated. Father Jamby went pale. The desert below was a blur and after five minutes the monastery was in sight. The ship touched down about ten kilometres outside of town kicking up a cloud of dust and sand that looked like a mini sand storm as it landed.

"OK folks, we're hear. If Datch and The Pack take the monk home. Then Shiner and myself will help the tribe with their tents."

"Timbo, do we have anymore beer?" asked Tank.

"Yes, I have seven more cases."

Fred was about to say where from but changed his mind.

"I had better take three then. It's going to be hot in the inn."

"You could stay here?" Said Dag.

"Yes, but if Father Jamby needs us, we need to be close by."

"OK, but take this. If you need help just yell and we'll be there in a hurry." Said Dag.

He tossed a communicator over to Tank who put it in his pocket and then followed the rest of them to the cargo bay. After moving the bikes outside and loading up the extra beer supply. They mounted up and headed off in the direction of the town.

The Start

The town was quiet as they entered it. There were the normal stares as they flew down the street to get to the inn. It was hot and dusty and the air was filled with the smell of smoke. They landed in front of the inn and Peebop came walking out to meet them.

“You guys took some time. Me and Faberfab have drank all the beer.”

“Who is Faberfab?” asked Tank.

“Oh, that’s the owners name. I’ve been learning to talk in the local tongue.”

“How’s that going?” asked Carina.

“Well, I can order chicken and rice, oh and some strange coffee that makes you see things.”

“OK. Note to everyone, DO NOT ORDER the strange coffee.” Said Fred.

“How did you get on with the you know what?”

“We’ll tell you later, we need to get the monk back with his bits.”

“Datch do you and Carina want to do the honours and take him back with the wine?”

“Yes, no probs.” Said Datch.

“Wine? Hope we have some to go with the chicken.” Asked Peebop.

“No, and trust me you don’t want it.” Replied Tank.

“Look, just come inside. We have three cases of cold beer.” Said Fred pointing at the pack that Tank was picking up from the back of his bike.

Datch and Carina walked up the street with the monk.

“Are you sure this will help your planet?” Asked Carina.

“Yes, once the gem is in place then the energy will flow and the world will be good again.”

“What if you get a bad monk again?” Asked Datch.

“The order has taken care of that. Only a monk that pass a number of tests can be part of the Tones sect and they can only lead the Tones once before stepping down.”

“But if you haven’t had the gem, how do you know it will work?”

“We do practise it every ten years just in case.”

“Well, Let’s hope it goes well. How will we know if things are, OK?"

"I’ll send one of my monks to see you at say four bells if everything has gone to plan. Tajiquay did say the wine should keep them asleep for hours.”

“Yes, it should be a while before they wake up.”

They arrived at the gate and the gate keeper opened it.

“Thank you – Datch and Carina, it’s been a very enlightening outing. Let the gods watch over you.” He winked and went inside.

They turned and started to head back down to the inn.

“You sure the monk will be, OK?” asked Carina.

“Yes, I think we can trust him, there is no one else to trust anyway.”

“I suppose you’re right.”

They carried on walking down the street and about halfway back they could hear someone humming out aloud.

“Well, it’s started. It won’t be long before the whole place is happy town.” Said Datch.

“Won’t it give the gem away?”

“It might but Jamby said he can keep the monks distracted so they won’t notice.”

“And what about everyone else?”

“They will all be doing the same thing so they won’t care.”

They arrived back at the inn and the rest of The Pack was sitting outside with cold beers along with the owner who now had a big grin. Datch wasn’t sure if this was due to the gem or the imported beer that he had in his hand.

“Did the monk get back OK?” asked Fred.

“Yes. he went in and the doorman was none the wiser.” Replied Datch.

“Good, Faberfab please can you get a couple of glasses for Datch and Carina.” Said Peebop.

“Yeas sier, err sir.” he said getting up.

“He speaks Bellatrixian?” asked Datch.

“He’s trying.” Said Peebop.

“So, what do we do now?” asked Tank.

“We chill and try to stay incognito for two days.” Said Datch.

“And just how are we going to do that?” Said Tank.

"Yes, it's a bit like asking a tiger not to eat meat." added Peebop.

"Can I suggest something." asked Hagger.

"No, we can't blow anything up!" said Fred.

"I wasn't going to say that. It's just that the tribe know all about what is going on and are having a party in the desert so why don't we go and join them?"

"That is a good point, we don't need to be here now that the monk is back safe and sound." said Dapo.

Just at that point Faberfab came back out with the glasses and two cold beers. They looked at him. He had a big smile on his face and looked as if he was the happiest man on the planet with his new friends.

"Well, we can't leave him like that, it wouldn't be right." Said Tish.

"No, I suppose not." Said Datch.

"Why don't we stay here tonight and then take him and his family with us to the ship tomorrow?" added Tish.

"That would work." added Rosey.

"It will give me chance to do the reconnaissance we were talking about. The roof looks like a good spot." Said Fred

"That's decided then." Said Datch.

"How big is his family?" asked Fred.

"Well, There's his wife, daughter and two sons. One of the sons is only just over six months old."

"So, four of them and a baby."

"Yes."

“We had better get Dag to bring his truck.” Added Datch.

They carried on drinking outside and watching as the people passing by got happier and happier. By the time dinner was ready the population were all humming and had a spring in their steps.

That evening Faberfab introduced them to his family. Datch asked them if they would like to see a real spaceship. His older son got quite excited along with his daughter. Faberfab said that they needed to stay for the guests. Datch volunteered Fred to stay and therefore Faberfab didn’t have much choice but to say yes.

Fred would stay behind to make sure the inn was OK. What they didn’t say was that Fred was going to work out the access point for Datch to place the gem in position. From the roof of the inn Fred could get a clear view of the top of the obelisk. Datch needed to have detailed images of the top and Fred had brought a small drone to go and reconnoitrer the area but he needed a clear line of sight for it to work OK. The rest of the evening was a bit on the strange side as Faberfab started humming and then Datch put some music on his clothing. Well, on the sound system that Rosey and Tish had built into them anyway. The inn started to get the locals coming inside and by halfway through the evening the inn was full of people and The Pack were all playing the music on their clothes that seemed to entertain the locals. Luckily for The Pack the sound systems in the clothing synchronised with each other and therefore the inn was filled with music. The party carried on until late and it was after midnight before finally The Pack got to bed.

The next morning just after two bells Dag turned up outside in his truck. There were a number of conversations between Clax, Faberfab and Fred about how to take care of the inn while they were gone. Fred said it would be fine and after all it was only overnight. They finally got in the truck and took off for the ship. Datch turned to Fred.

"You're sure the drone is, OK?"

"Yes, I checked it out last night while everyone was chatting. All its systems are fine. I'll send it up there as soon as you give me the OK from the ship."

"OK, See you at the monastery in two days."

"You be careful Datch. No dying this time."

"That's for sure. Carina would kill me if I did it again." He smiled.

Datch got on his bike and took off in the direction of the ship.

Fred had just got a coffee and was sitting down when the communicator bleeped. It was Datch giving him the go ahead. He finished his coffee and headed through the kitchen out into the small area at the back of the inn. There going up the back of the building were a set of stairs. They were sandy and not very wide but also easy to climb. He went up to the second floor. This floor was Faberfab's apartment and at the side of it was another set of stairs. These were even smaller than the last ones and were right up against the side of the building next to the inn. He headed up squeezing past a pile of boxes half way up. Finally, he made it to the top.

The roof had a small garden area with the vegetables growing in it and over at the side was a water extraction unit which was busy acquiring what little moisture it could get from the air. The water would then flow into a holding tank and any extra would then flow into the garden watering the plants. Fred walked over to a small patio area and sat down on one of the two chairs placing the small case he had brought with him on a little table in between them.

Fred opened the case and inside was a small circular disc shaped object with little cylindrical thrusters around the outside. It had a vid on the front with a small scanning array above it and on the back were two small thrusters. He removed it from the box and placed it on the table. He then removed a little vid comm from the box and placed it next to the little drone. He tapped a couple of buttons and the screen lit up and at the same time the little drone started humming. He had used this little device many times before for insurance assessments back at home and had brought it thinking it may come in handy. He didn't think however that he would be casing a monastery with it.

He connected to the vid comm with his implant and then the little drone took to the air. The obelisk was just two streets over and it didn't take long for the drone to get there. Fred flew it high up so as not to bring any unwanted attention to it. Soon it was heading up the side of the obelisk towards the top. There were bits of wood sticking out the side here and there where the wooden steps used to be. The rest of surface was smooth and looked like dark green marble.

Fred flew the drone around the obelisk in an upwards spiral so as to scan every millimetre of the surface. As the drone got near to the top the ancient writing could be seen and it was also glowing even in the sunlight. Soon, the little craft reached the top. There were two golden metal clamps sitting open either side of a depression. Fred tried moving one of the clamps with the drone. It seemed to move easy enough. The depression was the right size for the gem but had sand in it so Datch might need to take a brush with him but it looked easy enough to put the gem back in place.

He then took the drone down towards the base and the platform for the ceremony. It was a large flat area and had four parabolic mirrors carved out of stone. One in each corner and each of them had a small green gem mounted in the centre on four golden rods, he noticed they were glowing dimly. Other than that, the platform was deserted and only had a single set of large wooden doors coming from the main building. He moved in a bit closer for a better look just as one of the doors opened. He flew the drone over to the eves of the building and watched as a handyman came out and started sweeping the area. Fred had to think fast and flew the drone up onto the roof before gaining height. He had got all the information Datch needed so he flew it back over the roof tops to the inn. It landed on the table and he cracked open a beer before reaching for the communicator.

Datch had arrived to what could be described as a barbeque come beach party. The tribe were a very happy bunch of people and so were Faberfab and his family. As Datch touched down they were just being introduced to the tribe and also now had kababs in their hands. He walked over to them.

"Ah, here is Datch." said Tajiquay.

"Hi all, I see you have introduced everyone."

"Yes, you like Kabab?"

"Not just yet thanks, but I'll have a burger if there is one going later. I've promised to give Faberfab and his family a tour of the ship with Dag."

"Very good for them, oh don't forget sunglasses."

He turned and stared walking over to Timbo.

"Timbo, what's a burger?" Tajiquay was heard saying.

Shiner coughed.

"Why sunglasses?" Asked Datch.

"Well, you know the gem, it seems to be getting a lot more excited shall we say."

"How excited?"

"Err... If you want to get it out of the box, you're going to need welding glasses on. You need major sunglasses on just to go in the reactor room."

"It's in a metal box."

"Yes, a metal box that has become translucent."

"Oh."

"OK. We'll miss out that part of the ship out then."

With that Datch turned to the Faberfab family.

"Who wants to see the ship then?"

Soon Datch and Dag were giving a guided tour of the ship while the others set up deck chairs and sun umbrellas that Timbo had found from somewhere. No one was going to ask him were things kept coming from but just accepted that he had got them from some place only he knew about. The free bar which now had become 'The Party Shack' had also come with them and now seemed to have been extended and included bar staff, an Ice-cream maker and nuts. A bottle of Old Man's Boots had also appeared on the rapidly expanding shelf at the back and Timbo seemed to be very happy making cocktails behind the bar.

After the tour Datch brought them over the desert version of a beach front and got them a drink. Bottles of Gruck had also appeared for the younger members of the population. He had just settled down in a deck chair when Shiner came over and told him the call he was expecting had just come through. Tank, Peebop and Clax got up and followed Datch inside.

They arrived in the coms room and there on the vid screen was Fred.

"Hi folks. I have the information you need Datch."

"Cool, let's have a look."

Fred played the images from the drone and they sat watching as it flew up the side of the obelisk to the top.

“You might need to take a brush with you.” said Fred as the drone reached the top.

“Is it just me or are things getting more complex?” said Tank.

“Why?” said Fred.

“Well, the gem has started to glow a lot more. It’s now shining through the solid metal box and Datch has to clean the top of the obelisk before he can put it in place.”

“Ah, that could be a problem. we’ll have to think how to do it.”

“Don’t welding glasses dim automatically?”

“Well, normally but I’m not sure it will work with the gem.”

“OK, we’ll do a few checks at this end and get back to you. What about the area below?”

Fred carried on playing the footage from the drone. It dropped down showing the platform.

“Well at least that looks OK. If we put Timbo on the other side of that door, we should be pretty secure.”

“Yes. I agree. Datch can fly down to us once the gem is in place.”

“Do we know the time of the alignment?” asked Fred.

“Yes, it’s in thirty-nine hours forty-three minutes and counting.” Replied Shiner who had followed them in.

“OK. I take it that’s ship board time?”

“Yes. just under two days.” Said Shiner.

“Right, I’ll see you folks tomorrow and the rest of you the day after.”

Fred closed the link and took another sip of his beer.

Back at the ship the others sat looking at each other.

"Well, we need to find a way to handle the gem without Datch going blind." Added Clax.

"Let's all think about what we can do and try them out tomorrow after the Faberfab family has gone back to the inn." Said Tank.

"Sounds like a plan." said Datch.

They headed outside to the party and sat in the shade under a large parasol. Datch looked at it for a while and decided not to ask where it came from. Later that night they came up with a plan while doing some strange dance called a limbo that involved a very low pole which you had to go under without digging the sand out first or falling on your bum.

The gem was certainly having a big effect on the tribe and the Faberfab family. Faberfab and Tajiquay where currently in discussions about an expansion plan for the inn along with a profit-sharing plan for the staff. Datch sat watching them all. It was amazing the gem could do this. It was stimulating their desire to do better and their will to make life full. It was then he heard it. Faberfab's daughter was humming Star lovers. She had not been anywhere nearby when they had played it. Datch had to ask.

"Hey, that tune. Have you heard it somewhere?"

"No. It's in my head." she said.

"What do you mean?"

"What I said, it's in my head singing to me." She replied and went off into the crowd.

It was then Datch realised it was not just the emotion the gem was amplifying but the music and their thoughts. What they did in two days would spread across the planet and affect the whole population. He told Timbo to call The Pack together quietly, they needed to talk.

The next morning most of The Pack and the Faberfab's headed back to town. Carina stayed with Datch and the plan was that she would help him to put the gem in position as it would be easier with two of them.

They watched as Jep took off in Dag's truck and the rest followed on the bikes.

Datch walked back inside with Dag. Carina and Shiner were busy at work in the heart of the ship. They were both wearing welding glasses and the ships replicator was doing overtime as was the ships reactor that was supplying it power.

They had the gems box open and were currently placing squares of material over the top of it. Datch and Dag opened the door and closed it again very quickly before putting on a set of welding glasses themselves. They then opened the door again and went in.

"So, any luck?" said Dag.

"Well, we have tried all the normal stuff and it was like waving a piece of paper at it. We have now moved on to the more exotic material and are currently trying titanium." Said Shiner

"What is up next then?"

"A five-millimetre-thick gold plate." Said Carina and slowly placed it over the top of the box.

It sort of worked, but the gem could be still be seen glowing in the centre.

"Hmm, that's not bad but when we're near the monastery I suspect the intensity will go up." Said Datch.

"Well, we could try iridium but it will hammer the replicator and reactor fuel if we need to make a box from it." said Shiner.

Dag thought about it.

"Datch, if we do this, we could end up getting stuck on this planet. It will deplete the reactor core."

"Can't you get more fuel?" asked Carina.

"Not on this world. She might be an old ship but she uses high quality fuel rods."

"What if I got some shipped to you from off world?"

"It still means we would be stuck here for at least two or three weeks. If we need a rapid exit, it won't get us to the next planetary system."

Datch thought about it. He knew the gem would work but Dag did have a valid point.

"Hmm… let's do it. I'm sure it's going to be OK."

"OK. I just hope things go to plan. Shiner, make an iridium box."

"OK boss."

"Err… sorry to be a pain but can we make it so the gem sits in it with the pointy bit down and have it so it opens at the bottom?" Asked Datch.

"I can, but why?"

"If I can hold the bike steady and clean the sand from its base then Carina can just put the box on top and pull a pin or something and we can lift the box off and knock the clamps into place before heading to the platform."

"You have already thought this out, haven't you?"

“Yes. I always do.”

“Well, if we get stuck, we can always open a bar next to the inn that Faberfab and Tajiquay were talking about.” he said in a slightly sarcastic tone.

It took most of the reactor fuel to make the box and after it was finished, they tried it for size the gem fitted perfectly and more to the point the light didn’t spill out when it was closed.

“Do you think we should leave it open for now, a little bit anyway?” Asked Carina.

“Yes. It might be an idea. We don’t want to upset the population around here. They’re such a happy bunch now.” said Dag.

They left the bottom open so the reactor room was filled with a nice green glow and went back out to party in the sun. Datch was starting to realise that whatever happened the next day, the planet would never be the same again. Fred and Tank both thought that it would be for the better as they may start getting decent beer in the hotels. When actually just decent hotels would be a start. Maybe they were right. Datch sighed. He knew that there was no turning back now and what would be would be.

He put his head on Carina’s shoulder. She turned to look at him.

“You OK, lover boy?”

“Yes. I was just thinking what a big day it is for us all tomorrow. The destiny of the planet is in our hands.”

“Yes, but let’s make it our best day ever.” She gave him a kiss and he smiled.

“OK babes. We will. Love you loads.” He returned the kiss.

They sat chilling out under the parasols until it started getting dark.

In the town the little inn now was getting very busy. Quite a lot of the locals who had been staring at them a few days before were now having a knees up biker's fashion. There was quite a bit of merriment happening. Jep turned to Fred.

"Err, should we be doing this?"

"What?"

"Having a party?"

"Why not?"

"Well, these people don't party. They are normally boring."

"Duck!" shouted Fred.

"Why?" said Jep as a balloon hit him in the ear.

"I look at this way. If Datch is right, everyone on the planet is going to be motivated and be in party mode tomorrow. All we are doing is giving these folks a head start."

Jep thought about it for a moment before deciding that Fred's logic made sense and picked up another beer.

"OK?" he said taking a sip of his drink and then went off to find the owner of the balloon.

The morning was just like any other desert morning with the sun rising into the sky and radiating down its energies. Today though, there was a strange feeling in the air. It was just a hint of something magical and everyone at the camp was up and getting ready for the day ahead. Tajiquay had got twenty of his men together and they were sorting out the mounts in the shade behind the ship. Datch watched them out of the command deck window as they put guns in holders on the saddles. Dag walked up behind him.

"Looks like they are getting ready." he said.

"They do know not to shoot anyone, don't they?"

"Yes, they are just for show I think."

This didn't really put Datch's mind at rest but at this point things just had to happen.

"I think I'll just remind them." said Datch.

He got up and walked off outside. Dag watched him go and thought to himself how young Datch was to have so much on his mind and yet he didn't show it.

Datch came out of the cargo bay and went over to Tajiquay.

"Hi Tajiquay, What's with the guns?"

"They are to make sure no one is silly."

"You're not going to shoot anyone are you?"

"Oh, no Datch, don't worry we won't but they don't know that do they." He grinned at Datch.

He knew that grin. He saw it in the mirror just before a plan came together.

"If people don't like what we do and try to stop us, we point gun at them and my man over there shoots the wall next to someone and makes them jump. This makes them do what we want. Yes"

Datch could see how that would work.

"Well, try not to do it when the music is playing."

"As soon as the music starts everyone will stop."

"What do you mean?"

"It's the gem. It makes everyone happy."

"Oh… OK. Carry on then."

He went back inside.

"Dag?"

A head stuck out from between two of the seats

"What's up?"

"We have an army."

"Yes. but trust me it will be fine. I'll keep an eye on them. These are good people and will make sure we succeed."

"How?"

"Well, you don't think we came empty handed did you. when your dad said you might need our help, he also said to be prepared for anything. I now know why."

"You will have to come to one of dad's reunions. You and Shiner will fit right in."

Datch turned to head back down the corridor.

"Datch."

He stopped and turned to look at Dag.

"You just do your thing. We will do the rest. Don't worry!" he smiled.

"OK. I'll do my best." He headed down to the rec room where Carina was waiting.

In the monastery the monks were having breakfast when Father Jamby walked in followed by a number of other monks. They carried trays with glasses on.

"Fellow followers of the gem. I have been reading the texts all my life and this week I found a text that I had not seen before. In it was a toast to the gem and the alignment. We don't have the gem but I felt it was fitting to have the toast on the day of the alignment. Please join me in the celebration of this day."

He put the tray he was carrying down on the table in front of him and the other monks took their trays and handed glasses out to all the other monks.

"Are you sure about this?" asked the head of the order.

"Yes sir. It didn't say what wine though so I went for red. If you like I shall show the text after breakfast."

"OK. I'm not one to say no to wine even if it is at breakfast. Carry on."

Jamby had been hoping for this. With the backing of the head of the order no one would refuse.

"Sir, I hope it is OK but I used a couple of bottles from a very old vintage, I thought it was fitting."

"Quite right. Please proceed."

He waited until the wine was handed out and all his monks had returned to his table. If this didn't work, he could always get a job as a conman.

"Fellow monks. This blessing is a little odd but please bear with me."

He started to sing.

"This is the day; this is the time to let to sparks fly. We welcome the light and the fire within. Come on baby light my fire. Let the flame grow higher. Let the planets align and the green fire flow." The other monks were all looking at him but he carried on. "Now let's raise a toast to the gem and the stars."

He lifted his glass.

"To the gem and all the planets."

They all lifted their glasses and in true monk style knocked it all back in one go.

It was then he realised that they were all still looking at him.

"What?" he said.

"Your sparks" said the head of the order "They're green!"

There was then a sudden sound of breaking glasses as all the monks passed out apart from the group around Jamby

"Father Tucpin – Go to the inn in the town and tell Fred the monks are sleeping and the plan is a go. Father Tippy when father Tucpin goes out the gate put the cloth I gave you over the gate keeper's mouth and it should send him to sleep. Then look after the gate until father Tucpin gets back. OK?"

"Yes sir."

The two monks went running out the door. The rest stood looking at him.

"Let's make the rest of the brethren comfy." They were still looking at him.

"What?"

"Why are your sparks green?" asked one of the other monks.

Jamby realised it was the gem that was having an effect on him.

"It's the gem. I told you it was nearby. Now please lay the others in a more relaxed position so we don't have to put up with people limping around for the next four weeks complaining about aching joints and bad backs."

With that the other monks set about making sure the other monks were sleeping OK and picked up all the broken glass. They then headed towards the main hall and the steps heading up to the platform. Jamby placed a monk here and a monk there on the way to make sure The Pack found their way OK.

Tank was sitting outside the inn having a coffee and enjoying the lunch time sun when a monk came running down the street. By the time he reached the inn he was somewhat out of breath and very red in the face.

"Fred?" he panted.

"No. He's in the toilet, I'm Tank"

"Need to tell Fred." he said struggling to get his words out.

"Look, just sit down and get your breath back he'll be out in a minute. You're not being chased by anyone are you?"

The monk shook his head and sat down. Two minutes later Fred came walking out.

“Fred?”

“Yes.”

“Father Jamby said all is good and the monks are sleeping.”

“What about the gate keeper?”

“We did the cloth and he’s now snoring a lot.”

“Cool. You stay there and I’ll get you some water.”

Fred went back inside and picked up the communicator that Jep was looking after.

He pressed a button.

“Dag, Dag?”

A voice came back from the little unit.

“Yes?”

“The monks are good so the operation is a go.”

“Copy that, the backup is on the way. Dag out.”

With that Fred picked up a bottle of water and went outside. He was really starting to enjoy this secret agent type stuff.

The monk wasn’t quite as red now and the panting had calmed down. He gave him the bottle of water and sat down.

“Err, don’t we have to go?” the monk asked.

“Not just yet. We have friends coming to help. They will be here in about half a bell. Father Jamby knows the plan.”

Fred sat down and called the others over.

“The plans a go, get your heads in the game folks. We have a gig to do so let’s show this planet how to party.”

The others went inside and took their tops off before turning them inside out. Moments later they came back out. The monk wished he had sun glasses. The Pack looked like well, ‘The Pack’. They had light grey shirts with bright orange and yellow flames. Reaching up to the lapels. On the right breast there was ‘The Pack’ in bright green letters and on the left one their names. The collars were bright green again with bright orange and yellow flashes. The back had the same flame design but had the words ‘The Pack on tour, we rock planets!’ In bright green letters. Then below was a black square with small bright red letters spelling out the words ‘Free beer welcome!”.

“What do you think folks?” asked Rosey.

“Works for me.” said Fred.

They all agreed that Rosey and Tish had done a good job and the only down side was they weren’t leather which given that they were in the middle of a desert was also a good thing.

The monk and Faberfab were blinking at the blaze of colour. They sat waiting outside for the rest of the raiding party to show up.

At the ship Datch and Carina mounted Datch’s bike. In her hands was the black box containing the gem. Around them the tribe’s men climbed on their mounts with Tajiquay at the front.

Dag came out with a backpack on.

“I thought you were staying here?” shouted Datch.

“What, and miss all the fun. No way!”

Shiner was staying with the ship in case they needed a fast exit.

“OK Tajiquay, let’s move out.” shouted Datch.

The party started to head across the desert, as they did the sand was thrown into the air causing a cloud behind them.

“Carina, this is going to be one hell of a gig. Are you ready?”

“Yes. I’m with you.”

“I think the others should be getting into the zone. Let’s play some tunes to do the same.”

“Good plan. What about Wild Wind?”

“OK.”

The sound system burst into life. Datch left the system on external as well so everyone could hear it.

By the time the town was in sight Wild Wind, Rocking the City, No Place to Hide and Bikers Dream had all been played and as they approached the towns gates Datch put on Supernova. The party were now so pumped up that they could take down a city if they needed to.

At the inn everyone was waiting for the arrival. Faberfab was waiting but didn’t know why. The monk was waiting but didn’t know what to expect. The Pack was waiting and knew what was coming. Then the sound of music could be heard coming up the street.

“Sounds like it’s time to go. Get ready people!” Said Tank getting up.

The monk looked at him and then at the others. They were starting to move.

Down the street came the sound of music and the rumble of large animals on the cobles. Then they could see the approaching party. A stampede with a cloud of dust ahead of it. It got closer and closer until the lead animal stopped in front of Timbo. It was either that or knock itself out. Tajiquay looked down.

"Timbo!" he said.

"Yes." said Timbo.

Then something inside him told him to say.

"Are we ready to rock?"

"Yes." said Tajiquay.

Datch and Carina landed next to Tank.

"OK Fred, we'll head up to the roof top and wait there until you tell us to place the gem."

"I'll call as soon as we're in place."

"Right, let's do this." Datch said and put his hand out.

The rest of The Pack put their hands in.

"One, Two, Three. Let's party" They broke hands.

Datch and Carina headed to the roof and put the bike in hover and the rest headed up the street. Timbo was now pulling a big cart behind him.

"Timbo, What's in the cart?" as Fred.

"Just some stuff." Said Timbo.

"What sort of stuff?"

"Stuff we might need." Replied Timbo.

Fred knew when not to ask any further and went with OK instead. Knowing Timbo if they needed something, he would have it covered even if it was a small planetary cannon or something.

The group moved slowly up the street trying not to bring attention to themselves but seeing as it was a small desert town and there were over thirty of them. It was pretty much impossible to avoid the odd scream form a resident who picked the wrong moment to go out or hadn't noticed the rampaging horde closing behind them. They reached the main gate and knocked on the door.

"Hello. Who is it?" said a little voice from behind the door.

"It's us." said Fred.

"Who is us?" said the voice.

"You do know that you're meant to open the little hatch, don't you?" said Tank.

"Oh."

There was a scraping sound from behind the door and then the little hatch opened and a pair of eyes peered out.

"That's better. Oh, it's you Father Tucpin."

The eyes disappeared and another scraping noise was heard followed by a large bolt being pulled slowly backwards. The door finally opened to reveal a very short monk that also had a habit on that was at least two sizes too big for him. They went inside and Tajiquay told two of his men to stay with the monk on the door.

They started to advance up the path to the courtyard with a rumbling noise behind them. They spotted another monk near the entrance. The monk peered at them before waving them to come over. They crossed the courtyard and Tajiquay and his men dismounted. The rumbling noise stopped just behind them.

“Which way now?” asked Fred.

“This way but there is a monk we missed.”

“Where?” said Tajiquay.

“He’s standing just inside to the right. He was looking for the others I think.”

“Don’t worry, we’ll sort it.”

Tajiquay waved at four of his men. The men crept through the door and went inside. Inside was a large hall with bookshelves on both sides and behind them more bookshelves and little areas to sit and read. These formed two more corridors running down either side to a junction where corridors went off the left and the right. Straight ahead was a set of large doors.

Two of the men headed down behind the books to the left and the other two did the same to the right.

“Father, if you would walk right up the centre to flush him out, please.”

“You’re not going to hurt him, are you?”

“No, but he’s going to get a surprise.”

The monk went inside walking up the centre of the chamber. Sure enough, the other monk came walking over to him and stood with a very annoyed look on his face.

“You’re one of Jamby’s lot aren’t you. Where is Father Tiki?” he asked in a very cross tone. The monk looked at him.

“You’ll be in a lot of trouble if you don’t tell me.” he added.

There was a click behind him.

“I might to be able to help you there.” Said a voice.

The monk spun around straight into the barrel of a gun.

“What the hell do you think…” the second man put a cloth over the monk face and then caught him as he fell.

“There you go Father, sleeping like a baby.”

“Oh. I hope he’s not going to be cross with me when he wakes up.”

“Maybe, but if you give him a nice cushion and a comfy chair, he might not be mad for too long.”

The monk kicked the unconscious monk in the ribs hard and smiled.

“Oh, I see.” Said the man with the gun.

They waved at the others to come in and a rumbling sound came down the corridor behind them.

“Where now Father?” asked Fred.

“Down here.” said the monk.

They followed him to the junction and then to the right and up a flight of steps. The rumbling made banging sounds as it went up the steps.

“Timbo, are you going to take that all the way to the platform?” asked Fred.

“Yes. We need it.” said Timbo. It wasn’t an answer but more of a statement.

“Oh, OK.” Said Fred making a note not to ask again.

There was another set of doors. The monk put his head through first to check and then went in. The rest followed behind him after they got the nod. There was a bang as one of the doors found out it was not a good idea to try and close if a Timbo is coming through. They entered the grand hall with rows of seats on either side and a large raised platform at the end. There were ornate carvings on the walls and a high roof with skylights in it shaped like the gem. The same theme ran through the large windows on either side. All the glass was green in colour bathing the room in a bright green light.

At the back of the large platform was another group on monks. Standing in front of a large set of doors. Fred spotted Father Jamby at the front. They walked up to him.

"Hi Father, What's up?"

"We think the cleaner ran off with the key."

"And?"

"We can't find the spare. These doors lead to the platform."

"Do you know where he went? We can send some of Tajiquay's men to bring him back."

"No, he must have seen something and has left the monastery. We can't find him anywhere."

"We can shoot the door locks off." Said Tajiquay.

"It's a fifteen-thousand-year-old door. You can't go blowing it to bits." Said Jamby.

"Don't worry. We have something for to fix stuck doors. Timbo, please can you open the door for us?" said Dag.

Timbo looked the door up and down.

"Yes sir."

Timbo walked backwards a few metres and took a run up. A Timbo at a full run was like watching a speeding locomotive. He hit the doors with his shoulder and there was a splintering of wood as the doors decided what to keep, Hinges or locks.

The locks lost and the doors swung open with a loud bang. Behind them was a now unconscious cleaner laying on the steps at the back of them and looking like he had been hit by a train. Which wasn't far from it.

"We've found the cleaner." Shouted Hagger.

"Hmm, do you have a first aid room?" asked Rosey.

"He'll be fine, he just has a couple of bumps, that's all." said Dag checking him out.

They propped him up against the wall with a cushion and left one of the monks to make sure he was alright. They closed what was left of the doors and Tajiquay positioned his men to guard the hole where the locks had been.

They walked up a number of steps and onto the platform. It was a large flat open area and on the opposite side was the base of the obelisk. Timbo pulled his truck over the rubble of the doors and started to unload. The Pack went over to help.

"Timbo. It's a PA rig." Said Fred.

"Yes. we're doing a gig."

"We're on a planet that doesn't have music and who's main line of excitement is watching paint dry. Yet you have somehow got a PA rig."

"Yes. we're doing a gig."

Fred couldn't argue with that but where he had got it from in the middle of the desert, he had no idea. They laid out the kit and set up a portable generator that had come with it. Then Timbo opened another box and inside were a set of instruments.

"Sorry, these are not very good but they look OK."

"Wow, thanks Timbo."

“How long we got?” asked Fred.

“About fifteen minutes.” shouted Father Jamby.

Fred grabbed the communicator.

“Datch! You’re up. Fifteen minutes until alignment.”

“Copy that. On our way!” Said Datch.

Across the town the sound of the bike’s engines rattled the windows as Datch increased the power.

“Here we go babes. Hold on.”

Datch flew the bike towards the obelisk getting higher and higher as they went. People below came out to see what all the noise was about and stood looking up at the bike. That is apart from the ones who had seen The Pack coming up the street. They were still hiding in their cellars.

“OK babes, get ready!”

Datch manoeuvred the bike into position alongside the obelisk and got out a stick with a brush on the end. He brushed the top of the pit clearing the area of sand. The thrusters on the bike were blowing the sand away as he did it. It didn’t take long for him to get it clean. There was a larger stone chunk in the bottom and he had to use the other end of the stick to get rid of it.

“Datch. the box is glowing.”

“Oh wow. OK put it in place and then we’ll put our glasses on. I’ll set the bikes autopilot to take us to the platform as soon as we put the clamps in place.”

“OK!”

Carina placed the box over the pit. They both put their welding glasses on and then Datch put his finger on the autopilot engage button. Carina lifted the box. A bright green light shone across the sky. The glasses were working but it was still very bright and hurting their eyes. Carina managed to knock the clamps into place on the second attempt and Datch hit the button. The bike banked hard and dropped down sharply. From the platform they could see the light from the gem shining brightly. Datch's bike touched down on the platform near the doors. They jumped off still blinking and trying to see.

"You two, OK?" said Fred running over.

"Yes, I think so." Said Datch.

"Me to. But I have a very large gem shaped image in the middle of my vision."

"How long?" asked Datch.

"Three minutes." shouted Jamby who had now got a clock from somewhere.

Timbo gave Datch a guitar and Carina a set on bongos

"Everyone, take your places!" shouted Fred.

They all got ready to play.

"Now!" said Father Jamby.

"Timbo. Announce us please."

"Ladies, Gentlemen and aliens give it up for 'The Pack'."

Star Lovers rang out across the platform and the gems in the corners lit up like bright stars. Then a beam of green light shot up from each of them and hit the gem. The light from the gem grew brighter and brighter as the song played. The Pack then entered party mode and the beams intensified. Monks started glowing bright green and then Datch and Carina kissed. As they did the sky exploded like a supernova with a green light shooting to all parts of the globe. The other obelisks around the planet burst into life amplifying the gem's power and passing it on to everyone on the planet. It was a tidal wave of energy and emotion touching every soul on the world. In the middle of it all was Datch, Carina and the music. Everyone on the planet was now part of the song. People stopped in the streets and started moving to the sound in their heads. The second song started and the gem got brighter still, sending ever greater waves of energy across the sky. The monks were just bright green columns of light. Tajiquay and his men were lit up like roman candles and The Pack was now shining brighter than the sun. The strange thing was that The Pack could still see each other and the feeling felt great. The third song started and now light was everywhere. People came out into the streets with streams of light flowing down from their heads and were now dancing and singing along to the chorus even though they didn't know the song. The Pack finished playing and Datch shouted.

"Be happy, look after each other and party on people!"

As they stopped the gem gave out a final massive burst of energy and light before dimming down and just sending out small pulses of energy every couple of seconds. The monks who had been in a total trance slowly came out of it and stopped glowing quite so brightly. The Pack on the other hand now had a very bright green aurora around them that wasn't fading. Father Jamby came back to reality first and went over to The Pack.

"Oh Wow. I feel so good and so positive about the future. I also seem to have an urge to party."

Fred, Tank, Peebop and Clax all looked at Datch.

"Well, it had to be said." he said defensively.

"What did?"

"It doesn't matter. Anyway, what happens now then?" asked Datch.

"I'm not sure, it's been so long none of us know. I expect we need to do some sort of ritual or something. Maybe have a party, yes, a party that seems like a good idea."

Just at that moment there was a crash from behind them as the monks that had been sleeping came staggering out through the broken door, blinking in the sun light and still in a daze from the gem's energy.

The head of the order looked up and his jaw dropped open.

"Oh, it's… the gem!" he said staring up at it in a partial daze.

"Yes." said Father Jamby "Err, Sorry about the sleeping thing Father Tiki but we had to do it to get it up there."

He was waiting to be told off but it took Father Tiki a few moments to take his eyes off the gem. Instead, he just said.

"It's OK. We needed a nap, I think. Did you put the gem there by yourself?"

"No, Datch the music warrior and his friends did it. I just helped them do it."

"Thank you so much, all of you."

"Where did they find it? We thought it had gone forever."

"They brought it to me from space sir."

"You mean the prophecy was real and you're the monk in it?" He stopped for a second thinking about what to say "Your very clever to do all this. Thank you to all of you. Jamby did I ever tell how much I think of you?"

"Err… No."

"Well. I do."

There was a loud crash from behind them. He turned to look at the door. The hinges on the right that had managed to survive the Timbo attack finally had given up and the door fell off.

“Oh, and sorry about the doors.” Added Jamby.

“Hmm. Don’t worry, they were really old and needed replacing, I think we need to do some remodelling anyway. What about a barque and a wickerwork trellis to keep the sun off? In fact, why don’t we have a party here tonight to celebrate the return of the gem. Oh, all of you will come as guests of honour of course, won’t you?” he said waving at The Pack and the rest of them.

“Yes. We would be honored sir.” Said Datch.

“Good, good. We’ll see you at nine bells then. You must excuse us but we need to do a bit of cleaning up. Jamby you can tell me the whole story while we get this place shipshape and ready for a good knees up.”

Father Tiki then put his arm around Jamby and walked over to the other monks leaving The Pack alone.

“Well, that might have been the shortest gig ever but we got an after party.” Said Tank.

“Wow. That’s all I can say.” Added Jep.

“Does this normally happen at your gigs?” asked Dag.

“No, not always.” Replied Datch.

“Anyone fancy a beer?” Said Clax.

“Not half, lead the way.” Said Dapo.

“Anyone know how long I’ll be glowing for?” asked Tish.

“Don’t know, but it looks cool.” Said Dapo.

“It doesn’t go with the new fashion line though.”

“Maybe do something in blue?” added Hagger trying to be helpful.

“What about Yellow?” said Tank.

“Hey, it will look good at the next gig. The Barbers is going to go nuts.”

“What, more nut’s than usual? I’m not sure that can happen unless they remodel the bar again.” Said Peebop.

“The beers are calling guys.” Said Clax turning towards what was left of the doors.

They said their goodbyes to the monks. Jamby and Father Tiki were in deep conversation about seating and put their hands up as they went past. Tajiquay volunteered his men to help with repairs and setting up the evening’s reception. He then joined The Pack and they headed out of the monastery in the direction on the inn. People were in the streets laughing and singing. As The Pack walked down the street people started waving at them and saying things like “party on dudes!”. This came as a bit of a shock because thirty minutes ago most of them wouldn’t look at The Pack. Now, not only did they speak to them but did so in Bellatrixian and quite fluently at that. As they approached the inn, music could be heard coming out of the bar and as they arrived Faberfab came running out.

“It was you, wasn’t it? You are the music warriors.” he shouted excitedly.

“Err… Yes.” said Clax.

“I want your names; I want to put up big sign on wall.”

“Just call us The Pack.” Said Datch.

At this point the street started to fill with people who came up and started touching them and shaking their hands. One woman fainted when tank shook her hand. Soon there was a large crowd outside the inn. Timbo and Tank were having to try to be bouncers and the rest of The Pack had retreated inside. Tajiquay looked at them and went out to Tank and Timbo. There was a very loud bang and it went quiet. Then there was a moment of yelling in the local tongue before it went quite again. Timbo stuck his head around the door.

"Err… I think it safe to come out now." he said.

"Why?" asked Carina.

"Err… Tajiquay just had a word with them and they are now behaving."

"He didn't shoot anyone did he?" asked Tish.

"No, but the house across the road now has extra ventilation upstairs."

"Oh."

"You're sure it's safe to come back out?"

"Yes. I don't think they will cause any more problems."

Datch got up and looked outside. The chairs near the inn were now clear of people who were instead now standing on the other side of the road. Tajiquay was sitting in a chair at the front with his gun leaning against his arm. Datch picked up his beer and walked outside follow by the rest. There were cheers and shouts of excitement but other than that the crowd stayed on the opposite side of the narrow street and was behaving themselves.

"This is like home." said Datch sitting down.

He then looked across the street and two people fainted.

“What, having a gunman holding the crowd at bay.” Said Rosey.

“No, remember when we did the fountain gig and I got my shirt torn off. “

“Yes, and we had about thirty security officers stopping the fans from having everyone else’s clothes off as well.”

“Maybe we needed Tajiquay.” Said Fred sarcastically.

Rosey gave him a look that could have stopped a rampaging bull.

“I’m joking.” He added.

“Tajiquay, what did you say to them?”

“I told them it was very rude of them after you just ended the dark times and they should give you space.”

“Oh, OK. Cool. Let’s just chill for a bit then.”

“Well at least we won’t need lights tonight.” Said Dapo who was poking the halo around his head to see what would happen.

It turned out his finger would glow green for a while.

Just then two shuttles came thundering overhead heading to the monastery.

“What’s all that about?”

“I don’t know, maybe they suddenly got hit with the gems power and came to find out what’s going on or it could just be the furniture for the party turning up.”

Another larger shuttle flew in and hovered before landing.

“Hmm. Must be the furniture. It’s going to be a good after party that’s for sure.” said Tank relaxing with a beer.

There was another scream from the crowd of people.

"Who did that?" asked Datch.

Hagger went red.

"Hagger, stop it. Leave them alone." Said Carina.

"He will. Won't you!" said Rosey glaring at him.

"Err… sorry and yes." he said.

"You do realise they will be copying our every move, don't you?" Jep pointed out.

"Yes, so Hagger don't pick your nose." Added Tank.

Hagger went red again.

"By the way, what time is nine bells?" asked Tish

"About seventeen hours I think."

"We've got plenty of time then." Said Hagger.

"Cool, I want to freshen up before we go." Added Tish

"Me too. Err Dag can I use your ships shower."

"Sure, I need to move the ship closer now anyway. Anyone else?" a round of hands went up.

"You had better be quick folks the flight only lasts a couple of minutes."

"Can I bring my tribe too?" asked Tajiquay.

"Sure, it'll give these folks time to have a shower while we load up. I'll tell Shiner to let them know we're coming and to get them to start packing it up."

Timbo, Tank, Clax and Fred stayed behind and went for a cold shower out the back of the inn. It didn't have a bathroom as such and the shower consisted of Faberfab's son pouring water down on them from the first floor using a watering can with a sprinkler attachment. They took it in turns to have it and then spent the next couple of hours having a drink and chilling in the sun while waiting for the others to come back. Faberfab now also seemed to be able to get whatever they wanted within reason and had even managed to find some nuts from somewhere. They looked like nuts anyway.

Back at the ship there was a long queue down the main corridor for the shower. They had put a time limit on it of five minutes each. This was to make sure they didn't take all day and miss the party. The girls moaned about it and got an extra five minutes to do their hair and to ensure there was no arguing, the ships computer was told to control the shower.

Outside the camp was dismantled and put in the cargo hold. Even with half the men missing it only took twenty minutes to get the tents down and stowed in the cargo bay and that included the makeshift bar. Dag went up to the command deck and the yelled down the corridor for everyone to hold on a for a minute or two. The ships thrusters fired and the ship lurched into the air. There was a loud scream from the shower followed by a lot of expletives that even made Jep blush. The screaming and cursing had just about stopped when the ship landed with a bump and there was another barrage of words from behind the door. Rosey opened the door and stuck her head out. It was dripping wet.

"Have we stopped?" she said in a tone that could have silenced a city block.

"Err... Yes?" Said Hagger.

"Good!" She went back in and shut the door.

Just at that point Carina came out of one of the rooms with Datch. The others were standing looking at each other

"What we miss?" said Datch.

“Err… let’s just say Rosey wasn’t impressed when Dag took off while she was in the shower.”

“Oh. Is she OK?”

“That is unknown at the moment and I’m not going to ask.” said Jep.

“Me neither.” Added Hagger.

Dag came walking back down from the command deck.

“Err, everything alright?” his said.

“I would avoid Rosey for a bit. She was in the shower when you took off.” Said Tish.

“Oh... Hmm. Computer, tell Rosey that I’m sorry for the take off and she can have an extra five minutes to make up for it.”

“Time extension applied and the occupant has been informed.” Said the ships computer.

The shower room started singing and everyone breathed a sigh of relief.

Soon everyone was showered and feeling a lot fresher. They came out of the cargo bay and found that Dag had parked the ship right outside the main gates. It was about a two-minute walk from the ship up the road to the inn. Tajiquay walked up with them leaving the tribe to finish off setting up camp site.

The After-party

Outside the inn, the bikers sat with a number of cold beers, a bowl of nuts and some things called dates. They had tried the dates and decided they needed something adding. Because of this, the dates on the table were in fact a bit hotter than normal after having chilli added to them also some had salt on them. To go with them, there was also a small bowl with something that resembled soya sauce which appeared to be steaming. It also seemed to work and they were filling the hole in their stomachs until the party. The crowd had died down a bit now but there was still a large number standing opposite the bar and also people would wave at them and shout 'party on!' as they went by.

Datch and Carina were at the front when they arrived outside.

"Well, it looks like you guys are happy." Said Datch.

"Yep." Said Peebop taking a sip of beer.

"Faberfab, more beer please, Datch and the gang are back." Tank yelled at the door.

There was shouting inside the bar and moments later Faberfab came out with a load of glasses and a pitcher of beer. It turned out the kitchen was now missing a large measuring jug and that the glasses took just over a quarter of a litre of beer.

Another shuttle flew overhead.

"Wow. They must be doing a lot of remodelling." said Hagger.

"Well, Timbo did break a really big door." added Rosey.

"No. there's something going on. The security forces contacted me when I took off."

"What did they say?" asked Clax.

"They asked me what I was doing in the area. I told them I was bringing you to the party."

"And?" said Fred.

"It was really odd because they said it was restricted air space and then I heard someone mutter something and then the officer said Datch the music warrior?"

"Datch the music warrior?" added Fred.

"Yes, so I told him it was him and the other music warriors were with him."

"What happened then?"

"They told me I could park where I liked."

"Oh. Looks like we're all VIP's again." Said Datch.

"Do you think we should put our normal clothes on?" asked Rosey keen to feel normal again.

"I think it might be an idea. We're certainly not in Cognito anymore that's for sure." said Clax.

"I'm with that, these pants are starting to chafe." Said Dapo.

"Ladies in Datch's room, Gents in Hagger's and Dapo's," said Fred. Timbo stood looking at them.

"Timbo?"

"Mine are still in the other hotel." he said.

"I've got something that I think will fit him back at the ship." Said Dag.

"OK, you sort Timbo and we'll get changed. Tajiquay, do you mind guarding the beer for us while we nip inside?"

“No Problem, dudes.” he said cheerfully.

Datch gave him a sideways look.

They all headed inside. Ten minutes later they were back out and had shorts on with their normal T-shirts and jackets except for the girls who now had short skirts on.

Tajiquay looked at them and then at the girls twice.

“That is a really different look.” he said.

“Do you like it?” said Rosey who had been the main influence in the band’s current outfits.

“Yes, it is very err… party on I think?”

“Well, that’s one way of putting it.” said Tank laughing.

They had just sat down with their drinks when Timbo and Dag came walking up the road. Timbo now had shorts on and a T-shirt that could easily have been someone’s tent. Luckily, he didn’t have a jacket to go with it or he would have looked like a mobile nomad camp.

“What time is it?” asked Carina drinking the last bit of beer out of her glass.

“About eight and a half bells I think.”

“Shouldn’t it be getting dark?”

“Err yes.”

They looked up and realised that the sun had gone down. The gem was shining down and pulsing brightly against the darkening sky.

“They’re not going to need the lights on tonight that’s for sure.” said Datch.

“I think they can throw them away with that light.” Added Carina.

“Yeh, it’s a town with a midnight sun.” Said Dapo.

“We had better make a move.” Said Datch.

“Yes, we don’t want to be late.” Said Dag.

They finished their drinks and headed up the street in the direction of the monastery along with a small band of followers in tow, some of which were now asking for autographs. They reached the monastery gates and standing outside there were two large security officers. Fred walked up to them.

“We’re here for the party. Datch and The Pack.”

“One minute please.” Said one of the security officers and then pressed his comms badge.

There was a brief conversation which they didn’t hear but ended up with both officers saluting and the door opening.

“Please go in. I believe they are waiting for you.” he said.

The Pack went in and up the corridor to the courtyard. There were three shuttles parked in the cobbled area of the courtyard with officers standing outside of each them. The shuttles looked new and they were not the normal type. Datch had seen this type before. They were military shuttles similar to the ones on the starship Carpaycus. They crossed the courtyard to the big doors on the other side. There were two more officers standing next to them. They saluted as they approached.

“Hey, this is like being on your dad’s old starship.” Said Carina.

“Yes, it is a bit. Why do they keep saluting us though?” said Datch.

“Don’t knock it, at least we’re not being shot at.” Said Dag.

They walked through the doors and there were more officers inside. Datch saluted them back this time and they smiled.

“Do you think we should all do it?” said Tank.

“What, salute?” said Dag.

“Yes.”

“Hmm. Why not.”

With that they all saluted and smiled. They carried on until they reached the doors going out on to the platform. Considering they had only been gone for a few hours the doors were hanging back up and the locks had been reattached even if it was by nailing bits on wood over the holes. There were four officers stand at the door, one of which was clearly a higher rank and was also wearing a dress uniform. Datch walked up to him and saluted.

“I am Datch and this is The Pack plus three.”

The officer saluted back.

“Please follow me music warriors. They are waiting for you.”

Datch looked at the others and shrugged his shoulders.

The doors opened and they followed the officer up the steps and on to the platform. It had been given quite the makeover with seating around the edges and make shift barbeque in the corner where it looked like half a Jaxx was being cooked. At the base of the obelisk was a long table and sitting at it was Father Jamby, Father Tiki along with a hand full of other monks. Also, a group of four other people all dressed very smartly. In fact, there were quite a few other smartly dressed people sitting on the other tables along with the rest of the monks and Tajiquay’s men. The officer cleared his throat.

"Minister Prime, Ladies and Gentlemen and honored guests may I present The Music Warriors, Datch and The Pack plus three."

Datch raised an eyebrow.

Everyone stood up. Father Jamby got up along with two of the other men who were smartly dressed and walked over to them. Father Jamby smiled at them.

"Datch, may I present the Minister Prime, leader of our planet."

The Minister Prime held out his hand and Datch shook it.

"It's an honour to meet you sir."

"The honour is all mine. You and your fellow music warriors have brought our planet out from twenty thousand years of darkness. People are dancing in the streets of the capital and now we feel good about the world again. Please come and feast with us. I'm told you like the imported beer so we have shipped some in. Please could you introduce me to your fellow warriors."

Datch took Minister Prime along the line introducing each member in turn including the plus three. They got to Dag and Tajiquay and Datch explained how they had helped them. When they reached the end the Minister Prime turned to them all.

"Please come and take your places at the table. Maybe later you could play for us? We have set up a stage for you."

He pointed to the corner where a stage had been set up with their gear on which now looked more like the real deal and the PA rig had been improved a lot.

"I thought we couldn't play music in public?" Asked Datch

“Ah well, I used my ministerial powers and rescinded that law four hours ago. It was an archaic law anyway.”

“Well, I’m sure we can do a couple of numbers for you all.” Said Datch.

They walked across to the table with the Minister Prime leading the way.

“It’s a bit quiet.” said Tank.

“Yes, we need some sounds.” Said Peebop.

“I have a music player I can plug into the PA system.” said Timbo

At this point Fred couldn’t wait anymore and had to know.

“Timbo, where do you keep getting all these things from?”

“I’m using my implant!” he said.

“Oh. I see.” Said Fred a little taken a back.

“Yes. I see you need something so I order it and a shuttle brings me it.”

“Why didn’t I think of that.” Said Clax who had been listening.

“Because that’s my job.” said Timbo.

“You can’t put it any better than that Timbo.” Added Clax.

“Err, Minister Prime. Could we put some background music on? It makes a nice atmosphere.”

“Yes, feel free. I can’t think of anything more fitting. Oh, and call me Widfab please.”

“You don’t have a relative who owns an inn by any chance?”

"No, I don't think so anyway. Why?"

"Oh, I just wondered that was all." He turned to Timbo.

"Timbo, please go and plug it in. Chill out tunes only please."

"No problem." he said and went over to the PA rig.

"You mean there's different types of music?"

"Yes, ours is called rock. But there's a whole list of them. If you try listening to them all you'll find the type that you like the best."

"Oh... Please, tell me more."

Datch carried on explaining the types of music to Widfab while they were getting seated. Background music came on and a soft up beat tune with a Latino feel filled the air. The gem responded by increasing and decreasing brightness to the song's rhythm and pulse to the beat.

They sat down next to Widfab and his aides.

"Err, Datch. We hope we have got this right, our limited research showed us that plastic knives, forks, paper plates and plastic glasses were correct for barbeques?"

"Yes, that's about right, you can use your fingers too, my dad normally has some bowls of water and little paper towels to clean your hands with as well."

"Oh, what a good idea." he said and waved at one of the officers near the doors.

He came over and Widfab whispered in his ear.

Five minutes later little bowls and paper towels appeared.

“Let’s eat. Datch, you’re our honored guests, please lead the way.” said Widfab, he leaned closer to Datch and whispered in his ear.

“Also, we’re a little new to this so if I copy you, I’ll get it right.”

“OK.” said Datch smiling.

The food and drink flowed and The Pack were being watched by everyone and then copied. Soon the party was in full swing and people were getting the hang of things. It was then time for The Pack to do their bit.

Datch called them into a huddle.

“I think we should do a full set. It is the leader of their planet after all.”

“Yes, that sounds OK but what songs?” said Carina.

“We need to be careful; the gem is over there.” Said Fred.

“What about the first set we do at the Barbers?” said Hagger.

“Yes, but I think we should include Star Lovers as we did it earlier, So Star Lovers, Space Dust, Wilde Wind, Rocking the city, Hot city nights, Planet Rock and to finish with Supernova. How does that sound?” said Datch.

“Are you sure about Supernova? We don’t want the planet exploding.” Said Peebop.

“Yes, especially as we’re still on it.” added Tank.

“It’s a feel-good song.” Said Hagger.

“OK, but if we all go bang it’s your fault, OK?” said Tank.

“OK, OK guys, let’s just do it. Are we ready to party or what?” Said Datch.

He put his hand out and the others followed suit.

"One, Two, Three. Let's Party!"

The Pack ran on to the makeshift stage and Datch grabbed his mic.

"Hello Welly, it's time to party!"

As they started to play the gem obliged with a light show and soon people started to get up and dance. It was strange but people would start by making a few nervous steps and then the music would just take hold of them. Before long they had a crowd in front of them which also included some of the monks.

Datch gave them a shout out and they waved their hands in the air. The music got louder and the gem got brighter. The Pack didn't notice but the gems light was nearly as bright as during the alignment and was now strobing along with the tunes. Even the officers on the doors were dancing. Sparkles flowed from everyone as the music filled the air. They ended up doing three encores before putting some rocking tunes on the music player and sitting down. They sat drinking cold beer and cooling off. Datch looked at The Pack. They were one again and were also glowing very brightly. He then noticed Jep had a far off look on his face and went over to him.

"What's up Jep?" he asked.

"I was just thinking how I'm going to explain to the principal that we have totally changed a planets culture in a matter of hours and all the lectures we have been giving for the pass five hundred years are now wrong."

"Well. Just tell him we showed them how to party."

"Yes, that's what I'm afraid of."

"If all else fails you are now the only professor that knows the up-to-date details on Welly four culture and as such every school or university on Bellatrix will want you."

"True." he said with a sudden realisation.

"So, let's chill."

He brightened up and started smiling again. The party carried on with various different types of music being played and The Pack explaining to people what it was called and what it was about. Some of the town's council members came along with their husbands or wives. Also, the whole of Tajiquay's tribe came in. The platform was packed out and everyone was sparkling with a green glow.

The Pack still had a very bright green aura around them which Datch found very handy when he went to the toilet. The party went on until the next morning and then someone realised that the sun was in fact up and it might be time for bed.

"It's been one heck of a party dudes." Said the Minister Prime as they left for the inn.

They arrived outside and Faberfab was just sweeping the area around the chairs. He had a big grin on his face when he spotted them coming.

"You want coffee?" he said.

They nodded and after a couple of minutes he came out with a tray of drinks. They sat in the chairs and decided just to sleep outside as no one could be bothered to go to bed.

That afternoon after The Pack had regained consciousness, they sat eating a sort of Faberfab fried breakfast which was fried whatever it was. They had fruit juice with it which seemed to help reduce the grease and aid the digestion process. Datch was just about finished when a security officer turned up with another man who turned out to be one of the Minister Primes aids.

"Err, Hello. I have a message from Minister Prime."

Datch slowly turned to look at him. He was missing the blue nanobots in his pack that were currently in the other hotel and was having to deal with a hangover for a change.

"Yes?" he said quietly.

"The Minister Prime would like you to do a world tour with him."

Datch looked at the others and they sort of nodded.

"OK, but we have our trip home booked on the star liner Tar Gee in eight days' time. Is that alright?"

"Yes, we can do that. We'll just do the three major cities and the large town of Jabby before coming back to the capital for another open-air party and then a reception for you at the citadel. If we come for you tomorrow around nine?"

"Works for us. Any chance of finding us good hotels with showers and en-suite?" Said Clax.

"I'm sure we can sort it."

"Oh, and the rest of our gear is at 'The Bucket' any chance of picking it up for us? Tell them we'll transfer payment to them as soon as we can."

"Yes, I'll send some officers right away and don't worry about the bill, we'll take care of it. While I'm here, could you sign this for my wife."

He went around to all of them in turn and they signed the card for him

"Thank you. Well, I can see your busy recovering, see you tomorrow." and with that he left.

“Looks Like a full week of gigging then?” Said Datch.

“And you said it was going to be boring.” Added Rosey.

“At least we get VIP treatment now.” said Carina.

“That’s true.” added Peebop.

“Well, Let’s wait and see. Just remember this was the most boring place in the universe until yesterday!” said Tank.

That night they told Faberfab and Tajiquay what hotels were like on Bellatrix. They both took a lot of notes.

The next week was spent touring the planet with the Minister Prime. Everywhere they went people would come out into the street just to see them and as the week progressed the places got brighter and more colourful as people brought the planet back to life. Houses were being painted and people started to wear brightly coloured clothes. They did a gig almost every night and each time the people would leave looking like roman candles. The gems in the obelisks would light up brightly transferring the energies around the planet.

The end of the week arrived and they were taken to the citadel in the capitol which was the seat of power for Welly four. It had three obelisks surrounding it each with a small gem at the top.

They were given the highest honour the planet could give at a big event which also involved a gig which almost set the sky on fire as the three gems energised together and then focused the energy on to another gem mounted on top of the citadel. That was followed by a very good after party and lots of people wearing sunglasses. Also, they each received gold chains with a small green gem in a clasp so that they could carry it with them wherever they went.

Dag had his ship refuelled but decided to hang around and help Tajiquay and Faberfab sort out their new hotel which had now expanded into a resort complex with a spa.

Father Jamby was now very busy writing a new text called 'The Music Warriors of Light' which he had promised to send Datch a copy of when it was complete. Finally, it was time to catch the star liner home.

The Minister Prime came to see them off along with a lot of dignitaries and they were taken to the space station by military shuttle which didn't shake and was a lot nicer than the old crate they had on the way down. As they approached the space station, they could see the moon with the base on it. It now seemed to have got power back and all the lights were now on even if some were now half buried in moon dust.

They docked with the space station and the inside of it was being given a makeover. All the piles of junk had disappeared and the lighting had been fixed also a new coat of paint had been applied along with it being given a good tidy up.

The security officers carried their bags for them and they were escorted to the Tar Gee. Datch tried to thank the officers but they were told it was a great honour to be able carry the Music Warrior's things. They said good bye and boarded the liner.

The Home Coming.

They sat in the star lounge watching Welly four slowly disappear as the ship pulled away. They had changed the world and now were leaving it to a new destiny. Soon it was no more than a small speck of light and then it was gone.

"I'm going to miss that place." Said Hagger.

"Yes, me too" added Rosey.

"I think we all will." said Datch.

"Quite the adventure." Said Clax.

"So much for boring. Jep, I think you might need to update the school's information a bit." Said Carina.

"Err, yes!" added Tish.

"Well, quite a lot actually." said Rosey.

Jep was looking a bit down.

"What's up?" asked Datch.

"I don't know what the principal is going to say about all this. Also, I don't really want to go back."

"Why?" asked Carina.

"We were having so much fun there and it was nice not being known, well not till the end anyway."

"I know what you mean." Said Tank.

"You do realise that the whole universe is going to know about us now, don't you?" said Fred.

"Yes." Jep said and sighed.

"How long we got left at school?" asked Datch.

“About thirty weeks by the time we get back, I think. Why?” said Dapo.

Datch had a grin on his face.

“I know that grin, what are you thinking?”

“Just thinking, that’s all.”

Everyone was now looking at Datch.

“When you grin like that, we know a plan is coming?”

“Not at the moment just the start of an idea. What about Solar Ball, I need to get some practise in.”

“What is it then?” asked Rosey.

“Wind.” Datch said still grinning.

“Really?” said Tish.

“Solar Ball.” Said Datch.

They gave up at this point. He would tell them at the right moment and with maximum impact as normal. They got up and headed off to the Solar Ball suite. That is except the bikers, Jep and Timbo. They voted to stay at the bar next to the pool, especially now as Welly four was paying for the trip home in full.

The next two weeks went by very fast. It was nice having good food and also drinks that tasted like drinks. Along with the pool, Solar Ball and proper implant connections, it felt good but there was always Welly four in their minds.

The Tar Gee entered the Bellatrix star system and dropped out of interspace fifteen minutes from the space station. The Pack watched from the star lounge as the ship manoeuvred through the busy traffic lanes, full of ships coming and going from the space station. Behind the station was home. It looked so good with the green tint in the atmosphere and the oceans below. And most of all it was home.

The Tar Gee docked and they headed across the docking port to the space station. It was an hour before the shuttle home so they went and had a drink in the planet bar. They watched as the world below unfolded before their eyes.

"So, we going home first or to the Barbers?" Asked Fred.

There was a moment's thought and then.

"The Barbers!"

"We want the big table." added Hagger.

"I'll put a call through to Jim to get it ready. It might be an idea to call your folks and let them know we're home." said Fred.

The all reached for their vid coms and called home.

The Barbers inn was its normal daytime self. A few people were having food and Jim stood cleaning glasses at the bar when the sound of bikes made him look outside. There was The Pack. He breathed a big sigh of relief as the bikes stopped outside and then picked up a glass and started filling it. The Pack walked in and Datch put his hand up to Jim. Jim pointed up the stairs to the big table. The Pack were back.

"I've missed this table." said Hagger sitting down.

"Yes, me too." Said Rosey.

They had all just sat down when Jim came upstairs with the drinks.

"I'm glad to see you guys are back. The snowmen are a good band but they don't have your sparkle."

"Well, we have even more sparkle now." said Carina.

"Yes, it's been all over the news about Welly four and how you brought them out of darkness. They are calling you the Music Warriors."

"Yes, we know." said Datch.

"Apparently the galactic press spent two weeks looking for you on Welly four before they realised you weren't on the planet."

"Really?" Said Carina.

"Yes, apparently on Welly four they have opened up sixty-eight nightclubs already and have another seven hundred under construction."

"Wow, that was fast." Said Tank.

"They're busy little buggers, I'll give them that." Said Fred.

"So, come on. I've seen the news but what really did happen?" asked Jim.

"OK, sit down and we'll tell you." said Datch.

Jim waved at one of the staff to take over the bar and sat down. The next hour and a half were spent telling Jim the story and then another twenty minutes going over all the bits that Jim didn't get the first time around.

"That's a pretty cool story. So, you could end up sparkling on stage?"

"It is a possibility." said Datch.

"Hmm. Talking of the stage, I don't want to push you but when can you do a gig?"

Datch looked at the others. It had been a very long trip but a relaxing one and everyone looked ready to take on the world again.

"What about tomorrow guys? And then maybe one in four days' time at the weekend?"

There was a general nodding and agreement from everyone.

"That's great I'll go and make some calls. Oh, lunch is on me, a sort of welcome back thing."

With that Jim went back down to the bar. 'Lunch' Datch thought and looked at his vid com.

"It's only thirteen hundred."

"Yes, we were on ship time remember." Said Fred.

"Does that mean we were drinking at eight this morning?" asked Tish.

"Yes." said Fred.

"I was thinking it's nearly dinner time." said Datch.

Just then the door opened. Behind the bar Jim pointed up to The Pack before he went back to ordering supplies on his vid. Moments later Datch's mum and dad appeared at the top of the stairs. Datch got up so fast he nearly knocked the drinks for six. He went trotting over and gave his mum a big hug then another hug for his dad.

"Well, I see you missed us." said Tansya.

"Yes. I did."

"So, do I still call you Datch or are you Datch the Music Warrior?" asked Dechow.

"Just me dad." Said Datch smiling.

Tansya laughed.

"I take it you've heard then. Did Dag call you?"

"Err, no. I contacted him after you appeared as the headlines on all the news bulletins. He was still on Welly four and had gone into partnership with some guy called Faberfab and another called Taj I quay?"

"Tajiquay" corrected Datch.

"Yes, anyway, apparently, they are building a resort complex, health spa and a night club. He just said to tell you Jamby is still glowing and Father Tiki has opened a bar at the monastery and it sells kebabs?"

There was a lot of sniggering from around the table as they came and sat down next to Carina.

"We had better tell you what really happened then. Not the news headlines." said Fred.

Two hours, three buckets of fried Hacks, six bowls of fries and lot of drinks later they finished.

"Well." Said his dad sitting back "You sure know how to have a holiday."

"When are you gigging then?" asked Tansya.

"Tomorrow night. It should be a good night." Said Carina.

"And what if you sparkle?"

"It will be an even better night." Added Datch.

With that The Pack went to play Solar Ball and the bar staff ran for cover, but they were smiling when they did it.

The following evening Datch picked Carina up from her house and headed for the Barbers inn. They were told to use the back door which was normal for the gigs these days. Jim had taken the time to build a proper room at the back of the stage for them. That way he didn't need to put loads of bouncers on the front of the stage until the music was about to start. When they arrived the rest of The Pack were there apart from Jep who was on his way but had been delayed at the school.

Jim came through the door with some drinks.

"Hi folks. Joni Jabi is upstairs and has brought a crew down. He wants to record the gig and broadcast it on his Yuckiday show. he said he would pay the normal fee plus an extra thousand credits each if you give him an interview afterwards. Is that, OK?"

"Sure, sounds good to us." said Fred.

With that Jim disappeared back into the bar.

They sat drinking a cold beer and five minutes later Jep came in.

"So, how did it go?" asked Datch.

"Well, the principal has tasked me with rewriting the syllabus on Welly four and the third moon that they are going to convert to a low gravity party resort."

"They are?" said Carina.

"Apparently so. They are also sending a diplomatic party to Bellatrix to set up an embassy with a night club attached."

"Really?" Asked Tish.

"Yes. Oh, and they have put a statue of us up in the capital city outside the citadel."

"Wow. So how long were you at school for?" asked Datch.

"I went in at ten this morning. It took until mid-afternoon to explain what happened to them all, then I had the meeting with the principal."

"Are we in trouble?" asked Tish.

"No. apparently the school has been given an offer to be twined with the University of Light in the capital on Welly four. Therefore, the principal feels that it is a good thing and we just have to give a lecture about life on Welly four now."

"Wait, we do?" Said Hagger suddenly realising he was going to have to do something educational.

"Yes, you don't think I'm going to do it on my own do you. Oh, and by the way its next Yuckiday and also one on Tinderday for the first years. I think we need to meet up tomorrow and work something out."

"Anything else we need to know?" asked Datch wondering if they had been roped into anything else.

"No. I think that's about it."

"Right. Well, we had better get our heads in the game. Ten minutes till show time." Said Fred.

"Does everyone have their gems on?" asked Datch.

There was a general round of nodding a part from Tank and Jep who fetched them out and put them on.

Jim stuck his head through the door.

"You guys ready. We have a full house and street I think."

"They must have missed us."

"They did and they're hungry for you."

"Well, let's not keep them waiting."

Jim ran out on stage and Datch put his hands out

"One, Two, Three, lets party!"

The Pack ran onto the stage and the bar erupted.

They started to play the first song and the gems energised around their necks. Soon, a green aura started to appear around The Pack getting steadily brighter and the fans loved it. Then as people started singing along to the songs green sparkles would appear around their heads. By the end of the first set Datch and The Pack were surrounded by columns of light and headed to the back to cool down.

"Well, that was different." said Carina sitting down.

"Yes, you could say that, we're glowing brighter than the lighting rig. The people at the front were wearing sunglasses!" added Rosey.

"Well at least we know now. These little gems do the same as the big one but on a lot smaller scale." Said Datch.

He was starting to wonder what effect it would have. After all this was Bellatrix and not Welly four. By the look of the crowd people were certainly happy if nothing else.

"Did you see the people sparkling?" asked Hagger.

"Yes, it was amazing."

"I hope they don't all decided to go and open night clubs." Said Clax.

"I'm not sure that will happen, they are only sparkling not glowing. When it happened on Welly four everyone became columns of light. This is more like the first night at Tajiquay's camp." Said Fred.

"That was a really good night." Said Carina.

"Well, let's see if we can make it happen here then." added Datch.

The second set started and soon the bar was resonating to the sound of The Pack. On the main dance floor people were dancing and singing with sparkles flowing from their heads then came Star Lovers. As the song went on the intensity of The Packs glow got brighter and brighter until Datch and Carina kissed. There was an explosion of light which shot up and hit the roof. Then beams of light hit everyone in the bar and even some people outside. Everyone screamed with delight as they suddenly felt really good about the world.

The whole bar was now glowing and The Pack went straight into Planet Rock. Everyone was now up and dancing even Jim was strutting his stuff behind the bar. The bar reverberated to the rhythm of the music with everyone moving as one. After the fourth encore The Pack finally made it off stage. They sat down around the table cooling down. You could say they had an afterglow but it was more like they had been sitting too close to a nuclear reactor.

"Did you feel that?" said Datch.

"Yes, it was like we were on Welly four." Said Tank.

"Wow." Said Carina and Tish at the same time.

"Wow is an understatement." Said Fred who was staring at the glowing aura around his hands.

They sat for a few moments taking in what had just happened.

"Do you think they will be, OK?" asked Carina.

"I think they will be happy people for a few weeks." Said Datch.

After ten minutes they were taken up stairs to Joni Jabi. He had sparkles flowing from his head as well.

“Hi all.” he said “That was one heck of a gig. It must be the most amazing gig I’ve been to.” He gestured to the chairs.

They sat down.

“Wow. Look at you guys, you really do have a glow around you. Let’s not hang about I don’t want to miss any of this!”

“OK, but we will be glowing for a while.” said Datch.

“Well, shall we start?”

They all nodded.

“OK, start the vid.”

“Hi folks. I’m here with The Pack. They have just finished the most amazing gig I’ve seen in all my years in the business. Can I ask first why are you all glowing and come to that why am I, Datch maybe you would like to start?”

The next fifteen minutes were spent talking about Welly four, the gem and the residual effects thereof. Finally, they got to the end and Joni closed by asking.

“So, are you still The Pack or do we call you the Music Warriors?”

“Well Joni, we will always be The Pack, Music Warriors is just our Welly four title.” Said Datch.

“Thank you all for a great night and this wonderful interview.”

“You’re welcome, Joni.”

“There you go folks The Pack AKA the Music Warriors are back.”

He waved his hand and the vid landed on the table.

“That was great folks, thanks again. Err, just one thing. How long will I be glowing for?”

“We don’t know. I think it just wears off after a week or so dependent on how much you got into the music.” Said Datch.

“Yes, the more you sing and join in with us the more our gems boost the effect”

“What, you have gems?”

“Yes, we were given them by the Minister Prime on Welly four. Their only really little ones though. The main gem is the size of a football.” Datch showed him the tiny little gem on the chain around his neck. It was glowing brightly.

“That is very small” Joni said squinting to see it against the light it was giving off.

“Yes, they only amplify what is within us.” Said Fred.

“The gem on Welly four has charged us up somehow and the little gems boost it.” added Datch.

“So, they’re not like the big one then?” asked Joni

“No, I gave it to my mum to try on. It didn’t do anything when she started singing.” Said Carina.

“You need to have been very close to the gem on Welly four for it to work as far as we can tell.” Added Fred.

“We seem to have been given a gift to make people happy and we want to spread it about.” said Datch.

“Does it work if we broadcast?” asked Joni.

“I don’t know, we’ve never tried.” Said Fred.

“Well, what about this weekend?” said Datch sitting back.

“This weekend?” asked Joni.

“We’re doing another gig.”

“Where?”

"Here. Starting at nine at night. It's sort of for Jim to make up for the time we were at Welly four."

"Hmm, maybe, we'll try getting a crew here and broadcast the start of the second set live. We'd only be able to do maybe three songs before the ad break but I could do a message competition asking people to say how they are feeling, why and if they were sparkling."

"Yes, we could give you a couple of signed T-shirts and pictures for the prize. You must tell us what you find out though." said Fred.

"Sure, It's a deal."

With that Joni and his crew left leaving The Pack to look down at all the people now sparkling away below. There was a real difference in the feel of the bar. Everyone was still bubbling over with joy. At this point of the night, normally people would be heading home happy but it would have calmed down. These people were still bouncing off the walls with the joy of life and it didn't look like they were stopping anytime soon. To add to the atmosphere, Jim was juggling and singing behind the bar along with the staff.

"I hope this doesn't do the same thing as beer." Said Dapo.

"What do you mean?" said Datch.

"You get drunk, have a great time and then wake up with a hangover in the morning."

"That's down to the lack of alcohol in your body. Not lack of happiness. I don't think the gem works like that." Added Fred.

"I hope so." Said Dapo.

"Anyway, the effect lasts a lot longer." added Datch.

They watched as a group of about twenty people formed a conga line and headed out of the bar singing at the top of their voices and headed off down the street.

"Well, I have a feeling we're going to be on the news tomorrow again if nothing else." Said Fred.

"Why do you say that?" asked Datch.

"The guy at the front of that conga line was the channel twelve anchor man."

"Oh... Was he sparkling?"

"Yes, quite a lot in fact."

"He'll be smiling in the morning that's for sure."

"Well, at least it gives us a chance to see how long it lasts." Added Clax.

"Yes, all we'll need to do is watch the news every morning and check the sparkle level." added Jep sarcastically.

"Now that's a plan." said Hagger who didn't know how to spell sarcasm let alone know what it meant.

Datch sighed. He had seen this so many times that he knew what was coming.

"Right, Hagger do you watch the news?" said Fred.

"Sometimes, why?" replied Hagger.

"OK, well done, you're our sparkle monitor." Said Dapo.

"So, I have to watch the news. That's OK. When is he on?"

"Between six and nine in the morning." Said Fred with a grin.

"That's a bit early. Are you sure six in the morning is a real time? If it is, I'm sure they don't have much news at the time?"

“At six in the morning what time is it on the other side of the planet?”

“Err…” Hagger stopped and asked his implant.

“Oh…”

“Make sure you have a good look as well. The studio lights may hide them a bit.”

“OK, OK.” Said Datch wading in. “Let’s all try and watch it. That way we won’t miss anything.”

The others stopped before Datch said something else. If they upset him, he would stare at them and it was the sort of stare that would make you run and hide for a very long time. The only person who didn’t get it was Carina. Only she could stop Datch in his tracks.

“Yes. Good plan.” Added Tank.

They had another round of drinks before heading home. When they left Jim, he was still singing and the people left in the bar were still sparkling.

Weekends Sparkle

It was time to give their first lecture to the second years. They had been given a good talking to by the principal about changing planetary cultures where Datch had pointed out about the legend and therefore it wasn't their fault. The principal then tried to carry on moaning but Datch stared at him. The result was that they could do the lecture however they wanted and the principal went off to have a lay down.

The lecture theatre was full. Word had got around that The Pack were going to do a lecture and even those who weren't fans came as this had been the first-time students had ever given a lecture. It was also the first time the students knew more than the lecturers and therefore all of the lecturers were crammed in as well. The Pack had brought Timbo and Timbo had brought the PA rig. When everyone was in Datch sounded the bell and walked to the front of the stage.

"I bid welcome to my class mates and lecturers as well. The story I'm about to tell you started when the spider was in the city... That was when myself and Hagger found the cube..."

The next hour was spent with telling the story and each member of The Pack took a turn telling a part. Even Timbo was given a part in the tale. Eventually they reached the part where they first sang to the gem and sparkles started to appear around the room. Then arrived at the part of the story where they were on the platform. They walked across the stage picking up their instruments and started to play turning into columns of light and as they did. Everyone else started to sing along and sparkle. The principal put his head around the door and started to think about closing the door but the music took hold of him. He couldn't help himself but to go in. By the time the songs had finished the whole school was sparkling and had big smiles on their faces. They went on to explain how the population became one with the essence of the music and how they are remaking the planet with the images and ideas inside the heads of The Pack. Then Datch walked to the front of the stage.

"We have been given a gift to bring joy and happiness through our music. We are called 'The Music Warriors' on Welly four but here we are 'The Pack'. They say we were called there by destiny. I don't know if that's true but we are now part of the legend and part of us will always be there. That's the end of our story about Welly four but is it the end of the legend? I don't know. Thank you all for being such a great audience and if you have got tickets, see you tonight at the Barbers."

The room applauded and The Pack walked off the stage and back to their class mates. They were all in party mode.

The principal came over to Jep.

"That was a pretty amazing tale."

"Yes sir, it was pretty amazing being there, sir."

"I've been thinking about the Welly four twinning, they want a member of our faculty to go there. I was thinking maybe you would like it?"

"Sorry sir, but I have the band now and not to be disrespectful, but I make a lot more credits with them than I do here, sir."

"Yes, I suppose you do."

"What about Windle sir?"

"Windle? Don't you think he's a bit old?"

They turned around in time to see Windle showing some of the year two's how to table dance.

"Are you sure sir?"

"I see what you mean, I'll put him on the list."

At that point Datch came over.

"Sorry to interject, but is it OK if we all head down to the Barbers, sir? We have a gig in a little over five hours and want some food and a bit of a break."

"Yes, I think that should be OK."

Datch waved at the others, they came over and started to head out the door. Just as they went out, they heard the principal shout 'Windle can I have a word?'

Timbo stayed behind to move the gear for the gig. He got some of the other pupils to help him carry it to the truck outside and in return gave them a free ticket each for the nights gig.

The Barbers Inn was busy when they got there. It was still five hours before the gig. They waved at Jim as they walked in and pointed up to the balcony. He nodded and started pulling drinks and mouthed 'food'. Datch nodded as they headed for the stairs but then had to stop and sign an autograph for one of their groupies on their way. The rest of the afternoon was spent chilling, eating and having a beer. As the time of the gig approached, they sat watching as people started to fill the bar. In amongst them were people with sparkles around their heads. Datch watched them closely studying them. They seemed happy and still full of energy.

"What you doing?" said a voice.

It was Carina.

"Watching. I want to make sure people here are OK when they get exposed to the gems power."

"And?"

"Well, they seem happy enough."

“That’s good then.”

It was soon time for the gig and they were escorted down behind the bar and along to the backstage dressing room.

“Are we ready for this?” asked Fred.

“Yes. It’s time to make people happy.” Said Tish.

Datch put his hand out and the others followed suit.

“One, Two, Three. Let’s Party!”

The Pack ran out on stage to cheers and whistles from the crowd. The first song started and the crowd roared. As the first set went on and people started to sparkle, The Pack’s glow got brighter and brighter. They spotted the vid crew come in from Joni’s show and head up the stairs. The gems around The Pack’s necks were shining like little suns and the beams of light from them were combining above the dancefloor into waves of light that flooded across the floor and out into the street. By the end of the first set the bar looked like it was full of roman candles all dancing away in time to the music. The set finished and The Pack headed back to the dressing room for a breather.

They were sitting having a drink when Fred’s Vid bleeped. It was Joni so Fred put it on party mode

“Hi guys, we have just gone to the ad break so I have about five minutes, how’s it with you?”

“Hi Joni. Yes, we will be about ready. We’re just finishing off the drinks.” Said Fred.

“OK, After the ad break, I’ll announce the competition before coming to you live, Datch my crew are going to plug in to your PA rig if that’s alright. You’ll be able to hear me and I’ll be able to do the same. I'll cross to you in ten minutes. Make sure you're ready."

"That's fine. We'll be ready."

"Cool, talk to you in a bit. Joni Out."

"Well, you heard him let's get ready."

The Pack finished their drinks and headed back out on stage to cheers and whistles. Datch walked to the front of the stage.

"We have something special for you now in a minute we will all be live on the Joni Jabi show and the planet. So, let's make some noise."

The bar screamed at them and then Joni's voice came over the PA.

"Good evening, Barber Inn. You're now live across the planet."

There was a massive roar from the crowd.

"OK Datch. Take it away."

"Thank you, Joni. Welcome to the Barbers Inn. Are we ready to rock?"

There was another massive roar from the crowd

Datch nodded at Tish and Star Lovers started to play. The crowd went mad. What happened next was the gems around The Pack necks got as bright as the main gem had back on Welly four. The dancers at the front started to glow as well as sparkle and the light at the centre point in the bar then exploded with waves of energy pulsing out of the bar and across the city. They finally finished the second set and after the third encore they finally went back to the dressing room to recover. As they sat down Fred's vid com beeped. It was Joni.

"Hi Joni." Said Fred.

"Hi guys, that was incredible and we stayed with you till the end."

"I thought you could only broadcast three songs?" asked Datch.

"I know. The Network boss kept us on air when they saw the waves of energy spending out across the city. Apparently, his daughter was watching, she started sparkling and now has a very big grin on her face."

"So, do you know how far the energy went?" asked Fred.

"A far as I can tell, it covered the whole city but only affected people who were watching you."

"Cool. So how many?" added Datch.

"About fifteen thousand in the city we think."

"Oh wow." Said Carina.

"And from the messages they all feel really good about life."

"So, who's won the gear?" said Fred.

"No one yet, I thought it might be nice if you did it. The crew are still there. If I get them to come to your dressing room you could do it live."

Datch thought about this and then had a second idea.

"Joni, what if we do that now and then the winner can come to the Barbers next week to receive their prizes and we let them come on stage with us."

"That would be amazing, I'll get a crew down to you."

Joni turned away from the vid for a moment and said something to someone they couldn't see.

“OK the crew will be with you in a moment. Just chill and when they get there, I’ll get five of you to give me a number between zero and nine. I’ll type them into the system here and it will give me the winner.”

“That sounds easy.”

“So, which of us are going to do it?” said Carina.

There were a few moments of thinking before Datch reached for a piece of paper and tore it into eleven bits. On five he put an x and the others he left blank before folding them up. He grabbed an empty wine cooler and put them all in it.

“OK, Everyone, take one.”

“Yes, good call.”

They all took one and the winners were Carina, Hagger, Tank, Jep and Tish.

“OK, think of a number folks.”

Just then the vid crew were brought in and after a few seconds Joni came back on the vid com.

“Are you ready?”

“Yes, Joni.” Said Datch.

After a bit of an intro Joni turned back to Datch.

“Can we have the numbers please Datch?”

“Yes, Carina?”

“Number One”

“Hagger?”

“Number Three.”

"Tank?"

"Number Two"

"Jep?"

"Number Eight"

"Tish?"

"Number Five"

"And the winner is…" there was a moments tension before "Lusa from Yuland City."

"Cool, Thanks guys."

The vids shutdown and the crew exited and left them on their own. Then before they could order another around of drinks Joni called Datch's vid comm.

"Hi Joni."

"Hi Datch, that was great guys, Thanks again. I'll sort out the details with Fred and talk to you during the week."

"OK, Thanks Joni."

The Next Step.

The following weeks gig went really well. Lusa had been ecstatic about winning and after going on stage was taken back to the dressing room with them before being taken home in a big limo that had been supplied by Joni Jabi. The following morning The Pack sat eating breakfast outside the cake shop.

Datch was a bit quiet and sat looking into his coffee.

“What’s up lover boy?” asked Carina.

“I miss space.” he said after a moment’s pause.

The others all looked up.

“Yes, I know what you mean.” said Carina.

“It was fun up there.” Added Rosy.

The others all agreed.

“We’ll have to go again soon and somewhere where we are not known.” Said Datch.

“That’s going to be hard to do considering we have gone down in galactic history as the people who recreated Welly four in our own image. Let’s be honest, if you had a planet and found out we were coming, you would make sure you knew where we were.” said Tish.

“Yes. I know.” Datch replied.

Datch went back to looking in his coffee so Carina changed the subject.

“Does anyone know what we are doing at school this weekend?”

“You mean Triday and Hadday, the other two days we have been given off because of a gig in the city down near the emerald sea.”

“Oh yes. I forgot about that.”

“I’m not even sure why we have to go on the other days anymore?” added Hagger.

“It’s because we have to be there because of the law, that’s all.”

“Oh.”

“Talking of law. I wonder what ever happened to the guy who tried to kill the president?” asked Rosey thoughtfully.

“He was mind wiped and now works as a street cleaner in the capital.” Said Dapo without thinking.

“How did you find that out?” asked Hagger.

“Oh. It was on the news the other day.”

“Well, serves him right.” added Rosey.

“So, where are we staying in the Emerald Coast?” asked Tish.

“We’re in the Palace in the centre about ten mins for the gig which is in the stadium.”

“We stopped there last time. It’s the one with the pool on the roof.”

“Oh, that one. I want the seat at the end of the pool bar.” added Hagger.

“OK, but I’m having the sunbed under the palm tree overlooking the sea.” Added Carina.

“I’ll go with that.” said Datch.

They finished breakfast and then headed up to see Clax at his shop. There was always something new in there and they would sometimes surprise people by serving at the counter. It passed the time until school and also, he had a really good coffee maker.

Datch wandered into the back room where Clax was busy opening boxes of stock, including some strange looking blue things.

“Err, Clax?” he said.

“What’s up Datch?”

“I was just wondering how hard it is to get a pilot’s licence? You’ve got yours, haven’t you?”

“Yes, why?”

“I was just thinking about learning to fly.”

“Oh, got itchy feet now you’ve been up there?”

“A bit, I want to be able to disappear with Carina when we want, if you know what I mean?”

“Yes, you just want to get away sometimes. I get it.”

“Yes.”

“Well, yes, I have my licence. It takes about six months of training and then a test to get your full license or if you’re on a ship as crew you can do on the job training, again with a test at the end.”

“Oh, can’t you teach me?”

“There is one problem with that. I don’t have a ship.”

“Can’t we buy a little one?”

“A little one as you put it will cost you a couple of million credits and that would be a fixer upper.”

“Oh.” Datch looked a bit down hearted.

“Can’t the captain help you out?”

“He’ll want me to join the IPSF and I just want to be able to have a break when I want one.”

“Hmm. Looks like you’re going to have to do it the hard way. Still, we can always go on a galactic cruise or something.”

“OK, Thanks anyway.”

“No probs Datch, anytime.”

Carina walked in just as they were finishing.

“Well, I’m not sure what you’re on about but I’m sure it will work out. After all, we are The Pack and you are Datch.”

She smiled and that made Datch smile with her.

“I’ll second that” said Tish as she passed by the door.

“Hey, did you see Welly four have asked to have an embassy in Yuland city. Apparently, they requested it because we’re here.” said Carina.

“Oh, where are they going to put it?”

“The government has let them have the old library building about six blocks across from the Barbers.”

“I hope they don’t want free tickets all the time.” said Dapo who had just appeared around the corner looking for another coffee.

They helped Clax put the stock out and then it was time to head up to school.

The next five weeks were spent going around the planet making people sparkle. They were in very high demand and barely had time to relax. It appeared that the sparkles would last about two to three weeks depending on how into the music people got. They didn't seem to be any after effects apart from people wanting to keep coming to gigs so they could sparkle again. Therefore, the bookings for gigs had gone through the roof and they were starting to get worn out. Datch decided they needed a break and Fred told all the agents that after the current bookings finished, they would not be any gigs, vid shows or interviews for two weeks. They all need a rest and it was also a school break so they could do what they wanted for two weeks. Datch had made a few calls to sort out a proper break but wasn't saying what he had planned.

The next three weeks went by with gig after gig and finally they did the last gig at Barbers inn.

The next morning Datch and Carina got up and went down stairs where Jim was setting out the big table for breakfast. They had decided to have breakfast in the bar as no one had the energy to walk to the pancake shop.

"So, come on, you can tell me now, where are we going?" asked Carina.

"I don't know for sure."

"What do you mean. You don't know. You've planned it." said Carina getting a bit annoyed.

"I might have planned it but I'm still not sure. Trust me, it's going to be fun."

"I still don't know why you won't tell me."

"Just wait and see." he said and grinned.

Carina looked at him. She knew that grin and it meant Datch knew more than he was letting on.

"So, when are we heading to your place?"

"After breakfast when everyone else is here and I get a message from my mum."

"Message?"

"Yes, I'm waiting for something to arrive."

"What?"

"I can't tell you. It will spoil the surprise." He grinned again.

At this point Carina gave up. If there was one thing she had learnt over the last two years, it was, if Datch didn't want to tell you something there was no way you could find out. Also, normally it would be something really good.

The others joined them and they all tucked into breakfast. The others tried a few failed attempts to find out what was going on during the course of breakfast to no avail but the food went down very well. About half way through the morning the bikers appeared and they were all impatient to get going and then Datch's vid comm beeped.

Datch looked at it. It was from his dad.

'Why is there something very big and black on my front lawn? I've also had to sign for it!'

Datch sent back. 'I'll move it when I get home. Love you lots x x :)'

He turned to the others

"I think we can go now."

The others all looked at him. He thought for a second and then.

"Let's mount up and move out."

They carried on looking at him. He looked down.

"OK, sorry, when we have finished the drinks."

The drinks didn't take long as everyone was wondering what the surprise was. Soon The Pack were on their bikes and airborne heading towards Datch's mum and dad's ranch.

They formed up behind him and Carina in a wing and then accelerated. Below the city scape changed from large buildings to small houses and apartments as they went over the suburbs. Then below the concrete jungle turned into trees and soon they were flying over farmland. Datch looked into the distance and there was the little village with the café where he would take Carina for a coffee. Then the ranch could be seen and as they got closer there in the paddock was a large black shape. Hagger was the first to spot it.

"Err, Datch. Is that what I think it is?" he said through the bikes comms system.

"It might be?" replied Datch. No one could see but Datch had a very big grin.

"It is. It's a starbird!" he said almost shouting into his headset with excitement.

Sitting in the middle of the paddock was a large sleek black spaceship. It had a long-curved hull leading up to a cockpit at the front that had black tinted windows to keep out prying eyes. On each side it had long drawn back wings that made it look like a large bird of prey and just above them were two curved bulges that covered the interspace engines. It sat on three landing struts pointing slightly upwards like a bird waiting to take flight. It also had green flames painted down the sides that went from the front of the wings to the rear where the main flight engines were and protruding out of its belly was the entrance ramp. It had been designed for people who wanted not to be seen and the designer would have had something to say about the flames no doubt.

They came into land just behind it. It was a lot bigger than Dag's ship and looked a lot meaner in a very subtle sort of way.

"That's like the ship the casino boss had." Said Rosey as she got off her bike.

Datch laughed.

"It's not like. It is it!"

"What! I thought it was going to be destroyed?" Said Hagger who was starting to drool.

"It was, but I called the president and asked him if he knew where we could get a cheap ship on account of now being sort of envoys for Welly four. he said that he had a ship we could have as long as he got a couple of things for it."

"How much did it cost?" asked Fred waiting for a large bill.

"Six free passes to all of next year's gigs, three thousand credits for the paint job another six thousand credits for the modifications and finally another two thousand for the ownership transfer and my provisional license."

"Bargain!" Said Carina walking towards it.

"Datch, just who is going to teach you to fly it?" asked Tank.

"Clax and my dad."

"I am?" said Clax.

"Yes."

"OK. When did that happen?"

"In your shop a few weeks ago."

"It did?"

"Yes."

Clax was still trying to work out when he had agreed to teach Datch when the doors at the top of the ramp opened and Dechow came walking down with Tansya just behind him.

"Hi Dad. Hi Mum"

"Hi Datch, why do I have a very expensive looking spacecraft sitting outside my house?"

"Err, It's mine."

"What? Now I know you are earning a small fortune with the band but this ship goes for over forty million credits and that's a second hand one."

"I got it as a favour." he said grinning.

"A favour!"

"Yes, it was going to be destroyed and the president said I could have it for a few tickets and some credits for the modifications."

Dechow looked at his son and wondered if the universe was going to survive now Datch was no longer tied to one planet.

"Well, I think it's very nice." Said Tansya trying to stop any arguments before they started.

"And just who is going to fly it?" Dechow asked.

"I've got my provisional licence and you and Clax can teach me."

"We can?"

"Yes."

Tish burst out laughing followed shortly afterwards by Peebop and Dapo.

“Can we go and have a look inside?” asked Rosey.

“Sure. Come on, follow me.” said Datch starting to head into the ship.

“Err, when were you going to tell me about this?” asked Carina.

“About now babes.”

Datch smiled, took her hand and walked up the ramp into the ships belly.

The top of the ramp led to a small cargo bay which had spaces marked out for twelve bikes and were set out with six on each side. The walls had a number of panels on them and high up near the roof were a number of holo emitters. Also, near the entrance was a box with a glass front marked space suits and inside little headset units could be seen. On the other side of the cargo bay was another door leading into the rest of the ship. They walked thought it.

The ships corridor was brightly lit with soft panel lighting running along the walls and the colour scheme was a combination of warm pastels. The corridor ran the length of the ship with a set of stairs half way down it. The first door on each side led into engine room which contained dual reactors, the main engines and interspace drives. There were a lot of panels and pieces of other equipment including life support, the waste and water treatment plants and a replicator unit.

“Wow, this is compact. How fast does it go?” asked Clax.

Datch pulled out his vid and put up the ship’s specifications and then proceeded to read them out.

“We should be able to get interspace sixteen out of it and a flight speed of eighty thousand six hundred kilometres per hour. It has a range of four hundred light years and has enough life support for a hundred days. Oh, and it’s just been serviced.”

"Very nice." Said Hagger grinning.

"And it's all yours?" asked Fred.

"Yes. I own it, but it's sort of the bands as well. I got it so we can go where we want when we want and not have to do the booking thing telling people we're coming." Datch was grinning "OK, next is the gally and eating area."

They walked along to the gally. It had a large table in the centre with fifteen seats and on one wall was a food replicator and also a small kitchen area with a cooker and food preparation area in case you wanted to make the food yourself.

"Why fifteen chairs?" asked Tish.

"Well, we might have guests." Answered Datch.

They came out of the gally and crossed the corridor. The opposite room was a recreation room. Inside it had several large sofas and a number of coffee tables. Also, there was a large vid screen on the wall and a fully fitted bar. The room was carpeted from wall to wall in a deep pile carpet and the walls were tastefully decorated to put you at ease and make you feel relaxed. Everything had an air of luxury about it.

"This ship is quite something but where is the Solar Ball?" asked Tish.

"It's in the cargo bay. I had holo emitters fitted so we could play when we wanted."

"Cool." said Dapo.

"That's nothing, watch this."

"Computer, please can I have a glass of Gruck's."

There was a funny noise from the computer.

"Please Identify yourself?" it said.

"Oh, I forgot about that. We need to register with the system. Computer I am Datch Thome."

The computer made another noise and then said.

"Please wait while I scan your implant."

"Identity confirmed. Welcome aboard the star ship Raven Datch. Please take your drink."

A light came on at the back of the bar and a glass of Gruck appeared. Datch walked over and picked it up.

"Why the Raven?" asked Clax.

"Because it sort of looks like a big black bird."

"Oh cool." Said Dapo.

"You had all better do the computer thing."

"I don't drink Gucks." Said Peebop.

"Not the drink. The ship registration!" said Fred.

"Oh."

"Computer please register Carina." Said Datch.

"Please state your name Carina"

"Carina Agi."

"Scanning please wait."

"Welcome aboard the star ship Raven Carina."

The next five minutes were taken getting everyone registered with the ships computer system. Datch was glad of the Grucks after all of 'Computer please register …' and finally it was time to carry on the tour.

They left the rec room and headed a bit further along the corridor. The next room was a store room and had a number of racks and shelves with boxes on. One had 'Old Man's Boots' printed on it. Hagger's face lit up.

"Is that for me?" he said.

"I thought you would like the real stuff instead of the synthetic." Said Datch.

"Oh yes, it has a far better taste."

The next six rooms were bedrooms all with large king size beds and their own on-suite toilet and shower room. Also, a large vid on the wall and they all had deep pile carpets. All looked like a president could live in them. At the end of the corridor was a smaller room and inside was a number of banks of equipment including the main computer system, Navigational systems and communication systems. They turned around and went back to the stairs. At the rear of the second story there was an access door to the top part of the engine room. Next to that was another storeroom and then there were six more bedrooms just like the ones on the lower deck. Moving towards the front of the ship was another dining room along with a room with seating and tables in and two large vid screens. Then they arrived at the cockpit. It had twelve seats six on either side and then two more at the front for the pilot and co-pilot. The controls looked like the ones in the shuttle Datch had flown and he recognised the different bits. Datch went and sat in the pilots' seat. It was plush leather. There was a cough from behind him and he looked around. It was Dechow.

"I know it is your ship, but you need to learn how to fly it before you sit there."

"I know but I just wanted to feel what it was like and this seat is really nice. I've done a lot of flight training on a vid simulator though so I do know what to do."

"Maybe but that doesn't mean you won't crash. OK." Said Dechow.

"So, what are we going to do now?" asked Tank trying to change the subject.

"I thought we could go and see my brother on Hamel Four, it's seventy light years away so about nine hours. I understand his city has a nice beach front with its own private landing area nearby for VIP's."

"You've already worked this out, haven't you?" said Fred.

Datch just grinned.

"So, let's load up. Clax is it OK if my dad takes the pilot seat?"

"Sure, I quite fancy trying the ships bar out anyway."

"Dad?"

"Oh, why not. If nothing else it will give your brother a surprise."

"I'll just go and get a few bits for the trip." Said Tansya grinning.

"Right let's get the bikes loaded." Said Fred to the others

Datch got up and Dechow sat down in the pilot's seat.

"I see what you mean, these seats are nice. Right, let's see what you can tell me about the controls and no cheating with your implant."

"OK dad." Said Datch sitting down in the co-pilot's seat.

They sat going through the controls and Dechow was impressed on how much Datch had remembered from the shuttle. He then asked him about talking to the planetary authorities. Datch had been reading up on protocols and how to work out flight paths along with a number of other things. They had gone through the flight controls and were just discussing orbital platforms when Carina came in followed by the rest.

"Do you think I could take off dad, then you can fly it."

"Are you sure you can do it?"

"Yes. Oh, the ship can do a dual pilot thing so you can take over when you want."

"OK then, but I want you to do the prefight checks first though."

"OK."

Carina sat in the seat behind Dechow so she could see Datch. Then Tansya came walking in with a bag.

"Which room are we in?" she asked

"Take the one next to ours. It's the third one down there." said Carina pointing down the corridor.

Tansya went and put the bag in the room and then came and sat down.

"Right Datch. Put your headset on."

Datch put his headset on. The computer told him that he needed a certified pilot to allow him to use the controls.

His dad put his headset on and allowed Datch to have control. Datch went through the pre-flight checks and all system were showing green.

"OK Datch. Off you go. Hold on everyone just in case."

Datch brought the thrusters online and dust could be seen blowing up past the window. He gingerly pulled back the thruster control and slowly the ship lifted into the air clearing the ranch and buildings. He then moved the joystick and the ship turned towards the desert he moved the thruster power control forwards and the ship started to move towards the sands.

Dechow went on the coms and told the planetary fight control that they had a learner flying the ship and that they were heading out over the desert and then up into space before heading towards the outer planets away from the main traffic lanes to do a bit of flight training. After which they were heading to Hamel Four. He was given clearance to procced.

“Right Datch point the nose up and increase thrust.”

“I thought you were going to take over?”

“Nothing like learning on the job as they say. Now watch in your heads up for other ships. Most of them should be well away from us heading to the spaceport or the space station. But just keep looking around and relax. I’ll be watching in my headset so don’t worry.”

Datch relaxed a bit and then increased power and the ship started to climb.

“Give it more power Datch, we’re going into space not a trip around the park.”

Datch pushed the power control further up and the engines started to roar. The ship accelerated skywards and soon the sky started to change from light green, dark green and then black.

“OK Datch, Bank to the left a bit on to heading 234.2 and 178.5”

Datch turned the ship until the numbers in his head display show the correct heading. They cleared orbit and stared to head into space.

“Datch, Give her full throttle.”

Datch did and the ship surged forwards into the inky blackness of space. He turned his head and could see the planet getting smaller behind them.

"Wow." he said.

"Right, before we go to interspace, I want you just to do some gentle turns, slowdown and speed up. Just get use to the controls and please don't make us space sick in the process."

"OK dad."

Datch moved the controls and the ship responded, it took longer than on the bike but he could turn making the ship follow his will. After about thirty minutes Dechow turned to him.

"OK, I think that's enough for now. Let's set the interspace drive and put the ship on auto."

"How do I do that?"

"Ask the computer to do it."

"Oh. Computer set course for Hamal four interspace factor sixteen."

"Course laid in." came the response.

Dechow nodded at Datch.

"Computer switch to auto pilot and engaged interspace drive."

"Command accepted; would you like an alarm thirty minutes before arrival?"

"Yes please."

"Engaging Interspace drive please stay still."

The ship turned by itself and then the interspace drive engaged. The stars in front of the ship winked out for a moment and then stared to flicker.

“Now cruising at interspace sixteen. You may now move about.”

“OK, Datch you can get up now, the computer’s got it.”

Datch took off his headset and let out a big sigh. He got up and everyone clapped.

“Well. Let’s go try the bar out.” said Clax.

“I’ll just have another Grucks I think.” Said Datch hoping to do a bit more piloting.

They headed off to the rec room and sat around trying out the vid and various other things such as the reclining sofas. Then it was time to try out the Solar Ball in the cargo bay. The cargo bay lit up and became a jungle with trees and a swamp. The bikers watched for a while and then went back to the rec room with Tansya and Dechow.

Seven hours and sixty-eight minutes later the ship comms beeped.

“Attention interspace drive will disengage in thirty minutes. please prepare for arrival.”

“Cool.” said Datch getting up excitedly.

“Take your time.” said Dechow “pilot first.”

Datch stopped and let his dad go first who also had to stop at the toilet on the way to the cockpit.

“I always take a leak before I fly. You don’t want to pee your pants if things get a bit scary.”

Datch thought about this for a moment and then went in after his dad.

They sat down in the pilot's and co-pilot's seats.

"I think we should let the computers handle the descent here as its quite a busy planet. So how do you think we do that?"

"Err… We tell the computer?"

"Not quite. We need to get clearance first."

"Right. So, we ask the computer to ask them."

"No, we have to do it."

"OK."

"Right, watch and listen to what I do."

"OK. Computer connect me to planetary control for the Hamel star system."

"Connecting."

His dad put it through the cockpit speakers so Datch could hear.

"This is Hamel control. Identify yourself please?"

"This is the star ship Raven on approach to Hamel four from Bellatrix five."

"Welcome to Hamel space Raven. State Arrival point Please?"

"We are heading to the VIP Beach landing area outside Jafuler. We have a reservation there."

He looked at Datch. Datch nodded.

"Please transmit your IDs for Immigration and come into orbit at a vector shown on your heads up."

"May we have automated approach please?"

“Certainly. Please instruct your ship’s systems. Beacon 213458. Have a pleasant stay.”

“Thank you. Raven Out.”

“OK Datch, instruct the ship to follow beacon 213458 and to transmit our IDs to planetary control.”

“Computer follow beacon 213458 and transmit our IDs to the planetary control.”

“Confirm?”

Dechow nodded

“Yes” said Datch.

“Locking on to Beacon 213458. Please wait……”

The computer altered the ships course.

“New course laid in. Planetary services now have your information. Planet fall in eight minutes. Please stay still while the interspace drive is disengaged.”

Datch pressed a button on his left to activate the ships intercom.

“Hey guys, you need to get up here or sit down where you are. We’re on approach for Hamel and the interspace drops out in about seven minutes.”

There was a shout somewhere below of ‘coming’ and then the noise of someone climbing up the stairs. Five minutes later everyone was sitting down looking out the window. In the centre of the view was a small circle of flickering light. They watched as it got larger and larger expanding into a bright blue planet and then the ship disengaged the interspace drive and light flooded into the cockpit.

“Wow!” said Carina.

“You can say that again.” said Rosey.

The ship banked to the right and then started to dive towards the planet falling in behind another ship and in front of that was another ship. Down through the atmosphere they went slowing as they descended. Up ahead they could see a large city and on its outskirts was a large spaceport. The ship followed the others and then as it approached the city banked left leaving the other ships courses and headed towards the sea.

“Beacon control will terminate in 30 seconds please be ready to take control.”

“Dad?”

“Just put your heads-up display on and rest your hands on the controls.”

Datch realised that the controls had moved to their current flight settings. Dechow watched as Datch got ready.

“Pilot control in 10… 9… 8… 7… 6… 5… 4… 3… 2… 1… Datch you now have control.”

“Datch, follow the vector in your heads up and as the lines change,”

“Yes, I slow down and the bring the landing thrusters online. Just like in the simulator.”

“What simulator?”

“The one on my vid com.”

Dechow watched as Datch followed the lines flying towards an open area with a number of other ships that also looked like they cost a very large amount of credits.

Datch slowed down until the lines disappeared and an arrow replaced them pointing down. He pressed a virtual button and the landing gear deployed. He moved his head to look down. Below he could see the landing feet. He decreased thrust and the Raven started to drop slowly and a readout in the centre of his view started to countdown. Datch eased the thruster control back a bit more gingerly until there was a slight bump. He put the control to zero and pressed shutdown. The engines stopped and he let out a big sigh.

"That was pretty good Datch, well done." Said Dechow.

"It was a lot easier than the simulator. I flew into a building last time."

"Really?" said Dechow who was now even more surprised and slightly worried at the same time.

"Well, only a bit of a building. But the ship was fine."

"OK. Why don't we talk about it over a cold beer on the beach while you mum calls your brother?"

"I'm there!" said Hagger who hadn't had a drink for at least three hours.

This was because they had found a large list of games on the Solar Ball console and after a few moments browsing they found a racing game and he had spent the last two and a half hours racing Clax, Tank, Dapo and Tish in the cargo bay.

They all got up and headed down to the cargo bay.

At the back of the ship the ramp dropped down on two hydraulic rams revealing the cargo door. Inside Datch pressed the door release and the door opened.

"Shall we?" he said.

"Lead the way." said Dechow.

They followed Datch through the door and down the ramp. Two smartly dressed men were standing just behind the ship and as they reached the bottom of the ramp, they turned to them and said,

“Welcome to the Jafuler private arena. We offer a number of ship services including refuelling, cleaning, waste removal and damage repairs. The main resort is over there and has a private beach, three pools, seven restaurants, six bars including two pool bars and a recreation centre. Before you go, we are all here to help you and if you need anything at all please ask one of the staff.”

Datch walked up to the man who had just spoken.

“Thank you. Can you refuel my ship please?”

The man looked at Datch and then at Tank who had followed Datch over and was standing next to him. Tank nodded.

“Certainly sir.” Said the man who had now gone a little pink.

“Thank you and add ten credits for yourself.” Added Datch who quite liked it when he caught people out.

“Thank you, sir.”

Datch then turned to the others.

“Come on then, the beach is this way.”

The party set out in the direction of the beach and bar.

The resort was nicely laid out with plenty of space and a number of very discreet staff who were almost invisible. The pools were carefully crafted to have a mix of shade and sun while being surrounded with palm trees and various bushes along with reflective shielding, all designed to make sure that no prying eyes could get through. The buildings were all low profile and soft relaxing music filled the air.

“Well, this is nice.” Said Carina sitting down next to Datch.

“Yes. I could get use to this.”

He leaned over and gave her a pat on the shoulder.

"We have two weeks before the next gig so let's make the most of it."

"Sure thing, lover."

At that point Tansya came walking over with her vid in one hand and a drink in the other.

"I'll called Dydinyon and told him we were here."

"And?" said Dechow.

"Well, after he wiped the coffee off his desk and was able to talk, he said he is going to come down after work in about three hours. I told him to ask for the Raven party."

"Sounds like a plan. I'll tell the staff to expect him."

The party had got a nice spot under a number of palm trees next to one of the large pools. They found out that the bars had a full waiter service so they didn't have to get up. The Pack sat watching the world go by. After half an hour Tansya turned to the others who by this point were playing a game called spot the VIP.

"Err, do you folks always do this when your away?"

"Yes, normally." Said Tank.

"Most of the time." said Tish.

"Why not?" said Dapo.

"I'll have another drink please." Added Hagger as one of the waiters came by.

"Yes sir." he said and headed off in the direction of the bar.

"Yes mum. Sorry, I forgot you hadn't been away with us before. We like the nice hotels as we don't get hassled."

“This way we can relax and not have to watch our backs.” said Clax.

“I thought Timbo did that?” said Dechow.

“He does but it can still get a bit over powering until we get back to the hotels.” Added Carina.

“Places like this mean we can just chill. We only look over shoulder to see where the drinks are and here, they appear to turn up before we order them.” said Fred watching a waiter coming over with another round of drinks on a tray.

“I bet the drinks cost a bit here.” said Tansya looking at the tray.

“Normally two to three times the price but it’s worth it.”

“Don’t you ask before you order them.” she asked.

“If you have to ask, you don’t come to places like this.” Added Tank.

Tansya sat back thinking about this. If someone had told her two years ago that her seven-year-old son would be earning ten million credits a year she would have laughed at them. Now here she was two years later sitting with him and his band having drinks in a very private club on another world. Well at least he was having fun. She looked at Datch again hoping to see signs of her little boy but now he was the adult Datch and had grown up faster than anyone would ever have guessed.

Dechow saw the look on her face.

“You, OK?” he said.

“Yes, I was just thinking how much Datch has grown up.”

“He’s his own person now for sure.”

They watched Datch as he grabbed Carina by the hand and took her over to the pool.

“They make a good couple, don’t they?” said Fred.

“Yes.” said Tansya as they jumped into the pool.

The game of spot the VIP was abandoned due to the fact that everyone in the private area was a VIP and all you had to do was say there’s one and point at a random person as long as it wasn’t a waiter. The rest of the afternoon was spent chilling by the pool.

The sun was just starting to set when a waiter came over.

“Excuse we but we have the gentleman you informed us about at the gate.” he said to Datch.

He got out a vid comm and showed them the gate camera. There was Dydinyon looking a little over dressed and a bit flustered.

“Yes, that’s him. Can you bring him over also can we get a large table in the restaurant that’s able to seat all of us?”

“Certainly Sir. How long will it be before you require it?”

“Oh, say an hour, it will give us time to get changed.”

“Certainly Sir. Dress code is smart casual, No shorts.”

“Understood. Thanks.” Datch gave him a ten-credit tip.

The waiter nodded and went off to fetch Dydinyon.

A couple of minutes later he came back with Datch’s brother.

“Hi bro.” said Datch casually.

“Hi Datch. hi Mum, Dad, hello everyone.”

There was a round of hellos before he went over and sat down next to his mum.

“I wish you could have given me a bit more notice. I only spoke to you yesterday, how did you get here so fast? You didn’t say when you called me.”

“Datch brought us.” Said Dechow grinning.

“He did. So what star liner was it? I’ve been on most of them.”

“Datch, your brother was just asking which star liner brought us here. I think you should show him and I need a shower before dinner.” shouted Dechow who had given Datch his flair for the dramatic.

“OK dad, let me finish my beer.”

Dydinyon got the feeling things were not how he thought they were and no one was letting on. He also had blank looks when he asked where they were staying. Ten minutes later Datch and Carina got up.

“Come on then let’s go get ready for dinner.” Datch said.

“I thought you were going to tell me how you got here?”

“I am bro, come on.”

Everyone got up and started to follow Datch and Carina back to the Raven. They left the pool area and headed to the ships landing area. One of the attendants came over to Datch and held up a vid com. Datch looked at it.

“That’s fine thanks” he said and pressed a button, it beeped.

“Datch, why are we going in here? This is an owner’s area. And what did that guy want?” Asked Dydinyon.

Datch didn't say anything but just walked over to the Raven and went around to its rear. He pressed his vid com and the rear door opened lowering the ramp.

"This is how we got here and also where we are staying."

"Wow, who's ship is it."

Dechow couldn't contain his self.

"It's Datch's."

Dydinyon's jaw dropped and he was silent for a few seconds.

"What, yours for real?"

"Yes, dad's teaching me to fly it."

"I heard all about Welly four from mum and the galactic press, did you get it from them?"

"No, I got it this morning from the Bellatrixian president and wanted to take it out on a little trip."

"Oh, how much did it cost?" there was a cough behind them.

"Sorry to but in but are we standing outside all night?" said Fred.

"Sorry Fred, come on let's go inside and I'll explain." Said Datch.

They headed up the ramp and inside the ship. After Datch gave Dydinyon the grand tour it was time for a shower before heading out for dinner.

The restaurant was busy but very spacious. The staff had set out a number of tables joining them together to make a large one. It had been set up in one of the large bay windows overlooking the sea and was in the shape of an arc. They sat down and looked at the menus.

"Err, this menu does not have any prices on." Said Dydinyon.

"Don't worry about it." said Tansya.

"Just get what you want. My treat." Added Datch.

Dydinyon was a little taken aback. Tansya noticed and nodded at him when he looked at her.

The evening progressed and dinner was soon over. It was then time to tell Dydinyon the story of the gem. Dechow had seen Datch's older brothers trying to get one over on each other but Datch was in a class of his own. There was no way that anyone was going to beat him and he was only nine years old. (About twenty in earth terms.)

They were just discussing the number of gigs they had to sort out when a waiter came over and coughed politely behind Datch. Datch turned around.

"Sorry to bother you sir but Mr Daco has asked if it would be possible to sign a picture for his daughter?"

Datch thought about it for a second.

"Can you point them out for me?"

"Certainly sir, That's them over there in the corner."

Datch followed the waiter's eyes to the opposite corner and there was a couple with a young girl about four or five in Bellatrixian years. They were looking across to The Pack and the little girl looked excited to see them.

"Guys we've been asked to do a photo. But I think we should ask them over. Everyone OK with it?"

There was a general nodding and Datch turned to the waiter.

"Tell them that if they wish we are happy for them to come over and have a photo taken with us."

"Sir, how do you wish to be introduced?"

"As 'The Pack' please."

"Certainly sir."

Datch watched as the waiter went over and told them. The little girls face lit up and she started jumping up and down excitedly. Her Father then tried to calm her down as they got up and were pretty much dragged across the room to them along with the waiter.

"May I present Mr and Mrs Daco of Daco industries and their daughter Annabel. This is The Pack."

"Oh, you're the best band in the universe, wait until I tell my friends that I've met you." shouted Annabel who was now so excited that a bathroom break might be required very soon.

"Hi Annabel, I'm Datch."

"I know. I have a picture of all of you on my wall."

She then proceeded to name everyone in the band before stopping at Dechow when her brough furrowed.

"Err..."

"That's my mum, dad and brother." Said Datch.

"Oh... err, hello." she said.

Dechow let out a little laugh.

They all had a picture taken with Annabel and signed things for her. After which Annabel had a barrage of questions for them and then a bit of small talk before her dad turned to Datch.

"Do you have any plans to do a concert on Hamel?"

"Not at the moment but we have been taking about performing off world after going to Welly four."

"Oh, please, please do. I would love to see you live and it would make my daughter's year."

Datch looked at Annabel and then at the others who gave him a look of 'I know what's coming next.'

"Well, we'll try to sort something out."

Annabel's dad reached inside his pocket.

"Here is my card. If you sort out a date and tell me what you need, I'll get my people to do the rest. I do have a very large business empire which can sort out nearly anything."

"Thank you. We are having two weeks off at the moment, a sort of holiday so it might be a few weeks before Fred gets back to you if that's OK?"

Fred nodded.

"That's great, if you want anything while you're here on Hamel just give me a call and I'll try to help."

"That's very good of you, thank you." said Carina.

"No, thank you. You have all just made my little girl's week and that means a lot to us."

They said their goodbyes before dragging Annabel back to their table.

"Does that happen a lot?" asked Dydinyon.

"Yes, quite a lot." Said Carina.

"Oh my. I just realised who that was. He owns one of the largest corporate empires on the planet as well as subsidiaries across twenty star systems."

"Oh, well at least we should get a good after party then." Said Rosey.

"Doesn't that phase you?" asked Dydinyon totally puzzled by their reaction.

"Err why would it?" Said Datch.

"He's one of..." Tansya put her hand up and he stopped

"Datch along with everyone else rub shoulders with Presidents, planetary leaders and media stars almost daily Dydinyon. They are normal people to him."

"Wow. How do you think like that?"

"We don't, we just have a good time." said Carina.

"At the end of the day. He gets up in the morning, has breakfast and goes to work just like you." added Datch.

Dydinyon had a puzzled look for a moment while he thought about it.

"Oh, I sort of see what you mean." he said.

They went back to normal chit chat and ordered a few more rounds of drinks. Dydinyon had to go work in the morning so left them just before midnight.

The next week was spent chilling on the beach or around the pool along with a bit of sightseeing which involved dark glasses just in case people spotted them. At one point they bumped into Annabel on the beach who proceeded to tell them that all her friends were very envious that she had met The Pack. Dydinyon came around a couple more times and then it was time to go home.

Datch entered the Raven's cockpit and sat down. His dad followed suit and sat in the pilot's seat.

"Do you want to do it?" Dechow asked.

"Yes please, dad."

"OK. Do your pre-flight checks."

Datch pressed a number of buttons and asked the Raven's computers to verify all the systems. Everything was good so Dechow contacted planetary control.

"This is the Raven ready for departure to Bellatrix five."

"Please wait Raven. Flight paths are all busy at the moment – flight path will be clear for you in five minutes. Do you require auto guidance to high orbit?"

"Yes please."

"OK Raven, hold at two hundred metres and lock on to Beacon 703183"

Datch pressed another button and the main engines started up.

"OK Datch. lift off and hover at two hundred metres."

Datch slowly pulled back on the vertical thrusters

The Raven slowly took to the sky and stared to hover. Datch told the computer to lock onto the beacon and the ship hung in the air waiting for planetary control. Then as if by magic the ship turned in the air and started to increase height picking up speed as it went. Soon, they were above the clouds and the main engines were at full thrust. The ship fell in behind a cargo ship and matched its speed. The blue sky turned to black and the stars came out.

"Raven, beacon will release control in one minute"

“Thank you, control.”

Datch rested his hands on the controls ready to take over.

“Datch when you get control head over that way. There is clear space there.”

“OK dad.”

“This is planetary control, Raven the ship is yours – have a safe trip.”

“Thanks control, Raven out.” said Datch taking hold of the controls

He banked the ship slightly right and headed in the direction Dechow had pointed to.

“Computer, set course for Bellatrix five – interspace sixteen.”

“Course laid in.”

“Engage.”

The ship changed course and then the lights dimmed. Outside the ship the stars started to flicker. They got up and headed to the rec room.

They had been lounging around for an hour and contemplating where to go next when the main screen flashed up ‘Message for Datch’.

“I have a message?” he said.

“It will be on your vid com Datch. It links to the ships comms so the ship will tell you when you receive a message or call. Calls can be a bit weird though due to delays in the interspace links.” Said his dad.

“Oh, I’ll go and get it.”

Datch left the room and went to his and Carina's bedroom. Datch had picked the one near the front of the ship and had it decorated in pastel colours for Carina. His vid com was lying on the bed. He picked it up and looked at it. There was a message from the president of Bellatrix. He read it, smiled and sent a single word reply 'OK' before going back to the others.

He walked into the rec room.

"Well, anything important?"

"No. just the president inviting us to be guests of honour at a party."

"Which one?"

"Some opening event in the city."

"No, which president?"

"Oh, the Bellatrixian one."

"What did he say?"

"Well, the Welly four delegation takes over the new embassy in Yuland city in four weeks and wants us to open it. It was meant to be next week but got put back because of modifications to the kabab house and night club."

"And what did you say?" asked Fred.

"OK."

"Was that it?"

"Err, yes why?"

"Well, you could have put we would be honored or something."

"Oh. I'll be back in a minute."

Datch left the room.

Two minutes later he was back.

"I've told him we would love to come. Is that better?"

"Yes. much!" said Fred.

They went back to discussing where to go when they got back and after a long discussion it was decided that a nice quiet resort island in Southern Ocean sounded good. It had its own landing area and Datch could take the Raven out over the sea for some flight training with his dad in the mornings. They booked a landing spot and after fifteen minutes it came back with a conformation.

They had some food and then went to play Solar Ball in the cargo bay. They were just in the middle of the fourth game when the ships thirty-minute warning sounded. Datch left the game and headed up to the flight deck. His dad was already getting into his seat and Clax was sitting behind him.

"Hi Clax, you come to watch me."

"Yes, and to see how she flies"

Datch sat in the co-pilot's seat and put his head set on.

After checking the systems with his dad, they decided to let Datch fly it to the outer atmosphere and then Dechow would take it down. The island they were going to didn't have automatic approach as it was in the middle of the sea so they had to fly the ship down. They had just checked the weather over the island when the five-minute alarm sounded. Dechow turned to Datch.

"OK Datch, you do the honours."

He pressed the comms button.

"Bellatrixian Control – This is the Raven on route from Hamel four requesting approach to the Southern Ocean."

"Welcome to Bellatrixian space please adjust heading to 274.34, 561.37 on exit from interspace. Be aware there are five other ships on a parallel flight path. What is your final arrival point?"

"The Island of Salar in the Southern Ocean."

"After planetary interface change to heading 327.1, 149.6 for approach. Below twenty thousand metres navigation is at your liberty."

"Copy that control. Raven out."

Datch got himself ready for manual control as the circle of light in the centre of view got the larger. Then the lights dimmed and the ship disengaged the interspace drive and there was Bellatrix five in all its glory. Datch moved the controls slowly and the Raven turned on to the new heading.

"Datch when it starts to get bumpy, I'll take control OK."

"OK Dad."

"And remember not to fight it."

"I know, stay relaxed like it says in the training vids"

Datch followed the flight path and approached the planet.

The ships shields started to glow and Datch reduced thrust pulling the nose of the ship up slightly. The ship slowed and the shields generated glowing lines of plasma. The ship slowed down dropping lower and lower. The Raven started to bounce a bit as it hit the outer atmosphere. Dechow took over and Datch relaxed. The Raven bounced and bumped as it trans versed the high clouds and after five minutes the bouncing stopped and the Raven dropped out of the clouds into a clear sunny sky.

Below them was the Southern Ocean glistening in the sun light. Its waves reflecting the sun like diamonds and here and there a ship could be seen riding on the water like majestic swans on a crystal lake.

"Datch, do you want to take her in?" Said Dechow whose confidence in Datch was now building.

"OK Dad, but my landings in the sim are still a bit shaky."

"You'll be fine. Just take it steady."

"OK Dad." Datch put his hands back on the controls and got ready.

"Remember, nice and gentle. OK she's all yours."

There was a slight shake as Datch took control and the Raven glided down towards the sea. He levelled her out at five thousand metres and headed for the dot on the heads-up screen. The water went rushing by below and Datch relaxed into the controls. Carina and Tansya came on to the flight deck. Clax put his finger up to his mouth and then motioned towards Datch. Carina nodded and they sat down quietly behind watching Datch fly the ship. In the distance a small point of green appeared in the sea. Datch slowed the Raven and dropped down to two thousand metres.

"Salar Control this is star ship Raven on approach requesting a landing beacon."

"Raven this is Salar Control lock on to beacon 273, your landing reservation is landing area forty-two."

Datch pressed a couple of virtual buttons and there was a beep.

"Salar Control, Beacon locked on. Eta three minutes."

The island got larger and larger. It was covered in palm trees and had a small town with a harbour. A few small hotels were scattered along the sandy beaches. The trees stretched in land, running up to the foot of a large mountain. Just behind the town was a landing area and the control tower.

Datch slowed the Raven to three hundred KPH and dropped to two hundred metres. The island got closer

"Datch go slow over the town, we don't want to take their roofs off."

"OK Dad."

Datch dropped the speed to fifty KPH as he approached the town and dropped the Ravens landing gear. He had a look of concentration on his face as he brought the ship in over the beacon. The landing thruster fired and the ship dropped gently down on the ground with the lightest of bumps.

"Raven – this is Salar control enjoy your stay."

"Thank you - Raven out."

"Not bad Datch, nice landing but just watch your approach speed. You could have come in a bit faster."

"I wanted to make sure I got it spot on."

"I know and you did very well but if you're over buildings you don't want to hang around. Maybe twice the speed would have been ideal. I'll teach you during the week."

"OK dad."

Datch pressed a few buttons and the engine systems shutdown. As Datch got up Carina and Tansya clapped for him.

"Well done lover." Carina said and gave him a kiss.

"OK, let's hit the beach." he said.

They got up and headed out of the ship. Dechow left them and went over to Salar Control to make sure the training flights were OK while the rest headed for a bar on the beach.

The next week was spent with Datch having training flights in the mornings which included one shore landing on a deserted island with everyone onboard where a lunchtime beach barbeque was in order along with a swim in the sea. He slowly got the hang of the Raven and found that if he was gentle with the controls the ship was very easy to fly. Soon, he was landing and taking off like a skilled pilot. His Dad was impressed how fast he picked it up and even had Datch try a couple of simulated emergency landings.

The afternoons were spent down on the beach in front of a bar drinking and relaxing under the palm trees along with cooling off in the crystal-clear waters of the Southern Ocean. Afterwards it would be time for showers followed by a trip to a local fish restaurant. It wasn't a posh or fancy restaurant but instead was very basic and had a very rustic shanty town type feel. However, the food was great and the atmosphere was very chilled. They could eat outside on the veranda and watch the sun go down. The evening air was warm and the sounds of the soft music was backed by the sea lapping on the shore. It was all a million miles away from the Barbers inn. Finally, it was the end of the week and they sat outside contemplating the following one.

Fred sat looking through his vid comm.

"Wow that's a lot of mail." Said Tank looking over his shoulder.

"Yes, I have three from my old insurance company asking me if I can do an advert for them, one about my utilities being turned off for a few hours last week and seventy-five gig offers along with five hundred and forty-eight fan mails."

"Oh. I think I'm going to leave mine till I get home."

“Talking of gigs, are we going to do the Barbers tomorrow?” asked Fred.

“I’m good with that.” Said Datch.

The others all agreed.

“I’ll put a call through to Jim and let him know. When are we doing that opening gig at the embassy?”

“That’s err... Three weeks’ time.” said Datch looking at his vid comm. “Better tell Jim that as well, we might need to chill out the following day.”

Fred got up and walked on to the beach to call Jim.

“So Datch, you ready to fly us home tomorrow?” asked Tank.

Datch looked at his dad for guidance and he nodded.

“Yes, I think I should be OK to do that.”

“Cool.” Said Carina and put her arm around him a squeezed him a little.

“It’s been a really nice relaxing two weeks Datch. Thank you.” said Tansya.

“Yes, it’s been great. Nice to just do our own thing and with these exclusive resorts we don’t get bothered by anyone.” Added Peebop.

Everyone agreed.

“So, what are we doing next week?”

“There’s the gig at the Barbers and then school. I expect a gig somewhere next weekend but I think we should talk to that guy on Hamel about a gig, maybe do an interstellar tour or something in a couple of month’s time.” said Datch.

There was another round of nodding with some comments thrown in for good measure.

“Have you thought about where to keep the Raven?” asked Dechow.

Datch already had some ideas about this.

“I was thinking about the space port but that costs a lot of credits for the ship to just stand there. I’m going to look and see if there is a private landing site nearby to store it when we’re not using it.”

Dechow looked at his son. He was certainly thinking on his feet and had been checking all the options.

“Well, How’s this for a deal. I’ll put a hard surface down in the field next to the barn and even put in external power cables to keep the ships systems running when the ships shut down. In return I want you and Carina to take me and your mum on holiday at least once per year and you need to help me build it. How does that sound?”

Datch looked at Carina and she smiled.

“OK Dad, it’s a deal.”

“Great, we get at least a week or two away from the band every year.” Said Tank laughing.

“Yes, I might actually get my decorating finished by next year.” Added Peebop.

“And I can clean the back of my shop.” Said Clax.

They all looked at him.

“OK, maybe not, but I have thought about at least twice in the last hundred years.”

Everyone burst out laughing.

“Does this count as time number two or number three?” asked Rosey.

“Err… Number two.”

There was another round of laughing.

They chilled out in the bar and watched as the sun set over the sea. They carried on drinking and relaxing until it was time to head back to the Raven for sleep.

Schools Out

The next morning, The Pack plus two got up from what was now their mobile home AKA the Raven and went for breakfast. They had spent the last two weeks together chilling out along with Datch's mum and dad. During which time Tank decided to make his room look better by adding a few extra bits from a local store and that started things off. The doors onboard the Raven now had little plaques on the wall next to them stating whose room it was and also, the rooms themselves had a number of nonstandard items added such as a large pink teddy bear or a sign saying 'Life's better on the beach' and also a rather nice duvet cover or two. The pink teddy was Tanks.

After breakfast it was time to head for home. Datch had the ship refuelled the day before so they didn't need to stop on the way.

Everyone headed up to the cockpit and started to sit down.

Datch went to sit in the co-pilots chair and his dad stopped him.

"You have done very well this week. You can sit there."

he said pointing to the pilot's seat.

"Really?"

"Yes, but remember what I've taught you. I want a smooth flight, OK?"

"OK Dad."

Datch was grinning from ear to ear which put everyone on edge before they realised what was going on.

"You ready Datch?"

"Yes Dad."

Datch put his heads-up display on and pressed a few buttons and the ships systems came online. He did a number of systems checks before looking at his dad. Dechow nodded

"Salar Control this is the Raven ready for departure on route to Yuland city. Request a cruising height of forty thousand metres and speed ten thousand KPH."

"Raven your flight path is clear until you are in Yuland city control range. You are cleared for take-off. Have a safe trip. Salar Control out."

"Thanks, Salar control. Raven out."

Datch increased thrust and the Raven took to the sky. He was really getting the hang of flying the Raven. The Raven banked as it climbed and headed into the sky.

The flight took about twenty minutes before they were handed over to Yuland control.

"This is the Raven in bound from Salar island requesting a vector for landing at 132.22, 732.4." said Datch.

"This is Yuland control. Please adjust flight path to vector 123.65, 453.23, descend to ten thousand metres and slow to one thousand KPH. Be advised that the main corridors are currently very busy and expect traffic to your right."

"Thank you Yuland city. Changing heading and dropping to ten thousand. Raven out."

Datch dropped the ship down into the new flight path and slowed the ship as they were now in the thicker atmosphere.

They crossed the coastline near where the great river Axecon flows into the sea. Down below a patch work of fields and forests spread out across the landscape. Here and there a village or town nestled in amongst the chequered pattern. In the distance to the north was the desert that Datch knew so well. Another ten minutes and they would be home.

"Raven this is Yuland control please drop to three thousand metres and adjust your heading to 120.2, 451.7."

"This is Raven, copy that adjusting heading to 120.2, 451.7"

Datch adjusted the Raven's heading.

"Raven, you are on a heading avoiding Yuland city central but expect heavy traffic to your right shortly."

"Thanks, Yuland control. Raven out."

The fields started to give way to the desert and soon they were flying above the sands with the river off to the left. Datch watched the navigation read out and started slowing down. The river was starting to move away from them now and in the distance the glistening towers could be seen.

"Yuland control, this is Raven on final approach."

"Copy that, Raven. Cleared to descend."

Datch descended to three hundred metres and slowed to one hundred KPH.

The desert turned into scrub land below and then the ranch was in sight. Datch fired the landing thrusters and dropped the landing gear. The Ranch got closer and closer. Dechow was studying Datch's every move as he brought the ship smoothly around for a gentle landing in the paddock.

"Yuland Control this is the Raven. We have landed."

"Raven. Have a good day, Yuland control out."

Datch turned to his dad.

"So, how did I do?"

“You did very well Datch, it was a smooth flight.”

“Thanks Dad.”

“OK. Let’s go get a beer.”

The party left the ship and headed into the bar before spreading out next to the pool. Tansya took their bags into the house with Carina and made some sandwiches for lunch. After lunch everyone headed home apart from Carina who was almost a permanent resident at the ranch now. Then it was just Datch, Carina and his mum and dad laying around the pool.

“So how long do you think it will take me to get my licence?” asked Datch.

“I don’t know but after this week maybe two or three more months.” Said his dad.

“That long?”

“Yes, you can fly her OK. That’s not the issue. You need to be able to handle her in an emergency. That training can only be done on a simulator.”

“Oh.”

Datch was a bit down hearted and wondered when he could fit it in. Dechow noticed the look on his face and decided to help.

“Look, why don’t I have a word with the captain and see if he could help. The Carpaycus does have a flight sim onboard.”

“That would be cool dad, thanks.”

It got to late afternoon and it was time for Datch and Carina to get ready for the gig. They were meeting the others in the Barbers a couple of hours before the gig to have some food. So, after a shower they got on Datch's bike and headed to the city.

The Barbers inn was its normal self with people milling around and watching the vid. Datch and Carina went in and headed up the stairs to the big table. Tank, Hagger and Rosey were already there and deep in discussion. After a round of Hellos, the conversation turned to gigs

"Are we really going to gig off world?" said Rosey.

"Yes, why not?" asked Datch.

"It just seems like a big step."

"I remember you saying that when we did our first gig in the capital. Just remember Traxsent. That was our first big gig and it went really well."

"I know but this is off world."

"So was Welly four. Look at what happened there. We had a whole week of gigging and we changed the planet."

"OK, point taken."

At that point the rest of The Pack turned up.

"So, what's going on?" said Jep sitting down.

"We were just talking about an off-world tour."

"Oh good, I was wanting to talk to you about that." Said Fred waving at Jim for a beer.

"Why?" asked Tank.

"I've been looking through the rest of my emails and we have at least fifteen really good offers including two from Welly four. I looked at the offers and eight are on route to Welly four."

"So, what are you saying?" asked Datch.

"Well, we could do four on the way there and four on the way back. Also, we could detour to Hamel on the way back and maybe two there."

"Err, why two on Hamel?" asked Carina.

"Well, to be honest I really liked that place we stayed at and wanted to go back."

There was a lot of agreement on that point.

"So, what do you all think?" Fred asked.

"How long would we be away for?" said Rosey.

"Maybe ten weeks now we have our own ship."

"That's not too bad. But I will need to take the flight costs out of the pot before we divide it up."

"Granted. How much does it cost to run the Raven anyway?"

"She took just over a thousand credits for the round trip to Hamel fuel wise. So, I would say about five thousand five hundred to get to Welly four. Plus, landing fees."

"That's not bad. If we take say two thousand per gig and put it in the Raven fund then that should cover landing fees as well."

"Yes, that sounds about right. Any spare we can spend on Beer."

There was a general round of agreement to this as everyone had enjoyed going in the Raven.

"So, when are we going to do it?"

"Well, we have to do the Embassy thing first and we should do a few more nights at the Barbers before disappearing again."

There was another round of agreement.

"OK, what about six weeks' time?" Asked Fred.

"That's when the school holiday begins." Said Hagger.

"Good point, at least we won't get any hassle from the principal." Added Datch.

"I think he's given up on even trying now. Whenever he sees me coming down the corridor, he just sticks a sign on his door saying 'Gone for a long lunch.'" said Jep and then added "Also he doesn't answer when I knock."

"How do you know he hasn't gone for a long lunch?" asked Dapo.

"He does it at eight in the morning!"

"Oh!"

"Just to be safe I'll slip a note under his door so he knows." Added Datch.

Just then Jim came up the stairs followed by two security officers and a tall skinny man with a beard.

"Err Datch?" said Tank as they came over.

Datch looked around just as they arrived at the table.

"Err, Datch this is the President's assistant and he would like to have a word with you folks." said Jim looking a little worried.

The tall skinny man turned to Datch.

"Hello, let me introduce myself. I am Mr Smom and have the honour of being the officer in charge of interstellar affairs."

Datch looked at him, he didn't look like he was going to tell him off.

"Hi, I'm Datch what can we do for you Mr Smom?"

"Let me get straight to the point. As you know it is the opening of the Welly four embassy in three week's time."

"Yes, we have a gig there." Added Datch.

"Well, the President has got to make a speech at the opening of the new embassy and also mingle at the party afterwards. He needs to know how to behave to the Welly four delegation and I'm afraid that all of our documents relate to before shall we say 'the end of darkness'."

"So how can we help?"

"Well, we're sort of hoping you can advise us. You did bring an end to the darkness and from what I can tell, you're also are responsible for the cultural revolution on the planet."

"I take it that you mean. Due to us the planets now a party zone and you need to know how to party their way which is actually ours." Said Clax.

"Well err... yes." he said looking a little awkward.

Datch looked around at the others who were either grinning, smirking or both at the same time which in itself was quite impressive.

"OK, well it's a bit bad timing now as we're going to do a gig in a little while."

"Oh yes, I know. I didn't mean right now. Oh no. Sorry."

Datch was starting to enjoy this.

"We could fit the President in say tomorrow around eleven ish but we'll have to clear it with school."

"Oh, don't worry about school, I'll take care of that. Where shall I send the transport for you?"

“Here please, we have rooms for the night upstairs.”

“That’s wonderful, thank you. I’ll leave you to your, err… gig and see you when you arrive at the Presidential Palace tomorrow. Thank you for your time.”

With that he left along with the two officers. Jim stood looking at them speechless for a moment.

“You guys are going to the Presidential Palace?”

“Err yes, why?”

Jim looked at them all sitting there as if someone had just said ‘I’ll see you in the café later’. It then dawned on him that this was normal to them and rubbing shoulders with presidents and other celebrities was just something they did.

“How can you be so calm about things?”

“Well, we look at it this way. The President gets out of bed in the morning, goes for a dump in the toilet, eats cereal for breakfast and drinks lots of coffee to wake up. We do the same so therefore he is the same as us.” Said Tank.

Jim couldn’t argue with that logic and decided not to ask anymore. He went back to the bar to prepare the Barbers for the oncoming onslaught. The Pack headed to the ‘back of stage’ table to prepare for the gig.

The following morning Jep got a call from the school to say that apparently the President had decided that The Pack didn’t need any more schooling and they had passed. They were welcome to come back if they wished but please could the school have advanced warning as they would need to put on extra security. Also, could they please attend the graduation to receive their diplomas. It would also be nice if they could do a couple of songs.

He repeated it all back to The Pack at breakfast.

“Did they say anything else?” asked Datch sticking a sausage in his mouth.

“Err yes.” Jep went a little pink which wasn’t normal for him

“Come on spill the beans.” Said Tank.

“Well, they asked me if I was going to come back or not?”

“Oh… what did you say?” asked Datch.

“Let’s put it this way I only have one line of income now and that’s you guys.”

“Well, it looks like the interstellar tour is on then. By the way Fred what are they offering?”

“Well, most are stadiums with three nights of gigs and some very posh hotels which are free of charge.”

“Wow!” said Carina.

“Yes, very nice, but how much?”

“Oh credits?”

“Yes!” they all said together.

“Err… Fifty thousand per night each.”

The table went very quiet while they all took it in. Datch sat there adding it up and worked out that they would get one and a half million credits each. It was a few moments before anyone said anything and then it was Jep.

“Can I call the school and tell principal to…”

“No!” said Fred “They need to get their diplomas.”

“And have our graduation party.” Added Hagger not wanting to miss out on a party.

“Good point. I can tell him then.” The grin on Jep’s face was somewhere between positively evil and very vindictive. It was not a good look for someone who was well over nine hundred and nearly due for a new body.

“I think you guys should call your folks and tell them. It will stop them worrying about you not being at school.” Said Clax.

“School, I think they will be more interested in the one and a half million credits we’re going to be getting.”

“Well, One million four hundred thousand. Welly four is only paying twenty-five thousand each per night. But I thought that would be OK.”

“That’s not a problem.” said Dapo and reached for his vid.

Hagger did no more than call Tank who was sitting next to him.

“Really!” said Tank and everyone laughed.

Everyone called their parents to tell them about the interstellar tour. The calls were ‘normal’ to start with and then a little excited at the end.

They finished breakfast and were just drinking their coffee when a shuttle landed in the street outside. Moments later a security officer came walking up the stairs with Jim in tow.

“Good morning. I’ve come to convey you to the Presidential Palace.” he said.

“We’ll be with you in a moment. Do we have time to finish our coffee?” Asked Fred.

“Yes, sir” replied the officer.

They finished their drinks before heading out to the shuttle.

An hour later they arrived at the Palace. It was on the shores of the Eastern Sea and was surrounded by palm trees swaying in the light breeze. The building was a large circular structure with marble towers around the edge. They exited the shuttle and the President's aid came running up to them.

"Welcome to the Palace. Please can you follow me."

They followed him through the main doors. Inside was full of ornate sculptures and fancy looking pillars. The floors were all polished marble and the main hall was lined with holograms of previous Presidents. They followed the aid along this corridor and down that one before going outside into the gardens. They eventually arrived in a patio area next to a swimming pool. The President was sitting in a chair next to a large table which looked out of place.

"There you are." he said getting up.

"Hi Coola, how's it going?"

"I'm good Datch thanks. Hi everyone please take a seat."

He turned to the adviser.

"Mr Smom, if you would take notes, please?"

The presidents aid gave a small nod and got out a vid comm and sat down discreetly in the corner.

"So Datch, after saving me you've moved up a level and saved a whole planet. That's quite some going."

"Well, it just sort of happened!"

"Things seem to do that around you. So, now you've saved the planet, What's it like?"

"Well, I feel quite good about it to be honest."

"No, not you, the planet."

"Oh, Err, it's sort of like us."

The President looked at them.

"Like you?"

"Yes, the gem took our emotions and thoughts when we were singing and passed them to the entire population."

"They sort of got our outlook on life." Added Carina.

"Your outlook on life?"

"Yes." they all said together.

The President took another long look at them.

"OK!... Well, what I need from you is to tell me how they will react when they arrive. I have to look after the delegation until the embassy opening when they move in and as you changed their 'outlook' on life. You folks are the best people to teach me what I need to know."

"Oh, OK." Said Datch.

"Well, let's start at the beginning. How do they greet each other now?"

Datch thought about this and then said.

"They were saying things like Hi dudes and dudets or how's it going dude."

"And good to meet you." added Carina hoping to give the President a bit more to work with.

"How's it hanging?" Said Dapo.

"They also said hello and good day, but that tended to be the older people." Added Fred.

"I see, how old are the population?"

"Well, they live to about two hundred and sixty."

"Is that it?"

"Yes, most of them don't have implants so they don't get new bodies and the med techs don't have nano bots on hand."

"Oh, I see. That explains the question in the mail then."

"What mail?"

"We've had a number of correspondents from the Minister Prime."

"How is Widfab?" asked Datch.

"He's fine apparently and asked about Nano bots and body engineering."

"Oh, I may have mentioned something about that at one of the after parties." Said Jep.

"One of them?"

"Yes, we had a lot of them!" added Hagger.

"We had a week of touring the planet with him and gigging most nights. So yes, as Hagger said a lot." Added Peebop.

"I see. Well, what do you think they would like as a gift then? They are bringing a gift to the planet when they come and I need to give them something in return."

They sat thinking for a while and then Datch had an idea.

"What about a new body for the Minister Prime and the information how to do it for themselves."

"Yes, and maybe some of the nanobots that fix your hangovers, they'll be needing a lot of them." added Hagger.

“That’s for sure.” said Rosey.

“Oh, I have a good idea! What about a large selection of music from all over Bellatrix?” Said Tish.

“That’s a good idea, they would like that. I know I would.” Added Fred.

The President smiled.

“OK. What sort of clothes do you think they will be wearing?”

“When we left them, they were expanding their clothing collection at quite a rate and it had a lot of bright colours in it.” said Tish with a grin on her face.

“Hmm, I wonder why?” added Dapo with a smirk on his face.

“So, not only have you changed the planets entire culture but you have given them a whole new wardrobe to go with it?” said the President in disbelief.

“Well, if you put it like that, then yes!” said Tish.

The President looked at them trying to work out how they did what they did. It was as if the universe had created them just to turn it into an endless party.

In actual fact when the creator of the universe saw Datch turn up it decided to move to another one and didn’t leave a forwarding address.

“OK, let’s have a drink and you can all tell me the story of your trip and try to think about the people and how they behaved to you and each other.”

He beckoned to a shadow near the door and a servant came over.

“Yes Sir?” he said.

The drinks were ordered along with some snacks and while they were waiting for them the president asked.

“So, have you been using the ship and how do you like it?”

“Oh, its fantastic thanks! We’ve called it the Raven.” Said Datch.

“We’ve taken it to Hamel to visit Datch’s brother.” Added Hagger.

“Yes, it was very nice of you to let us have it.” said Fred.

“Well, it seemed a shame to see it scrapped, it is a nice ship.”

“Datch has been learning to fly it.” said Carina who was quite proud of him.

“Oh good.” Said the President raising an eyebrow. He was now starting to wonder if any planet was safe now that The Pack was free to roam the stars.

Just at that point two servants came out carrying trays with the drinks. After they had gone The Pack started to tell the story of Welly four filling in all the details they could think of as they went. During which a number of buckets of fried Hacks and Fries were demolished along with an assortment of dips. It was late afternoon before they had finished going over all the information. They said goodbye and were taken back to the Barber Inn

That evening they sat around the big table wondering what to do. Normally team Datch along with Jep would have come down about seven in the evening and the rest of The Pack would turn up at some point around then. Now however, they were all there together which was more like a midweek session and not an everyday occurrence. Datch felt a bit weird about it.

“I don’t know about you guys but I feel a bit odd not going to school.”

“Me too.” Said Carina “It’s like we lost something.”

“I know what you mean.” Added Rosey.

“Listen to you dudes. Most people are glad when they finish school and have a big party. You lot are looking like someone just died.” Said Peebop.

“I know, but it just seems odd that’s all.”

“It’s like a part of life is missing.”

Fred looked at them for a moment before speaking.

“OK, look this may be a little blunt but I need to say it.”

They all looked at him.

“This is what we all do every day. We get up and do what we have planned and try to make life enjoyable for everyone. This is now normal life, well as normal as life can be with Datch around. So, let’s sit here, have a beer or two and try and plan the next few weeks out. OK?”

They sat quietly thinking about what he had said then Hagger spoke.

“You mean it’s a bit like losing my dad. I moved on and now enjoy life with all of you. We do good things together and now we can do a lot more.”

“That’s not quite what I meant but yes. So, you now have a free weekend apart from the gig so let’s do some other stuff.”

“I see what you mean. This could be really good.” Said Datch suddenly realising the potential of having more time.

“OK, so what do we do?” said Dapo.

“What about writing some songs?” said Datch grinning.

The thought did cross Clax’s mind at this point that it might be safer to stay in his shop. Song writing would no doubt involve lots of beer, unhealthy food and some very late nights.

“Err… what are we going to write about?” asked Tish.

“Well, all the things we’ve done and the fun we’ve had. I have a title for one. ‘The Music Warriors’.”

“It’s a good title and let me guess. Welly four?”

“Yes, we are the warriors. In fact, that makes a good line ‘We are, The Warriors!’, what do you think?” asked Datch.

“Yes, it works.”

“See, this is easy!”

“Well, we have four words of the song and no music yet. So, don’t count your hacks yet.” said Fred.

“Let’s just try it?” said Datch.

The others nodded.

“OK look, let’s chill tonight and then everyone meet up tomorrow after lunch at our studio. I’ll make sure we’ve got plenty of cold beers in the fridge.” Said Tank.

“I’ll do some burgers and chips if you like.” added Hagger brightening up with the thought of house guests.

“That sounds like a good idea.” Said Datch keen to get started.

“OK then, Let’s say you come around ours at about midday? That way we should all be awake.” Asked Tank.

There was another round of nodding this time with a bit more excitement as beer was involved.

The following few days were spent going to the studio at Tanks apartment trying to work on 'The Music Warriors'. It was hard work but the first song was starting to take shape. The hard part was getting the music to match the words and they finally started to get the workings of a powerful rock song down. They also agreed that if they could they would try it out on Welly four as this gave them plenty of time to get it right.

Mid-week arrived and it was gig time at the Barbers Inn and therefore they had that day off from song writing. The weekend was the same as they had two gigs each one day apart so nothing more happened with the song until the following week. Then it was the mid-week gig again which went down better than normal and there seemed to be a larger number of aliens than usual and also some people who were glowing a lot more than the rest. Datch suspected they were from Welly four but didn't get a chance to talk to them.

The week came to an end and it was time for the embassy.

The Embassy

Datch opened his eyes only to find something autumnal red and sweet smelling was blocking his view. He moved his arm and the object moved revealing Carina's face. She did smell nice. It was then he remembered about the shower!

'Oh yes,' he thought, 'that was why'. He gave her a kiss on her cheek. She opened one eye and looked at him.

"Hello lover boy."

"Morning babes. Do you want some breakfast?"

"Yes, Pancakes please."

Datch got up and headed down to the kitchen. When he got there his mum was sitting having a coffee and some waffles.

"Morning!"

"Hi mum."

"Did you sleep well?"

"Yes thanks."

"I take it you are clean?"

That was a loaded question and Datch realised that his mum had heard something.

"Err, sorry. Did we wake you?"

"No Datch, I was still awake and next time please pick up your towels!"

Datch thought about it and then remembered pulling Carina's towel off her and chasing her to the bedroom.

"Sorry mum, we were just getting clean."

"Yes, it sounded like it!" she said with a knowing look.

Datch went a bit red.

"OK, look this is our house as well as yours, please remember that when we go bed, we want to sleep so please keep the noise down."

"OK Mum. Sorry!"

"Lucky for you your dad was asleep."

Datch let out a sigh of relief.

"Err, mum?"

"Yes?"

"You know how we're going to go on an interstellar tour."

"Yes. It wasn't a surprise; I had wondered how long it would be. I know you guys have been making big news across the galaxy. So, when do you go?"

"I'm not sure yet, Fred's sorting it out. But it looks like we will be gone for around ten weeks."

"Where are you heading?"

"Well, it looks like a number of planets including Welly four and Hamel."

"Hamel?"

"Yes, that man we met there is going to sort it out so that will be the last stop on the way home."

"Oh, well what if me and your dad went to visit your brother and you gave us a lift back?"

"I'm sure it will be fine but I'd better just check with the others."

"So, are you ready for tonight?"

Datch let out a sigh.

"Yes."

"You don't sound too excited about it? It is a big thing for the city and the planet."

"I know mum, it's just that I just sometimes wish I could just chill with you on the weekends."

"You see us during the week instead."

"Yes, but they are just normal weekdays."

"You have a band and because of that your weekends are during the week. You do what you do and it brings so much joy to people's lives."

"I suppose so."

"Look, people work for weeks and weeks looking forward to seeing you and The Pack on stage. Some people have very boring jobs and going to one of your gigs is the highlight of their year. Datch don't over think things. You are lucky and can do what you enjoy for a job. Make the most of it while you can."

Datch thought about this and started to look a bit happier

"OK mum, I just didn't think I made that much of a difference."

"You do. Now, tonight make the magic happen for everyone there."

"I will mum." He smiled.

Just then Carina came walking in.

“So, what were you two talking about?” she asked.

“Nothing much.” said Datch grinning, he took their breakfasts and headed into the bar with Carina.

The rest of the morning and early afternoon was spent chilling by the pool. Around mid-afternoon Datch and Carina got ready to head to the Barbers Inn. The Pack was going to stay there overnight and had arranged with Jim for a late drink. The Embassy party was set to finish at about midnight and Jim had said he would stay open for them into the early hours so they could chill afterwards.

Datch arrived at the Barbers Inn with Carina and they went upstairs. The rest of The Pack was waiting for them.

“Hi guys, I’ve got the beers in.” said Clax.

“Thanks.” said Datch sitting down.

Jim came up with the drinks.

“So, what’s on the set list for tonight?” Asked Fred.

“I think we do the same ones as we did the night of the gem. I think they will like that.”

“I agree.” said Fred, “It will go down well.”

“Has everyone got their gems and new shirts?”

There was a round of nodding.

“OK, looks like we’re set. We’ve got about an hour before we need to get down there so I think couple of beers are in order.”

There was a lot of nodding and then a round of catch up before it was time to go.

They pack walked through the city towards the old library. The streets were busy and the city had a buzz about it. As they got closer, they came to a barricade manned by the security forces. The officers scanned their implants before they were let through and an officer escorted them to the rear of the old library where Timbo was waiting for them.

"Hi Timbo." Said Datch.

"Hi guys, I've got all the gear set up and you will need to put these on." He gave them all a lanyard to put around their necks.

"Thanks, so are we ready to go in?" asked Carina.

"Yes, but we all have to use the front doors." Answered Timbo.

"Oh, OK."

They walked around to the front of the building and were confronted with a large crowd. The officer who was still with them escorted them to the centre of the street after enlisting the help of some of his fellow officers and they were taken through the cheering crowd to a red carpet leading to the main doors.

"That way please folks." He pointed to the carpet.

As they started to walk down the carpet, vid bots circled them and the crowd cheered. Vid crews and reporters from around the galaxy were waving and shouting things like 'Can we get a few words please' or 'Smile'. They made their way to the doors and two smartly dressed officers opened them. Datch took lead as The Pack went inside.

As they went in, they were met with a very impressive sight. The room was a large open space filled with tables and chairs and a large staged area at one end. Above them hung huge chandeliers brightly lit and leading to the centre were four metal beams supporting something that was covered up. At the far end, a large table was laid out and Datch noticed that it had just the right number of places for The Pack plus one.

They walked up to a large man in a dress uniform who announced them to the room. A man came over and escorted them to the large table and on the way a lot of people came and shook their hands. The Minister Prime was there and came over to them.

“Hello Music warriors, I’m so pleased to meet you again and I’m so glad you could be here tonight.”

“We’re pleased to be here as well.” said Datch.

“I can’t thank you enough for what you have done for our planet. Our economy has gone mad and my people are happy again. I have a surprise for you later. Please take a seat. I will introduce you and unveil our gift to your planet at the same time.”

“OK. Thanks.”

They headed to the table.

“Well, that was a little cryptic.” said Fred.

“Yes, but its politics.” said Clax.

“True.” he said shrugging his shoulders.

They arrived at the table and sat down.

A waiter appeared and took their drinks order. They sat watching people come in and then Tank noticed it.

“Err Carina, your tops glowing.” said Tank.

They all turned to look. There was a dim green glow coming from the centre of her chest. Datch looked down his gem was glowing as well.

“Hey guys, our gems are glowing!” he said.

They all looked down and sure enough all their gems were glowing.

"We're not singing though?"

"It must be because we're near people from Welly four or something."

"Yes, they glowed all the time we were wearing them on Welly four."

"Maybe it's because the Minister Prime is here."

"Well, they will be glowing a lot more later." Said Datch with a grin.

They sat and watched as one after another, celebrities and dignitaries arrived. Some were big movie or Vid show stars and there were dignitaries from all over the galaxy. This was the first embassy off world for Welly four since the reawakening and every race had tried to get to the opening to see how Welly four had evolved. It was about thirty minutes before everyone had arrived.

The Minister Prime took to the stage.

"Ladies, Gentlemen, Aliens, dudes and dudets. I would like to welcome you to the opening of our first embassy for over twenty-three thousand years. Please accept this evening a token of our new found hospitality and friendship. I hope you enjoy the entertainment. Food first though."

He clapped his hands and waiters poured out of the doorways carrying plates of food including kababs. The next hour was spent eating and as far as The Pack was concerned playing guess the guest. This was really impressive especially when you consider that Hagger managed to guess the ruler of Riegeller two and when asked how did you know he replied 'because he's a short ass' which made everyone laugh including the table next to them.

It was then speech time and the Minister Prime took to the stage again.

“I would like to start by saying why we are here. We have chosen this world as the site for the first embassy because it is the birth place of the Music Warriors who I’m very pleased to say are here with us tonight.”

A spot light lit up The Packs table. Datch smiled and waved and the rest uneasily did the same. The Minister Prime continued…

“We as a planet have evolved to a new level thanks to these dudes and as such want to welcome all the beings of this galaxy and beyond to our world. We want to extend… “

The Minister carried on with his speech telling the gathered all about the new and progressive Welly four. Then it was the turn of the president of Bellatrix to welcome the delegation from Welly four and to say how the new alliance would help the interplanetary federation and how it had opened up new trading opportunities to the planet. Finally, the Minister Prime took to the stage again.

“Well, Ladies, Gentlemen, Aliens, dudes and dudets. That is the end of the speeches so it’s time for The Pack to take to the stage and get the party started, please if you would.” He looked at them and Datch nodded.

“Come on guys – party time!” They got up and headed to the stage where their instruments had been set up. As they got in position the Minister Prime continued.

“But before they start, I would like to give a gift to Bellatrix five. It is a part of Welly four’s prosperity and we hope it will be good for the people of Bellatrix five. Please unveil the gift!”

The cover was pulled off of the thing in the middle of the roof. It was a gem. The gem was half the size of the one they found and about the same as the one on top of the obelisks in the villages on Welly four. It was pulsating dimly and the gems around their necks were also pulsating with it.

There was a round of applause and Tank turned around,

“Oh boy!” he said.

“You can say that again.” Added Fred.

“Oh boy!” Said Clax.

“Really!” Said Fred.

“Well guys, it looks like we’re going to be making a lot of people happy tonight.” Said Datch.

The Minister Prime carried on.

“Please receive this gem as a token of friendship and let it bring prosperity to your world as it does to ours.”

There was another round of applause.

“So, without further ado, let the music begin!”

He turned and looked at The Pack.

Datch grabbed the mic.

“Hello Yuland city it’s time to party!”

They went straight into the first song and their gems lit up brightly sending out beams of light that hit the gem in the ceiling. The gem increased in brightness as The Pack played and then the room exploded with light and a wave of energy spread out from the embassy and radiated out across the city and beyond.

At the ranch Tansya walked into the bar to sit with Dechow only to see his head sparking and then realised hers was as well.

“Look at our heads!” she said.

Dechow turned to face her.

“Looks like they just started their performance.” he said with a grin.

Back at the embassy The Pack started their second song. The guests now all had sparkles flowing from their heads and the Welly four delegation had become columns of light. People started to get up and dance as the music took hold of them. Soon, the dance floor was full and then came Star Lovers. The gem in the ceiling increased in brightness and the gems around their necks became mini suns. The song built in intensity until the kiss. Then the gem exploded with light and a beam shot through the roof and into deep space, at the same time another wave of energy spread out through the city and into the villages and towns beyond. From the outside the embassy looked like it had an exploding star inside and people in the streets were now sparkling as well. Everyone had big smiles on their faces and looked ecstatically happy. The songs went on and people were cheering and generally having a great time. Finally, the last song finished and the Welly four delegation lost their columns of light but along with The Pack now had bright auras around them. The Minister Prime took to the stage and stood next to The Pack.

“Ladies, Gentlemen, Aliens, dudes and dudets. Put your hands together for the Music Warriors.”

Everyone cheered and clapped.

“OK, I believe it is now time to mingle. I will take this opportunity to thank you all for coming and hope you enjoy the rest of the evening. If you require anything please just ask one of the waiters.”

There was another round of applause and the Minister Prime left the stage followed by The Pack.

The Pack sat down and then people started coming over and talking to them. This was something new for The Pack as normally they were separated from people by a lot of bouncers.

"Err, what do we do?" said Hagger looking out of his comfort zone.

"Just remember the state dinner training you had at school and come to that, the state dinner when you saved the President." said Jep smiling at the ambassador from Sirus six who was just coming over.

"Err, I think I fell asleep during that one." said Rosey.

"Well, look at this as on the job training."

"On the job training? When did we get a job?" asked Dapo.

"Whether you like it or not, we're ambassadors for both Bellatrix and Welly four." Added Fred.

"Oh!" said Tank who was starting to wish he was doing some one's hair at that point.

"It's not hard. Just smile and make small talk." Added Jep.

"OK Folks! What Jep said. Let's mingle!" Said Datch.

They spread out and started talking to the other guests.

Jim was leaning on the bar in the Barber Inn talking to one of the locals. It had been a strange evening. The bar had been quiet until half way though the evening when a wave of energy hit everyone in the bar. The net result was that the sound system was turned up and the place filled up with people wanting to party. He even had to call in extra staff to cope with the influx of people that had appeared. They were very happy folks and were dancing and drinking till well after eleven. It was nearly midnight before they all left. It had calmed down now and there were just three or four people left. It had been a great night but Jim was hoping The Pack would get back soon as he wanted to shut the doors.

He was just saying good night to the last of the locals when the door opened and a security officer came in looking around.

“Err... We’re closing soon officer.” Said Jim.

The officer smiled, said “I know!” and then said something into his comms.

Jim got a little worried and then the door opened again. Datch came walking in followed by The Pack. Jim let out a sigh. The door stayed open and the President came in followed by a number of the Welly four delegation.

“Jim, I hope you don’t mind but these folks are going to join us for a chill out drink. Get a round in on my tab please.”

Jim watched in disbelief as the bar filled up with two planetary Presidents, a number of dignitaries and ten security officers. After a quick sweep around the bar the security officers went and took up station near the door.

“Coola, this round’s mine.” Said Datch as he went to go to the bar.

“OK.” he said and headed back to the group.

“Err... I just sent all my staff home. This may take a few minutes.” said Jim starting to pull pints.

“No Problem.” said the President of Bellatrix. He waved at two of the officers.

They walked over to Jim and much to his surprise started to help pulling pints.

“So, this is where it started?” said Widfab looking around.

“Yep, this is where we started singing.” Said Carina.

“I’ll make a note to put it on our list of places to visit at the embassy.” He then let out a burp.

“That’s a good idea Widfab, I’ll get It added to the tourist information guides as well.”

Jim decided that if they had any more people coming through the doors, he was going to have to remodel the bar again and wondered if he could buy the buildings next door.

“So, how did you start singing?” asked the Minister Primes aid.

“We started singing Karaoke after school and people liked us.” said Carina.

“Yes, Datch dragged us all up on stage and then after a few weeks Jim asked if we would like to sing as a group.” Added Fred.

“How very interesting, Karaoke… what form of music is this? I don’t think I’ve seen it on any of the lists.”

“It’s not a music type. They have a music system call a Karaoke Machine. It has mics, vid screens and plays songs without the singing. The lyrics appear on the screen for you to sing along with. You choose the songs you want to sing and anyone can do it”

“Maybe we should get one for the Embassy?” said Widfab.

“It could be fun.” The aid replied.

Jim finally finished pulling the beer and carried them over to the party along with the security officers. He was just about to head back to the bar when the President of Bellatrix turned to him.

“Please come and sit with us Mr?”

“Err, Its Jim Mr president, just Jim.”

“Well Jim, I’m Coola and this is Widfab from Welly four. This is a very nice bar you have here. Last time I came it was a bit full and it was hard to see for all the people.”

“Well sir, it was a gig night.”

“It’s not sir, its Coola!”

“Err OK.”

“Now Jim, Datch has been telling us that you are the one that found them?” asked Coola.

“Well, I’m not sure about that. I think they found me.”

“So, this is where the legend began.” Said Widfab catching up with the conversation.

“Yes, this is where we started.” Said Datch.

“It’s a very nice place. Do you only sing here?”

“Oh no, we play Solar Ball.”

“Solar Ball?”

“Yes. Guys lets show him.”

The Pack got up, Jep, the Bikers and Timbo voted to watch. Jim went and got a helmet for each of the presidents.

Datch pressed the start button and the bar turned into a volcanic moon.

The Welly four delegation all jumped as their table turned into a crater full of boiling lava. Coola just picked up his glass and had a drink before putting it back in a stream of lava that was running across his part of the table before falling off the edge and disappearing between his legs. There were a few trial pokes from the Welly Four members and then amazement as they found it was just a light show and not real.

Datch stepped up to take his shot. The balls were all flaming rocks of different colours. He took aim and hit the white one into the purple one which flew across then knocking the green one into a net that in this case was a hole spitting lava with a number seven on it.

The virtual score board showed fourteen points to team A

Next it was team B's turn and Tish was up. She took her shot knocking the yellow into a cinder cone on the balcony for double points giving team B sixteen points.

The game ended with team B just winning by five points.

The Welly four delegation sat looking at them as they came back over to the table.

"Widfab, what did you think?" Asked Datch.

"I think we need to get one of these as well as a karaoke machine." he said with a big grin. "May I have a go?"

"Sure, whose team do you want to join?

"I'll come with you if you don't mind."

"Sure, we need someone else to balance things up though."

Five people stood up. Datch looked at the others who were also itching to join in.

"OK, anyone who wants to play come over here."

The rest of the delegation stood up and came over. The people were then evenly spread out between the two teams. Not to be outdone by another planet the Bellatrixian entourage joined in as well. Leaving just the bikers, Jep, Jim and Timbo sitting down with the security officers. This meant they now had two very large teams of twelve. Datch put game in super play mode. He had never used it before as you had to have two teams of ten people or greater to use it.

Datch pressed the start button.

The game changed and the bar turned into a jungle complete with a waterfall cascading off the balcony into a pool near the door. Which was right on top of a security officer who did not look impressed and moved into the alcove next to it. To add to the fun the balls were all fruits of one sort or another which had timers on and as timer reached zero, they would rot away and explode. Also, your team not only had to hit the white ball into the other balls but had a number of bonus holes to protect using pink balls.

The next hour went by very fast and after the third game they all went back and sat down to recover.

“That was a lot of fun.” said Widfab getting his breath back.

“I must say I agree, I haven’t had this much fun for years.” Added Coola.

“Well, you’ll have to pop in more often.” Said Datch.

“We will indeed.” Said Widfab.

Jim thought that he really needed a bigger bar now. Maybe with a private side for VIP’s and after the last game a much larger room.

“So, when are the Music Warriors returning to Welly?” asked one of the aids.

“We are just sorting out the dates now and it’s looking like fifteen weeks’ time roughly.” Said Fred.

“Oh, that’s excellent news. Mark it in my diary please.” said Widfab turning to one of his aids.

“I’ll message you when I have the exact date.” Added Fred.

“That’s great, thanks. Err, do you know where they are going to be?”

“I believe one is in the capital and we’re hoping to have another open air one in the desert near the actual gem.”

“I hear that Quaki is becoming very busy these days and is expanding at quite a rate.” said one of the aid’s

“Oh, well I hope they have a decent inn now, Faberfab was a nice bloke but the beer was not the best.”

“I think you may find that’s changed now.”

“Oh, cool, do they have Old Man’s Boots?” asked Hagger.

“Old Man’s Boots?” said Widfab.

“This. Try some.” he said passing his glass to him.

“I don’t mind if I do. Thank you.” he took a sip of the drink.

“Woooww, that’s good stuff.” he said in a hoarse voice.

After he had regained his voice, he turned to Jim.

“Get everyone a glass of this please.”

Jim walked over to the bar followed by one of the officers and proceeded to pour out a small amount of liquid from the bottle into a number of small glasses.

“Do you know if Tajiquay and Faberfab have started building their hotel yet?” asked Tank.

Widfab wasn’t sure and so one of his aids stepped in.

“You mean the tribe leader who helped you and the inn keeper?”

“Yes.”

“Oh, they are good dudes, we helped them and your friend Dag to get it started. It should be nearly done when you visit, I would think.”

“You really don’t hang around do you.”

“Well, we have twenty thousand years to catch up.”

“Hmmm. I can see how that would make you hurry things along.”

“Do you need any assistance at all?” said Coola and then burped.

“Well, if you can spare any techs, it would be handy. We have started making implants compulsory but we could do with skilled people to help get the planetary network up and running efficiently.”

At that point Jim and the officer returned with the glasses and handed them around.

“Bottoms up everyone.” Said Widfab and lifted his glass.

“Cheers all!”

They all lifted their glasses and took a good drink.

There was silence at first and then Fred said.

“I prefer the Dark Forest malt myself.”

“Oh, can we try some of that?” Said Widfab.

Another hour later the party finally finished as most of the top shelf of the bar took effect. Everyone either left, was half carried out or in The Packs case, went to bed.

Graduation

During the next ten weeks they did at least two gigs a week and the rest of the time they spent working in the new songs. They managed to get three songs completed, 'Music Warriors', 'Green Gems' and 'Black Spiders Die'. All of which were fast and powerful rock songs and they were talking about trying the first one out at their graduation on the weekend. Fred and Timbo had been working hard on The Packs first galactic tour and had sorted out all the dates, hotels and security along with a number of extra gigs that had been accommodated in the schedule. They were going to leave the day after the graduation in the Raven.

It was mid-week and Datch was checking the Raven over with his dad.

"So, this will be you first flight solo." Said Dechow.

"Yes, but Clax is going to be next to me. Thanks for sorting it with the captain so I got my licence."

"You earnt it son. You passed the exam after all."

"I know but the simulator in the Carpaycus really helped a lot and the report from Don really helped as well."

"He was really impressed by you. You controlled the ship very well even when it was falling apart around you. He sent me a couple of the simulations and you kept your head very well. If anything, he's a little disappointed that you're not joining the fleet."

"I know but I love my music, the stage and making people happy and the money helps too."

His dad laughed.

"Come on, the engine room systems are all good. Let's move to the stores."

"OK."

They moved to the store room.

It was full of racks and storage bins. The first rack was a refrigerated unit and had steaks, hacks wings, various other frozen meats and ice-cream. The next rack had a stasis field and contained fresh fruit and veg. Then there were six racks of beer, soft drinks and a number of bottles of spirits.

"Well, it looks like you have the important supplies!"

"Yes, I made sure I got plenty of ice-cream."

Dechow laughed.

They carried on looking at the racks.

"I think we're good." Said Datch looking at his list.

"OK, flight deck then."

They headed up to the cockpit. Datch sat down in the pilot's seat and started pressing buttons. Dechow got in the co-pilots seat and started doing the same.

"Datch."

"Yes Dad?"

"I haven't had a chance to ask you but how are you coping with all the fame? Both myself and your mum are concerned."

"I'm good, in fact I'm loving it. It can get a bit much sometimes but we look out for each other and the look on people's faces at the end of the night makes me feel good."

"Are you sure this is what you want to do?"

"Yes Dad. I love what I do and I get to have fun doing it."

"OK then, well as the bikers would say. Party on Dude."

They both laughed.

"OK, everything looks good over here." said Dechow.

"Yes, and over here."

"Let's go and get a beer."

"Sounds good but I'm putting my trunks on beforehand."

They got up and headed to the pool via the bar.

The weekend arrived and The Pack flew out to the ranch for midday. The graduation wasn't until mid-afternoon but they were doing a gig and the following day was the departure so everyone met up at Datch's.

They assembled in the bar and after everyone had got drinks, they sat down to discuss the events.

"I know we're all a little nervous about this afternoon and also about setting out on another adventure tomorrow. But let's go with having fun. If it's OK with everyone at the graduation I think we should do Music Warriors and Star Lovers?"

"You sure about Music Warriors?" said Tank.

"Yes. I think it's ready. Also, if we mess up it's only at school."

"Good point." Said Fred.

"OK, does everyone have their stuff for the tour?"

There was a round of nodding.

"OK, let's finish our drinks and load up the Raven."

"Sounds link a plan." Said Clax.

They finished their drinks and took all the bags out to the Raven and sorted out their rooms. Afterwards they headed back to the bar.

"Right, there is a large limo coming to pick us up in two hours and will bring us back from the Barbers later. I figured we'll need a drink after the graduation."

"That sounds good to me." said Fred.

There was another round of nodding.

They finished their drinks and grabbed their bags before heading out to the Raven and loaded up. Ten minutes later they were back in the bar.

"I know we're used to performing in front of fifty thousand people but I'm a bit nervous." Said Rosey.

"Yes, I know what you mean." Added Tish.

"I think we all are." Said Carina.

Datch looked at them all. He felt the same. It was one thing performing in front of strangers but these were some of their friends. He looked at them all. They needed something.

"OK everyone, look at it this way. The graduation is a warm up gig. It's two songs and then a party!"

Hagger started to grin.

Then everyone else followed suit.

They had another drink before team Datch went to get ready. Tank had brought his hair styling gear and did Datch's, Dapo's and Hagger's hair first as it was harder for the boys to mess theirs up. Also, the girls would take longer to do as they wanted perms and the like.

Just over an hour later they assembled outside near the pool and the six of them lined up for Tansya to take some pictures. The boys were all wearing smart dress shirts and trousers, they had even got shoes on instead of trainers. The girls all had long evening dresses on and also high heal shoes. Tansya took some individual pictures and also some group ones and when she had finished, she sent copies of the images to the other parents.

A taxi arrived to take Tansya, Dechow and the bikers to the school. Jep was meeting them there as he had been asked to give team Datch their diplomas. Apparently, the principle had now got a complex about meeting mega stars and didn't want to mix his words up. Tansya gave Datch and Carina a big hug.

"I'll see you there everyone. Remember this is your day." she said.

"Yes, I know you have been teaching the teachers but if nothing else it has given you each other. Make sure you have fun." Added Dechow.

"See you at the gig dudes." Said Tank getting in the Taxi.

"Later folks." Added Fred.

They watched as they all got in the taxi and it headed off towards the city.

"I never thought of it like that." Said Datch.

"Like what?" asked Carina.

"I never could see the point of school, but Dad was right, it gave us each other."

"I suppose it did."

They all stood thinking about it for a few moments then Datch spoke.

"Well, At least I have something for the speech now!"

“What speech?” said Rosey suddenly panicking that she hadn’t got one.

“Don’t worry. I was planning to do an impromptu speech after we got our diplomas. We are last up, so we can get our diplomas and then get the party started with the gig.”

Just then there was the sound of engines and a large limo came flying across the fields.

“Could we have got a bigger one?” said Dapo with slight sarcastic tones.

“Yes.” said Datch, “but I was worried the hot tub in the back would slosh around too much!”

They all burst out laughing.

The limo landed on the drive near the Raven’s landing area and the chauffeur got out.

They walked over to the limo.

“Mr Datch and Party?” he enquired.

“Yes, and it’s just Datch and no sir, OK?”

“Yes sir, Sorry Datch.”

“Also, please can you contact the school’s security on approach as they will need them to escort us inside.”

“Certainly Datch. I am aware of your celebrity status. In fact, a have been to a couple of your gigs.”

“Did you enjoy them?” asked Carina.

“Yes, very much thank you mam.”

“It’s Carina, just Carina”

Datch decided to introduce everyone so to avoid any more sir’s or mam’s

Afterwards the chauffeur turned to Datch

"Are we ready to leave Datch?"

He looked at the others and they looked back at him. It was strange but at that moment it was as if they were on the second day of school again all following him.

"Yes." he said.

The chauffeur opened the rear door for them to get in. Datch let the others go first before getting in himself.

The inside of the limo had thick plush carpets which went half way up the doors. The seats were very high-end luxury and were big enough to seat two. On the screen behind the chauffeur was a large vid screen which was displaying a message saying 'Just Ask'. Then to finish it all off the limo had dark tinted windows. Datch opened the drinks cupboard and inside was a selection of their favourite drinks.

"Well. I suppose this is the end of team Datch." he said grinning "Now we are just The Pack."

"I don't think 'just' is needed. We are The Pack!" Said Dapo opening a beer.

They all looked at Datch.

"The Pack!" he said holding out his glass.

"The Pack!" they all said and touched glasses.

The next twenty minutes were spent with messing around with the vid and generally trying to take their minds off things.

The intercom buzzed, Datch picked it up.

"Sorry to disturb you Datch but we are on final approach." said the chauffeur.

"OK, Thank you."

Datch turned to the others

“Here we go folks.” He held out his hand.

They all put their hands on top of each other.

“One, Two, Three, Lets PARTY!”

“YERRRRR!” they said.

The Limo reduced altitude and Datch looked out the window. There was a huge crowd of people around the school entrance and security barriers had been put in place. The limo landed at the edge of the parking area and the chauffeur came around and opened the door.

“Well, this is better than coming on my bike with my dad.” Said Datch.

“Wow, that’s a lot of people. Who are they waiting for?” asked Hagger.

“Us!” said Datch and went to the door.

“Well, let’s not keep them waiting!” said Carina following Datch.

Datch and The Pack stepped out into a circus of vid bots flying overhead and lights flashing across the path. The press were being held at bay by the school’s security who were being backed up by the local security services. They walked to the school’s doors amid shouts asking them to look towards the cameras which they did and smiled. They finally got to the doors and went inside.

The head of security was just inside the door and saluted as they came in. Datch recognised him from the nights when they would come back late.

He stopped and said “Hello.”

“Hello Datch. If you and your friends would please follow me, I’ll take you to the main hall.”

“Lead the way.” said Datch grinning.

“I can see why the principle didn’t want us back. They would have had to triple the security staff.” Said Datch as they followed the head of security up the corridor.

“Yes, we’ve had to call the security services for help today, I have all my staff in plus thirty more city officers.”

“Wow. All that for us. I know the gigs have a lot of security but I never thought about normal things.”

“You did save the President and change an entire planet as well as playing really good music.”

“You like our songs?”

“Well, it’s not my thing but my daughter loves you.”

“Hmm. Do you have a pen and a piece of paper?”

“Yes, Here.” said the officer stopping and fishing them out before handing them to Datch.

“What’s your daughter’s name?”

“Deelin.” he said.

Datch wrote on it ‘To Deelin Thanks for liking our music best wishes – The Pack’ and then they all signed it.

“Here you go. It’s not quite a signed picture but we don’t carry them.” he handed the officer his note pad back.

“Thanks, my daughter will love it.”

“Well, you did have to put up with us coming in late at night.”

“Yes, just a lot!” added Carina.

“Well thanks again. Shall we go?”

“Yes, lead on.” Replied Datch.

They went around the corner and the hall was in front of them.

The hall was a large circular room with a stage at one end and had a high ceiling with lights scattered about it in clusters. The walls had been decorated with flags and bunting which had also been placed carefully around the pictures of previous principals hanging on the wall. The room was laid out like an award evening with tables in a large arc around the room. Each team had its own table with the team’s name above it.

As they walked in the noise level in the room dropped as everyone turned to look at them.

“This way please.” said the officer.

He led them to the front where a large table had been placed. There at the table were their parents, the bikers and the captain.

“Thank you.” he said to the officer.

They all said hi and then Datch looked at the captain. He smiled and said,

“You didn’t think I’d miss this, did you?”

Datch smiled and sat down.

The main stage had two rows of chairs along the left side and a podium in the centre. To the right side of it was another stage with their instruments on and a PA rig. There standing at the back of it was Timbo. Datch waved at him and he gave him the big thumbs up.

The lights dimmed and the stage lights came up. The lecturers filed in along with Jep and the principle. They all carried a small black case with a star on the front. They went to sit down except for the principle who stepped up to the podium and waited for them all to be seated before clearing his throat.

"Ladies, gentlemen and students, welcome to all of you on this great day. Today you children have become adults. They have proven to us all they are ready to become part of society and through their hard work have achieved a high level of conduct. Some have excelled themselves and some have found it tough. But every one of them made the mark. It has been a long two years and we have all had obstacles to overcome even myself. These students have shown the lecturers a thing or two and some have even changed the course of planetary history. I have been honored to help get them ready for the rest of their lives and I look forward to hearing all the great things that I know will come from them. Well, I could talk all day but we have diplomas to give out and I'm sure the students want to party! So, without further ado, Mr Clots please get the ball rolling."

There was a round of applause.

The professor on the end chair got up and exchanged places with the principal carrying his small black case with him.

He announced his team and called them all up on stage one at a time to receive their diplomas. As they came up, he congratulated them and gave them a scroll from the case. After they went and stood at the back of the stage.

The rest of the teams went up one after another and filed to the back of the stage. Finally, it was Team Datch's turn. The principal took to the podium again.

"Last it is a very special group of people and I'm sure they need no introduction. But before they come up, I have to say that sadly this is the end of an era for the school. Their tutor Mr Doji is leaving us after many years with the school."

He turned to look at Jep.

“Thank you for your many years of service and we will miss you greatly. Please put your hands together for him.”

There was a round of applause and when it finished, he continued.

“Mr Doji. Please step up and give your team their Diplomas.”

He went and stood at the side of the stage and Jep took to the podium.

“Well, where do I start. Team Datch are a remarkable group of people and it’s been an honour to watch them become adults. If someone had told me two years ago, I would be giving up teaching to become part of a rock band and rubbing shoulders with planetary presidents, I would have laughed at them. Yet here I am. Team Datch has taught me how to live life to the full and at the same time be true to yourself. I’m sure I don’t need to tell what they have done as the press has done that for me. The best thing about team Datch is they have fun whatever they do and I’m proud to be part of it. Anyway, time for the diplomas. Carina, please come forward.”

Carina got up and walked up the steps onto the stage to a round of applause.

“Carina, well done.” he said smiling and handed her a scroll.

“Thank you, sir.” She said taking it and then stood behind him.

“Rosey, please come forward.”

Rosey walked on stage to more applause.

“Rosey, well done.” he said smiling and handed her a scroll.

“Thank you, Sir.” She said taking it and then going to stand next to Carina.

“Tish, please come forward.”

Another round of clapping.

“Tish, well done.” he said smiling and handed her a scroll.

“Thank you, Sir.” She said taking it and heading to Rosey.

“Hagger, please come forward.”

Hagger went up with another round of applause.

“Hagger, well done.” he said smiling and handed him a scroll.

“Thank you, Sir.” he said taking it before going to stand with Rosey.

“Dapo, please come forward.”

He got up and headed on stage to a round of applause.

“Dapo well done.” he said smiling and handed him a scroll.

“Thank you, Sir.” he said taking it. He went and stood next to Tish.

“And finally, their team leader. Datch, please come forward.”

Datch stood up to a huge round of applause. He stepped up onto the stage. Finally, the applause stopped enough for Jep to speak.

“Datch well done.”

He gave Datch his diploma.

“May I say something?” Datch asked.

“Of course.”

“Err, we’re doing Star Lovers and Music Warriors.” he said quietly to Jep’s ear and then turned to the mic.

Jep looked at the others who were all grinning. They nodded.

“Hi mums, dads, fellow students, lecturers and honoured guests. I want to say a big thank you to all the staff of the school who have been so supportive and to our parents and friends who have helped us along the way. The last two years have been one hell of a ride for all of Team Datch and The Pack. But now it’s time to party!! So, let’s make some noise!!”

There was a huge cheer and a round of applause. Datch turned to the others including Jep and pointed to the stage. They ran across to the stage and picked up their instruments. The bikers got up and followed them. Datch grabbed the mic.

“Are you ready to party!!”

“YES!!!!!” came the response.

Star Lovers blasted out from the stage and the room went nuts. The Packs gems lit up and energised the room. People got up and started to dance and as they did, they started to sparkle.

“Here is our one of our new songs – Music Warriors.”

Music Warriors started and people carried on cheering and by the end of the song were all joining in the chorus. Everyone was in party mode. When Music Warriors finish everyone wanted more. Datch pulled the others together on stage.

“I don’t know about you, but I think we should do one more song here and then see if Jim will let us move the party to the

Barbers and do a full set there with the rest of the new songs. What do you think?"

After a moment's thought they all agreed.

Datch bounded over to Timbo who was at the side of the stage

"Call Jim and see if it's OK to bring everyone to the bar for an impromptu gig and party? If it is, give me a thumbs up, OK?"

"OK Datch." he said pulling out his vid comm.

Datch went back to the centre of the stage.

"Supernova everyone."

Supernova blasted out and towards the end Datch looked at Timbo. He smiled and gave the 'OK' sign.

The song came to the end.

"OK everyone, the party carries on at the Barber Inn in thirty minutes where we will be doing a full set. Everyone is welcome!"

There was a huge cheer from the room.

They left the stage and helped Timbo pack the gear before heading back to their parents to see them before the party. The bikers and Jep along with security helped Timbo load up the truck with their instruments and other bits of kit before heading to the Barbers to get set up.

Datch went over to the podium and said into the mic.

"Party at Barbers in twenty let's go"

They went outside and the media were still there but this time all the other students were with them and swept through them like a tidal wave before heading the short distance to the Barbers.

Ten minutes later the wave swept through the doors of the bar and at its head was Team Datch.

Jep came running over.

“You have a round of drinks at the back of the stage. We’ve got it all set up and figured you would want to hit the stage straight away.”

“Sure thing.” Said Datch.

He went over to the stage and picked up his mic as wave after wave of students flooded into the bar.

“We’re just grabbing a fast drink and then we’ll get the party started again.” he said.

They headed to the stage and stood at the back getting their breath back and having a drink. They watch Jim and a couple of bar staff pulling beers like they were going out of fashion. Then another staff member managed to get through the door and ran behind the bar and started serving. They waited until people had got drinks, well some had and went into a huddle.

“I think we should do Space Dust, Black Spiders Die, Wilde Wind, Planet Rock, Shoot for the Stars, We Can't Get High Enough, Green Gems, Rocking the City and finish with Supernova.” Said Datch.

“Are you sure Green Gems is ready?” asked Clax.

“Yes, and anyway, we could play just about anything and they would dance to it.”

He looked at the others.

“OK, are we ready?”

They all nodded and put their hands in the centre.

"OK! One, two, three lets PARTY!!"

They all turned and ran to their places on stage.

"OK everyone are we ready to PARTY?"

"YEH!!!" came back the reply.

"I CAN'T HEAR YOU. ARE YOU READY TO PARTY?"

"YEEEHHHH!!!!!" came the response.

"LET'S DO THIS!!"

He turned to the others and counted.

"One, Two, Three."

"Black Spiders Die!" the sound blasted out cross the bar and everyone went nuts.

The next five songs blasted out and then Datch stopped after Jim stood waving at him frantically. He looked at him and he pointed to the end of the bar. Datch looked and Joni Jabi was there with two other guys. Joni waved and pointed at a small vid bot. Datch nodded and the vid bot flew up in front of the stage. He turned to the other.

"Smile folks!" he said and pointed at the vid bot.

The next four songs rocked the bar to its foundations. They finished the final song and went to sit down amongst cheers and whistles. Joni Jabi came over and sat with them much to the interest of everyone else.

"I wish you had told me you were doing this. I would have got here from the start. Is there any chance of a second set?"

He looked at the others and at everyone else. They were all having a great time.

“Please do.” said Zorm who was standing behind him.

“Hmm. OK Joni but instead of paying us I want you to do a DJ’s set for us. It is our graduation after all.”

Joni thought about it and checked his planner.

“OK. I’ll do a two-hour set.”

“Cool, let us have a fifteen-minute break and then we’ll do it.”

Datch got back up and went to the stage.

“Hi everyone, we are going to do a second set for you in fifteen minutes so get that beer down. Also, to keep the party going afterwards Joni Jabi of Channel 14’s Joni’s Music Movers has kindly offered to do a DJ set for us.”

A huge cheer went up from the bar.

He left the stage and went back to the table.

“Well, we had better work out the song list.” Datch said sitting down.

“Do you think Road to Happiness is ready?” asked Hagger.

“Hmm. Yes, we could give it a go but just watch the instrumental Dapo as we cross the stage.” said Datch.

“Will do.”

“I think we should do Music Warriors again and throw Green Gem in at the end and as an encore.” Said Carina.

“That sounds good. So, Planet Rock, Road to Happiness, Supernova, Star Lovers, Wilde Wind, Wind in Your Hair, Music Warriors, Rocking the City, Hot City Nights and Green Gems for the encore.”

Everyone agreed.

"Well Joni you're going to get the debut of not one but three songs. How's that?"

"I'm looking forward to them."

"Also here is some news for you. We start our first galactic tour tomorrow starting at Sirus six and finishing off at Hamel four in ten weeks' time a total of thirty-two concerts."

"Wow, that is news! What are the new songs called?"

"They are Music Warriors, Green Gems, Road to Happiness and we've just performed Black Spiders Die."

"That sounds great. Definitely one for the weekend show."

They finished their drinks and went back on stage.

The bar exploded again and word was starting to get around about the impromptu gig and people started dancing in the street. Jim had got the bouncers down manning the door to limit the numbers inside the bar. This meant it was basically just the students and friends inside. They finished the second set and encores. The party looked like a room full of roman candles as everyone had sparkles coming from their heads and The Pack had a very bright aura around them.

"OK folks that's it for us as we want to party too. Please can I get I huge welcome for DJ Joni Jabi."

A spot light came on and lit up a hastily constructed DJ booth and Joni waved to everyone as they cheered and whistled.

"Hello Barbers, Thanks Datch for that great introduction let's get straight to it!"

Music blasted out of the sound system and the lights flashed. The Pack went over to the table which took them a while as everyone wanted a picture of themselves with The

Pack. The atmosphere was amazing and it wasn't long before Team Datch were up and dancing.

The party finally calmed down after Joni finished his set and after another hour of drinking a lot of people started heading home. The Pack had moved up stairs and had been chilling with Joni until he had to go. Now it was The Pack and Team Zorm.

Timbo had already had the gear shipped to Datch's ranch and was now chilling with them.

"So, what time you leaving tomorrow?" asked Zorm.

"Oh, when we get up." Said Carina.

"No, I meant what time it your ship departing for Sirus?"

"When we get up." Added Rosey.

Datch looked at them and smiled.

"We have our own ship parked at my place."

"Oh Wow!"

"Yes, and it's a starbird!" Said Hagger who loved the ship.

"I've got my pilots licence now and Clax is helping me get experience. So, as we said when we get up." He smiled.

"When did you get time for that?" asked Jen.

"Err, we haven't been at school. The president told the principle that we passed about twelve weeks ago so we've had a bit of time to do things."

"The President?" asked Zorm.

"Yes, Coola gave him a call."

"Coola?" Asked Sadey.

The Pack were enjoying this. It was always fun when you name dropped.

"Yes, that's the Presidents first name."

"Wow!" said Zorm.

"I would love to meet people like that." Said Sadey.

"You've just sat here talking to Joni Jabi." Said Tish.

"Oh! We have haven't we."

"Yes!"

"But the President."

"He is the same as Joni. They are just people."

"Oh."

"Well, I'm feeling like food." Said Datch.

A very large pizza was ordered along with three buckets of Hacks wings with fries. Another hour passed and they decided it was time to head home. It was going to be a long couple of days. The limo pulled up outside and they left the Barbers leaving their fellow students behind. Yes, they would be back gigging but that was the last time they would be there as students. It had been a great two years and now the universe waited for them.

The next morning, they had breakfast and sat in the bar at the ranch watching a vid. After they had finished eating and drinking their coffees Datch turned to them.

"Well, I think it's time to go."

"Yes, the universe awaits." Added Fred.

They all got up and headed towards the door.

His mum came over and gave him and Carina a big hug.

"You take care of each other out there, OK?"

"Yes, Mum, we will."

She looked into his eyes and thought for a second before saying.

"You go get them Datch!"

He grinned and they headed to the Raven.

Datch went and sat in the pilot's seat and went through the pre-flight check along with Clax.

"OK folks, we're good to go. Everyone ready?" he asked.

"Yes." came the response.

"Yuland city control this is the Raven we are ready for departure. Requesting flight path out destination is Sirus Beta. Awaiting clearance for lift off."

"Good morning, Raven. Flight path is 216.3,175.2. Please be advised that there is heavy traffic to the left of you."

"Thank you Yuland city control. Flight path laid in."

"OK Raven you are cleared for launch."

Datch turned to the others.

"Here we go folks!"

Datch brought the thrusters online and the Raven took off before pointing her nose up. Then with a thunderous roar the Raven headed into the sky and the universe beyond.

The End... Until next time.

Other Books in the Chronicles of Datch Series.

Datch – The Great Adventure.

The Datch Pack.

Arcaneus.

The Quest for Earthly Delights.

Hunting Jackars.

The Orphaned World.

www.ingramcontent.com/pod-product-compliance
Lightning Source LLC
Chambersburg PA
CBHW070428170726
48291CB00002B/405